Echoes of Betrayal

Maya Hartwell (Quest for Justice)
Series Book 3

Gabby Black

ISBN: 9798863475059

Contents

Foreword

AUTHOR'S NOTE

Prepare to be captivated by the remarkable Maya, the protagonist of this series. Her backstory is as fascinating as her iron will and unyielding determination to uncover the truth, utilizing all the knowledge and skills she's accumulated throughout her life so far. Myself as a lover of suspenseful and thought-provoking entertainment media, particularly courtroom dramas, I've spent years refining my passion, and combining it with my background in the Justice System has led me to this moment. With a compelling narrative that keeps readers on the edge of their seats, the forthcoming books in the series will thrust Maya into increasingly intricate, nerve-racking, and suspenseful predicaments, both within and beyond the courtroom. Immerse yourself in a world that will thrill your senses and challenge your mind.

I warmly invite you to embark on this extraordinary journey alongside Maya and myself. I sincerely appreciate your time spent reading the third book in this 'Quest for Justice' series. Your interest and support hold immeasurable value, and I genuinely hope you relish the tale. To stay informed about

Maya's upcoming endeavors, kindly consider subscribing to my newsletter at **www.gabbyblack.com.**

Dear Reader

I would like to bring to your attention that this book in written in American English, which may differ in certain word choices and spellings from British English and Australian English. Throughout the narrative, you may encounter variations in vocabulary and expressions that are specific to American usage. I hope you find this linguistic distinction enriching, and that it enhances your reading experience. Thank you for joining me on this journey.

Warmest Regards
Gabby

Also By

BOOKS BY GABBY BLACK

Maya Hartwell (Quest for Justice) Series consists of;

Echoes of the Past Book One (Published on Amazon)
Room of Echoes Book Two (Published on Amazon)
Echoes of Betrayal Book Three (Published on Amazon)
Book 4 in the Quest for Justice Series Coming Q2 2024 or
sooner!

Available in Audio

**Echoes of the Past – available in US & UK https://books
2read.com/u/baq9O2**
**Room of Echoes – available in US & UK https://books2r
ead.com/u/m0WqvA**

Chapter 1

The old willow behind my childhood home had been hit by lightning at some point in the past but no one knew exactly when. Its branches were old and gnarled, some of them charred black as they knobbed and crooked, extended out over the lawn and shaded the grass below with weeping shroud of delicate leaves. I'd loved that old tree, loved its age and bearing, often pretending it could speak, like the old willow in that Disney movie about Pocahontas and John Smith. But what I'd loved most about the tree was the swing that hung from a thick branch—the swing and my father's hands.

Back and forth I'd sway, pumping legs that did little to help propel me through the air, leaning back on the upswing in anticipation of feeling my father's strong hands gently push me through a gentle crescent of motion that took me away only to return me back to him again.

Now, years later, sitting in my quaint little kitchen and waiting for the coffee to finish brewing, all I wanted to do was lean back and feel those gentle hands support me. The last few weeks had been agonizingly stressful, what with having volunteered to be a defense attorney in a murder case involving one of my best friends and dealing with the bureaucracy of the

United States military's version of justice. Not to mention the emails...

Closing my eyes and placing my palms on the top of my kitchen table, blocking out the noise of the coughing, burbling Mr. Coffee on the counter, I tilted back in my chair, thinking that maybe, just maybe, I'd feel something. Some sign that my dad was with me, that he was still here, that he—

An impatient *beep* from the coffee maker, as well as the footsteps of my houseguest walking down the hallway toward the kitchen, jerked me upright. Usually, I didn't jump out of my skin at domestic sounds—dealing with insurgents while in the Marines had heightened my senses, not dulled them—but only one of those noises led to a definitively positive result: my morning influx of caffeine being ready. The other...well, having a houseguest in and of itself was something relatively rare for me—my hectic work schedule at the law firm usually didn't allow for it—but having that guest being intent on helping me find the truth behind my father's death...that was something entirely different.

When he'd shown up at my door the day before, I'd felt a confusing mixture of surprise, happiness, and dread. We'd spent the morning catching up and then he'd spent the afternoon arranging my living room to look like a home office. Blinking routers and a wireless printer had been set atop my coffee table, with two laptops open between them. Manila folders were stacked randomly in the open spaces and I'd wondered at his organization and preparedness. It seemed he'd thought of everything.

"Morning, Maya," said Wren as he walked into the kitchen. My impromptu guest looked amazingly perky after the late night we'd shared—especially since those hours had been filled with tense conversations and repeated readings of my email inbox rather than with any activities that fell outside the realm of our platonic friendship. My eyelids felt grainy and I was sure my blonde hair was either plastered to the side of my head or poofed out from the disarray of early morning hours spent tossing and turning in my bed.

Experimentally pressing a hand to my head and mentally reminding myself to check with a mirror before leaving my bedroom now that I was sharing my apartment with someone, I replied, "Morning. You manage to get any sleep?"

"Plenty."

At my disbelieving look, Wren shrugged. "I've never really needed much sleep."

He did look remarkably put together this morning. His short, slight frame was covered with khaki pants and a comfortable-looking, salmon-colored linen shirt that accentuated the spattering of freckles covering his cheeks and the bridge of his nose. The hair sweeping across his forehead was thin and fine, the sandy brown color highlighting the vivid green of his eyes.

I stood, gathering my robe closer around myself in an attempt to hide my wrinkled, tan t-shirt and camo exercise shorts, a habitual dress code acquired during my time in the Marines that I'd never felt the need to break. Until now. "Coffee's ready."

I got two mugs out of the cupboard above the coffee maker and at his eager nod, filled both to the brim. A spoonful of sugar and a touch of cream was all I needed, while Wren took his black. We settled at the table, sipping contemplatively.

After several minutes of silence that was surprisingly comfortable, Wren said, "Any new emails this morning?"

I shook my head. "I haven't checked yet."

Bobbing his head, Wren stared into the middle distance, somewhere in the vicinity of my fridge. The emails he referred to were the reason he was here rather than at the library where he worked in Landsfield Ridge, a small town in northern California. I'd started receiving them during the last case I'd been working on, when an anonymous sender with the designation Concerned Citizen had sent me a message saying that they had evidence about my father's death. Six years ago, he'd died in a car accident. Icy conditions and fatal head trauma from not wearing a seatbelt was what the official report had stated as the cause of his death, and though I'd known at the time that it was very unlike my father to drive without a seatbelt as he'd always been something of a worrywart, there had been no reason for suspicion—at least, there hadn't been until the Concerned Citizen had revealed that my father had been murdered.

This confusing and frightening turn of events was made even more disconcerting when, with Wren's help, I discovered that some of the emails had been sent by an attorney I'd been working on a case with. The details were convoluted but Tom Braseford had admitted to being part of a government conspiracy to hack into my emails in an attempt to scare me, unnerve me enough that I dropped the case. Though finding out Tom had been scheming against me had been alarming, it wasn't until I received another email from the Concerned Citizen, one that couldn't have come from Tom, that I'd really started to feel shaken up. Started to dread opening up my inbox every day.

With half of my coffee gone and feeling fortified enough to start the day, I stood and went to the living room to grab my laptop, returning to sit at the kitchen table. Opening the computer, I could feel my heartbeat accelerate. It still had the email app open from last night's lengthy scrutiny, with the most recent email from the Concerned Citizen visible.

Long time, no talk, Ms. Hartwell.

If you want to know the truth about your father, then you're going to need more than a computer hacker to find me. Respond to my emails, follow my instructions, and the truth will be yours.
Concerned Citizen.

Even after reading it over and over again the night before, seeing the email still made the muscles between my shoulder blades tense. My change in posture must have been obvious because Wren leaned over and gently set his hand atop mine.

"You okay? Did you get another one?"

I swallowed, shaking my head. "No. Nothing new. I just can't believe...I mean..."

He mentally filled in the blanks. "I know. All this must be devastating for you. But I'm here for you, Maya. You can count on me."

Fighting back tears, I managed to quirk my lips into a smile. "I know. Thank you again for coming here."

"When you opened the door yesterday and I got a look at your expression, I thought you might not want me around and that I'd have to use my two weeks' vacation on an actual vacation. On a librarian's salary?" He thoughtfully tapped his chin with an index finger. "Where's the nearest campground?"

I returned his smile. "There's a nice park nearby. It's pretty popular with San Francisco's homeless population but I'm sure we could find you a nice bench to sleep on."

He laughed.

Hearing his deep, pleasant chuckle, I turned over the hand beneath his and grasped his fingers tightly in mine. "I'm so glad you're here, Wren. Really."

He squeezed my hand in return before releasing it and coming to his feet. "After you went to bed last night, I finished something I've been working on ever since you told me about the Concerned Citizen." He went into the living room, retrieved one of his laptops, and brought it back into the kitchen. Setting it on the kitchen table next to mine, he opened it and tapped on the keys, glancing up at me with a reassuring expression, before a welcoming note that was familiar from my own laptop booting up sounded and he hunched over, typing so fast his fingers blurred.

It wasn't long before he straightened and turned the computer screen toward me with a satisfied sigh. "Maya, I'd like you to meet my Trojan horse," he said, like a proud parent introducing a favorite child.

I leaned forward, frowning. The screen was full of computer code, which looked like nothing more than a series of random ones and zeros to me. "I see..." I trailed off, glancing from the screen back to Wren. "Is this some new kind of computer game I should know about?"

Shaking his head, Wren turned the screen back towards himself. "This is how we're going to track those emails you've been getting." He pointed at the screen. "I've created an email software embedded with a virus that latches onto any incoming emails received by your account. The virus is undetectable and when you reply to the incoming email it lies dormant until your reply is opened by the original sender, at which point it takes control over the server of the computer it's been opened on. With the virus controlling the computer, I can see the where the server is sending data from using the IP address, which tells us where this Concerned Citizen is hiding, who his or her contacts are, as well as giving us access to any incriminating evidence backed-up onto the computer's hard drive." He sat back in his chair with a self-satisfied exhale. "This computer hacker—I can't believe the Citizen called me a *hacker*, how insulting—just got us one step ahead."

"You're amazing," I said, filling my voice with the appropriate amount of awe. Narrowing my eyes, I peered at him. "Do you have books that show you how to do stuff like this at the library?"

Wren laughed and shook his head, but I thought the laugh sounded forced, his movements stiff where before they'd been relaxed. "No, I'm a nerd with no social life. I have to fill my time somehow."

I let it go. If he wanted to keep his secrets close, I wasn't going to push him. We all had parts of our lives that we didn't feel comfortable sharing. There were events and situations I experienced while in the Marines that I wouldn't want to burden him or anyone else with, so I wouldn't hold it against him if there were things in his life he didn't want to talk about. *But a Trojan horse email able to hack into computer servers? How in the world does he know how to create something like that?* Forcing down the incipient Nancy Drew tendencies that always seemed to get me into trouble, I smiled and patted his shoulder before returning my hand to my lap.

"Tell me more," I said. "What happens next?"

"The next time the Citizen sends you an email, we'll write him back asking for more information. When he opens our reply, TJ will insert itself into his hard drive and tell us everything we want to know about this guy." There was an edge to his voice that I'd never heard before. I liked it.

"TJ?" I asked. "And how do you know the Citizen is a guy? Women are capable of sending threatening emails too, you know."

"TJ is my nickname for the Trojan virus. And yes, I realize women are just as capable of being manipulative and corrupt as men—I just have this feeling that we're dealing with a guy." He shrugged. "Call it a hunch."

I nodded. "Okay. Sounds like a plan." As if on cue, my computer *dinged* with a new incoming email and my heart bounced from the bottom of my stomach up into my throat. I hurried over to my desk and leaned over my tucked-in chair, tapping the keyboard and opening my email while Wren hunched over his computer with an intent scowl, fingers again typing wildly.

At the same time, we said, "Grubhub ad," and broke into relieved laughter. Wren had given himself access to my email account during the Tom-blackmailing incident, so I wasn't concerned about him being able to check my email. It made me feel safe and secure.

"Speaking of grub," he said, closing his laptop. "What's for breakfast? I'm starving."

Standing, I walked over to the fridge and opened it, leaning down to look inside. "Hmm. Leftover Chinese takeout, half a bottle of white wine, ketchup, and a block of cheese that I'm pretty sure is supposed to be moldy." I straightened and looked apologetically at Wren. "I don't really cook."

Making a *hmphing* sound, Wren pushed himself to his feet and walked down the hall to the guestroom without saying a word. Half a minute later, he returned wearing shoes and a light jacket. "I'll be right back," he said, patting his pockets and nodding thoughtfully to himself before walking to the door and letting himself out.

Probably headed to the fast-food place around the corner. Shrugging, I took the opportunity to take a quick shower and make myself presentable. When I emerged from my room wearing a light green jumper and sandals, my shoulder-length hair swept back into a bun on the top of my head, I walked into the kitchen—and froze.

"What in the world..." I trailed off, too surprised and impressed to speak.

The top of my round kitchen table was covered in food. Croissants, loaves of crusty bread, jars of jams and marmalades, bunches of grapes and ripe figs, rounds of soft cheese, and folds of prosciutto. It was a feast for the eyes. My stomach rumbled, reminding me that while eye feasts were well and good, *real* feasts were better.

"Breakfast is the most important meal of the day, you know," Wren said, giving me a playful scowl. "And last time I checked, ketchup and wine aren't part of a balanced diet."

"It's really good wine," I protested.

"Uh huh." Wren started opening up the cupboards above the counter. "Plates?"

"Let me get them," I said, joining him. "It's the least I can do after you went out and got all this. How did you know where to shop?"

"My phone told me," Wren said, leaning against the counter and watching me set plates and silverware. "I figured it would know better than you where to find decent food around here."

"Hey," I said defensively. "Easy. I just made senior partner and have to work a lot and—"

Wren held up a hand in surrender, chuckling. "You don't have to defend yourself. Here," he took a plate from the counter, "let me make you a plate. Have a seat."

Still feeling a little prickly, I sat and watched him heap my plate full of bread and meat and cheese. As he spread a thick, dark red jam over a slice of bread, the warm homeyness of the scene eased the last of my tension and I felt my shoulders drop from where they'd been hovering stiffly near my ears. Having someone in my home with me, making me meals and taking care of me was...nice.

"Here you go," he said, pulling a chair out from the table and handing me a plate. "Bon appétit."

"Thank you, Wren," I said. "Really. Thanks for everything."

"That's what friends are for," he replied, gazing at me with a warm smile. As our eyes locked, I felt my cheeks redden. Breaking the connection, I looked down at my plate and picked up a fig.

He cleared his throat. "Eat. We're going to have a lot of work to do today and we need to keep our strength up."

I nodded silently, not wanting to share my fear that dealing with the Concerned Citizen was going to be very emotionally draining and time-consuming—more than either of us were prepared for.

Chapter 2

After breakfast, all I wanted to do was go back to bed and take a nap. The last few nights had been sleepless and my stomach was pleasantly full, my apartment unexpectedly cozy with the addition of Wren. Even though we hadn't known each other long—I'd only spent a week in Landsfield Ridge, where we'd first met and solved a decades-old murder together, and most of our correspondence since had been by email or text—sharing space with him felt comforting and familiar.

But I was working on a big civil lawsuit and one of the "perks" of being made a senior partner meant that weekends were nothing but two extra workdays, so I grabbed my briefcase full of depositions and case files and brought it to the living room couch, where I set up my laptop, started playing "The Piper at the Gates of Dawn," Pink Floyd's debut album, and got to work.

The case I was working on targeted a multi-billion-dollar pharmaceutical company that had committed criminal negligence when it had neglected to sufficiently spell out the adverse side effects of one of their products during testing. Though the human volunteers had agreed to the drug trial, they hadn't agreed to the seizures, heart failure, and death that had resulted from the company's failure to disclose and I was tasked with setting things right by making sure the victims who had survived and the families of those who hadn't were compensated for their medical bills and heartache. I didn't lose many cases and I certainly didn't plan on losing this one; I'd lost a parent, knew the devastation of grief firsthand, and while money couldn't bring back the loved ones who had died, it could help ease the futures of those left behind.

"What is this? I've never heard this music before," Wren said as he entered the room carrying his laptop in one hand and a croissant in the other.

"It's Pink Floyd. How are you still eating?"

He sat beside me on the couch. "I'm carb-loading for the day ahead. Like a marathon runner."

I watched him take a huge bite of the flaky pastry. "Right. You do a lot of running?"

Shaking his head, Wren set his laptop on the coffee table beside mine, opening it with one hand. "No, I hate running. I always get blisters and shin splints."

I smiled. "You're a strange man, you know that?"

"Yes," he said with a nod. Finishing the croissant and brushing the crumbs from his shirt, he scooted to the edge of the couch and placed his fingers on the keyboard of his laptop. "What are you working on?"

I told him about the case, feeling butterflies start to batter the insides of my stomach. Knowing the stakes was one thing, but telling someone else about how important it was for me to win was something altogether different. So many people were depending on me. *What if I lost?*

It wasn't until Wren said, "You won't. You're the smartest, most determined person I know," that I realized I'd asked that question aloud.

"Thanks," I said, bumping my shoulder against his. "What about you? What are you working on?"

"I'm currently developing code which, when opened in an email, will take control of the computer it's on, which will then allow me to find out who Concerned Citizen is and where they are located. The most important part of this is that no anti-virus software currently exists that will be able to detect it and—I'm sorry, how can you work with that psychedelic music playing? It's totally distracting."

I tapped a key on my laptop, lowering the volume. "Sorry. I got hooked on Pink Floyd after listening to it with my dad all throughout my childhood. While other kids were getting nursery rhymes, I got 'Comfortably Numb'." I shrugged. "He wasn't around much because he worked all the time, he was a lawyer too, but when he was home, this music," I gestured at the laptop, "was on the record player."

"Huh. That explains it."

Frowning, I turned my body to face his. "Explains what?"

He shrugged. "Why you live alone. Having to listen to that all the time would drive even the most devoted suitor away." Laughing, he dodged the punch I aimed at his shoulder. "I'm just kidding. When I have kids, I want them to be exposed to the LSD music of the seventies too." My next punch landed and he yelped, rubbing his upper arm and looking at me with playful reproach.

"You're strong."

Laughing and shaking my head, I turned back to face my computer. "I was a Marine. That's what you get for dissing Pink Floyd. Now, if you'll excuse me," I turned the volume up again, "I have work to do."

We worked in companionable silence for the rest of the morning, my music accompanied by the scratching of pencil on paper and the tapping of fingers against keyboards. Taking a break for coffee, we were in the kitchen mixing up cold brew when my cellphone rang.

I unplugged it from its charger and glanced at the screen.

Maman

I'd forgotten all about the Sunday phone call my mother insisted on every week. Grimacing, I debated on whether or not to answer. I didn't want to get into the same old arguments we always got into with Wren listening—I worked too much and dated too little—but I also didn't want to have her calling me on the hour every hour for the rest of the day. The debate was decided for me when the call went to voicemail; I'd waited too long. Mentally shrugging, I silenced the phone and silently promised to call her from work the next day.

"There's always tomorrow," I said under my breath as I handed Wren a glass of iced coffee.

"It's only a day away," he agreed with a knowing grin. After taking a sip and smacking his lips in satisfaction, he asked "Your mother's French?"

I raised my eyebrows. "How'd you know?"

"Maman," he said, pointing at my phone. "I've watched enough Hallmark channel movies to know that it means 'mother' in French."

I nodded, leaning against the counter. "Her and my dad met when he was in France on business. They fell in love and ended up living there until I was six, when we moved back to the US."

"You're lucky to have such an international background. I grew up on a farm in Iowa. Nothing but corn fields and cows."

I tilted my head. "How did an Iowa farmboy learn how to write computer code and track IP addresses?"

He opened his mouth to reply but was interrupted by a *ping* from the living room. We looked at each other, tension suddenly sparking between us, before hurrying to where our laptops sat.

Sitting on the couch, we simultaneously leaned forward and tapped at our keyboards.

"It wasn't me," Wren said, shaking his head.

I swallowed, clearing my throat. "It's me. I got an email."

There it was, at the top of my inbox. An email from Concerned Citizen. When I didn't make a move to open the new message, Wren laid a comforting hand on my back.

"Want me to read it for you?" he asked.

I shook my head. Taking a deep breath, I opened the email and read it aloud.

Ms. Hartwell,

There is no reason our relationship shouldn't be mutually beneficial. I have something you want and you have something I want. Let's start with you: you have the power to lose the case against AME Pharmaceuticals. And that's exactly what you'll do if ever want to know the truth about your father's death. Because that's where I come in. I possess evidence that proves your father was murdered.

Need proof? I figured a big-shot lawyer like you would demand to see verification so I've attached a short clip—a trailer, if you will—of a video starring your father and his murderer. The clip doesn't contain any damning evidence, so I wouldn't suggest you do anything stupid like take it to the police, but it does set the stage for the climactic death of your father.

Watch it. I'll be waiting.

Concerned Citizen

P.S. If you decide not to lose the case, I'll destroy the video and you'll never know what really happened. Could you live the rest of your life not knowing the truth?

My voice was almost intelligible by the time I got to the end of the email. Quivering lips and eyes brimming with tears made it difficult to speak or read; my whole body seemed to be reacting to the contents with a violent response that I was unable to control. I wrapped my arms around myself and tried to hold myself together as I closed my eyes. I wanted to cry and while maybe tears were forgivable when a daughter is faced with watching her own father being murdered, they weren't forgivable when that daughter is an ex-Marine who had seen and dealt out death.

"Can you believe the nerve of this guy?" Wren said. I could hear his fingers tapping madly against keys as he spoke. "Demanding you throw a case or else he's going to destroy the video? That's blackmail. That's illegal. What a..." This last sentence was muttered under his breath but I could still make out the expletive he used to finish it.

Wren's anger acted like a balm against my fear and doubt. I opened my eyes and unwrapped my arms, interlacing my fingers and snugging my hands into my lap so he wouldn't see how bad they trembled. I could tell he was watching me out of the corner of his eye, gauging my level of composure. He must've seen something positive because he asked, "Tell me about the case you're working on again. Maybe knowing more about it will help us figure out more about Citizen."

Clearing my throat, I answered. "It's a civil lawsuit against a pharmaceutical company that neglected to tell volunteer testers about all of the possible side effects. Some had heart attacks and some even died." I shook my head. "These were people hoping to find a cure for their diseases and ended up dying instead. AME was willfully and knowingly negligent and I have evidence to prove it. It's a huge deal at my law firm because billions of dollars are on the line when...if...we win." I hated the hesitation, the automatic self-correct my brain had substituted. Knowing everything that was at stake, I was disconcerted with how my "when" had become an "if" so easily.

"So what do you think Citizen's involvement is?" Wren's brows were drawn together, the vertical lines between them deepening.

"I have no idea. I mean, if he's working for the defendants, it would make sense for him to want me to throw the case. But how would he have gotten a hold of this video he says he has?" Now I was referring to the Citizen as "he"too. But Wren was right, it did feel like there was a man at the other end of these emails.

"Do you want to watch it? The clip?" Wren's voice was hesitant and careful.

I filled my chest with air, straightening my shoulders and untangling my fingers. *Get it together, Maya.* "Yes, let's watch it."

"First, let me check the attachment for viruses and spyware. He could be doing the same thing we're thinking of doing, putting some kind of surveillance program on your server. It may take a little while so I can let you know when I'm done if you have other things to do."

I did have other things to do. Standing, I vacillated between going through my case files and working on my opening statement for the coming trial or performing some of the housekeeping tasks I usually reserved for the weekend. In the end, I sat back down.

"I'll just sit here and wait." I knew I wouldn't be able to think about anything else in the interim and the thought of doing laundry right now was as unappealing as a trip to the dentist.

It only took Wren forty-five minutes to do a virus sweep of the video clip. When he sat up and rolled his shoulders, stretching his neck from side to side, my heart tried to leap into my throat.

"It's ready," he said, looking at me questioningly. "Are you?"

I nodded, unable to speak.

Wren clicked on the pad of his laptop and a video image popped up in the center of his screen. Tapping again, he pushed play and we both leaned toward the screen.

I instantly recognized my dad's car, even though the BMWs grill was smashed and mangled. Steam issued from beneath the crumpled hood, sending contrails of vapor into the darkened surroundings. It was dusk but the camera must have had some sort of infra-red technology built in too because the image was bright enough to make out small details, like the deflated safety bag that lay in my father's lap and the blood dripping from his nose. I swallowed when he moved his head and a stray beam of light illuminated the distinctive ocean-blue of his eyes. My chest ached with a heady mixture of grief and hope. Seeing my father after all these years, even within the confines of this video, was like having him come back from the dead. I kept wanting to turn around, as though he'd be there, standing behind me with his arms out wide and his blue eyes twinkling. *He's gone*, I reminded myself. *And he's not coming back.*

A dark blur entered the shot, obscuring one corner of the video. As the blur moved and the image sharpened, I could see it was a gloved hand, the fingers thick and black and somehow monstrous. As the hand neared my father's face, his eyes widened and his mouth opened as though to speak. Before any discernible words escape, the hand covered his mouth and fingers pinched his nostrils closed.

"No!" I shouted, jumping to my feet as the video cuts to blackness. My legs felt shaky, as though I was a newborn giraffe, and I sat back down when my knees threatened to give way.

"I'm so sorry, Maya," Wren whispered.

Closing my eyes, I let my internal emotions and thoughts go wild. *He was killed. My dad really was murdered. He didn't die in an accident. Someone purposefully ended his life.* These affirmations and proclamations helped me make sense of what I'd seen, helped ease the shock and pain of knowing that my father had survived the car crash that I'd been told had killed him—only to be murdered in cold blood. As my turbulent thoughts began to arrange themselves in an order that displaced some of the panic I'd been feeling, I took a deep breath and opened my eyes.

I knew what I had to do. Turning to Wren, I asked, "Can you track it? Can you tell me where that video came from?"

Still eyeing me carefully, Wren nodded. "Yes. What I'm going to do is send Citizen a reply embedded with TJ. When he opens the email, TJ will invade his computer and tell us everything we need to know. But Maya," he faltered before continuing, "shouldn't we take this to the police?"

I shook my head. "What does it prove? That my father was in a car accident and that someone was there. The hand could've been helping, could've been trying to wipe the blood from my father's face."

"Yeah, but it's obviously not," Wren said with a frown. "Someone arriving at the scene wouldn't be concerned with wiping blood from your dad's face, they'd be calling for help."

"You have to think of it from a lawyer's perspective. All the video shows is that my dad was in an accident and that someone else was present. None of that negates the autopsy report that states he died as a result of head trauma. The safety bag was deployed. That's been known to cause fatal head injuries." I sighed, frustrated with the truth. "It's not enough to prove that my father was murdered beyond a reasonable doubt and Citizen knew that or else he wouldn't have sent the clip in the first place."

Wren nodded. "You're right." He blew out a long breath of air. "Well then, TJ is all we've got. What do you want to say in your reply?"

Biting my lower lip, I thought for a few seconds. "Let's stall. We need to figure out where he's sending these emails from. Write...that I need some time to think."

Wren's fingers flew across the keyboard. After he read it back to me, I nodded and said, "Send it."

With a *wooshing* sound, the email was sent. Our Trojan horse was in place. Now all Concerned Citizen had to do was open the reply and let TJ in.

Wren leaned into the back cushions of the couch, as though trying to distance himself from what we'd just seen. "How are you feeling, Maya? Are you okay?"

I shrugged. "I don't know what I'm feeling right now. I guess I'm alright." I pushed myself to my feet. "I'm going to get a glass of water." Walking into the kitchen, I finally allowed my expression to mirror what I felt inside. In the window above the sink, my reflection glared back at me with bared teeth. I'd lied to Wren. I knew exactly what I was feeling. A determination to right wrongs. A resolution to do anything in my power to bring those responsible for my father's death to justice.

Chapter 3

Bright and early Monday morning, I left Wren—and yet another extravagant breakfast—behind and went to work. My office is located in downtown San Francisco and while battling the traffic to get there is a hassle, the views from my office were amazing and more than made up for the inconvenience. The massive Golden Gate Bridge stood in the distance, spanning the strait that connects the bay to the Pacific Ocean, the lower half of it covered in a thick layer of marine fog that would burn off once the sun cleared the horizon. Then, the bay would sparkle and sailboats would dance atop the bluish-green water, propelled by the ever-present breeze that came in from the ocean, smelling of seaweed and salt. But for now, the thick fog coated everything, the trolleys and pedestrians forced to wade in the mist as they made their way through the city.

I only spent an obligatory half an hour in my office, answering the emails and phone calls that had accumulated over the weekend, before making my way to the courthouse. Today was the initial deposition of the AME suit, but I wasn't planning on examining any witnesses this morning—or allowing the defendants to do so either.

My intentions kept me occupied as I neared the imposing gray structure that housed the courthouse. Tall and peppered with arched windows, the entrance was situated on a busy intersection, the tip of a sturdy brick wedge that swept back for blocks. San Francisco had learned its lesson after the earthquake and resultant fire that had decimated the city in 1906; buildings were built to last, to withstand the tremors that habitually rocked the seaside, San-Andreas-fault-straddling metropolis.

After going through security, I made my way to the assigned courtroom and met with my two paralegals. Go-getters fresh out of law school and eager to please, Nancy and Tim did a lot of the heavy lifting that accompanied big cases like mine. They conducted research and produced copious amounts of printed notes pertaining to the technicalities of obscure statutes and mandates pursuant to my law firm's legal proceedings as the prosecuting party. After rehearsing our objective for today, we waited outside for the proceedings to begin.

Trying to mentally rehearse what I planned on saying to the judge, my thought process kept getting sidetracked by the video clip I'd seen the day before. Wren and I had talked about nothing else, discussing the minutiae of both the emails and the video until we eventually ran out of topics of conversation. There was nothing else we could do, no action we could take until the Citizen opened the email and triggered TJ. Now it was a waiting game—and I hated waiting. I was ex-military. I thrived on conflict and confrontations. Being on standby was tortuous.

At the appointed time, I shook off lingering thoughts of my father and strode into the courtroom, followed by the mincing footsteps of my two paralegals; they still felt in awe of the courtroom setting, while I felt nothing but the weight of responsibility.

Sitting at our respective benches, I surveyed the opposition out of the corner of my eye. I was looking for any sign that the defendants had something to do with Concerned Citizen's emails, that they were somehow behind the video and blackmail. I wasn't sure what exactly I was looking for. I didn't expect them to stare shiftily at me or mouth silent threats but I thought just maybe they'd send a weighted glance my way, don a meaningful expression of menace that would let me know they were the masterminds of yesterday's ultimatum. On the contrary. They ignored me completely, shuffling papers and tapping on iPads with a studiousness designed to look industrious and competent. I recognized it because I'd employed the exact same frowns of concentration, the scowls of engrossment, during many of my previous cases.

When the judge entered the courtroom, we rose upon command and waited until he was seated until resuming our own chairs. The Honorable Judge Stephen Cosman was residing today. A slight African American man with wire-frame glasses and short gray hair, Judge Cosman was known for being fair yet eager to deal swift punishment on those who delayed proceedings or made a mockery of the law. As I was intent on doing one of those things today, my heartbeat started pounding in my ears the second I laid eyes on him.

Introductions were made and the defending attorneys were invited to speak on behalf of their client. The lead, a tall woman with a bob hair cut that exaggerated the sharpness of her chin, stood.

"Your Honor, on behalf of my client, I motion that the case be dismissed based on the lack of validity in the supposed victims' claims and insufficient evidentiary submissions from the prosecution."

Judge Cosman immediately shook his head and said, "Motion denied." The lead nodded and sat down. "Does the prosecution have any motions to present to the court?"

I stood, smoothing the material of my pant suit and trying to swallow without overtly displaying my nervousness. While the defense had known her obligatory motion would be denied, I was hoping that mine would be granted.

"Your Honor, due to unforeseen circumstance, the prosecution motions for a continuance of two weeks' time in order to continue gathering evidence. As our expert testimonies are being given by qualified physicians who are extremely busy saving lives, the necessary corroboration has proved difficult to schedule."

The motion was partly true. It had been difficult working within the physician's hectic schedules but they'd been sympathetic to the case and agreeable when it came to making arrangements for our initial meetings. I was mostly concerned with buying more time to deal with Concerned Citizen and his demand that I lose the case.

The judge fingered his chin as he thought. While he'd expected the dismissal request, I doubt he'd anticipated one for a continuance.

"I'll allow it," he said after a long pause. "But Counselor, this case has been on the docket for too long and needs a resolution so I'm only granting a one-week continuance." He lifted his gavel. "Be ready with your first witness at 9:00 a.m. a week from today." With a bang, the gavel was dropped and the continuance I desperately needed was granted.

We rose as Cosman left the courtroom and waited until he was out of sight before filtering towards the exit. Nancy and Tim, who hadn't been anticipating my request for more time, followed me silently, exchanging confused glances that I caught out of the corner of my eye.

When we exited the courtroom, I turned to them. "Let's meet in my office in half an hour."

"Yes, Ms. Hartwell," Nancy said.

Tim nodded, a head bob that bowed the whole of his upper body.

As I watched them walk away, I had to push down feelings of guilt. Those two were counting on being a part of a winning case—this suit against AME would make their careers as much as it would add to mine, maybe more. Their job prospects would be boosted greatly when they included a win of these proportions on their resumes. *If* we won. A loss with this much at stake...I shuddered.

I returned to my office after stopping at the coffee shop—the fog was only ankle deep now and would soon dissipate completely—on the corner and sipped a latte while I went through my case files and witness testimonies. Even though I ached to call Wren and find out if TJ had been activated, I knew that I had to stay on top of the case. After the week was over, Judge Cosman would not be granting any more continuances and I had to be ready to present my case. When Nancy and Tim showed up, I told them that a personal situation had arisen and caused me to ask for the continuance, then gave them ample work to do in the hopes of keeping them so busy that they didn't have time to tell other paralegals about this new development. The other senior partners had paralegals too, and I didn't want gossip about how my personal life was affecting the case to spread to the upper echelon of the firm. I would have to tell my boss that the case had been delayed a week—but I didn't have to tell him why.

After sending them on their way, I leaned back in my desk chair and sighed as I rubbed my temples. Stress was radiating through my neck and jaws, a headache of epic proportions in the offing, but I couldn't take some aspirin and call it a day.

Being a lawyer isn't about trials or juries, it's about truth and justice.

My father's oft-spoken words ran through my aching head on repeat and gave me the strength to straighten and pull my legal pad toward me. I had depositions to write.

I had just put pen to paper when my cell phone rang. My heart fluttering against my chest, I reached over and turned it around to see the screen.

Maman

Blowing air through my lips, I thought about ignoring the call but pressed the answer icon instead. Like pulling off a band aid, it was better to just get it over with.

"Bonjour, Maman. Ca va bien?"

"Oui. je vais bien. Maya, why don't you ever answer my calls?" My mother's voice was strident but I could hear the relaxing sound of chirping birds in the background, the juxtaposition making her sound even more angry. I could picture her sitting in the vast garden she loved so much, pinching the heads of dead roses with aplomb.

"I'm very busy, *Maman.* I'm working on a very big case."

"You're always working on a big case. You're always too busy to talk to me. Are you dating anyone?"

The switch from accusation to inquiry was so abrupt I had to take a moment to process it.

"Maya? Hello?"

"I'm here. No, I'm not dating anyone right now. I told you, I'm too busy." For some strange reason, an image of Wren popped into my mind.

"*La la.* Always with the excuses. You're getting old, Maya. Soon you will be too old for children and I will have no grand-children to comfort me in my old age."

"Twenty-nine is not old, *Maman.*" I picked up my pen and scratched a note on my pad. These conversations were ha-bitual, repeated on a weekly basis; I usually didn't have to concentrate too hard to be able to keep up.

The put-upon sigh that issued through the speaker spoke volumes. "Listen," I said, "why don't we get together for dinner later this week. *D'accord?*"

"Very well."

We made plans and I managed to end the call without any further references to grandchildren or my love life. For the first time, I actually felt kind of appreciative of the talk with my mother; the familiarity of our conversation had been calming to my frayed nerves. *But if Dad was murdered, I'll have to tell Maman.* The realization raised goosebumps on my arms and I shook my head to dispel the thought. Better the devil you knew...I smiled, thinking of my mother as a denizen of hell. She wasn't *that* bad. Although constantly being reminded of my spinsterhood did wear on the nerves after a while. What was the alternative? Marriage and a life of childbearing? How was that better than freedom and autonomy?

"It isn't," I muttered aloud, doodling on my pad as I thought about the inciting experience that had soured me toward mat-rimony.

My platoon had been charged with a reconnaissance incur-sion into the stronghold of an Afghani warlord named Ahmad Ghulam, who was suspected of harboring a cache of weapons. The intel said that he was scheduled to meet with an associate outside of his closely guarded compound, an opportunity that allowed for me and my platoon to enter the compound and search for the cache. We'd gathered at the stone wall surrounding the perimeter of the compound, hiding in the darkness as we watched the warlord get into an armored Land Rover and drive away. I remember looking at my captain, waiting for his nod to move in on the building, and seeing his face suddenly light up.

We all ducked down as the purring noise of an engine and the flash of headlights passed by. What had happened? Why was Ghulam returning so quickly? When I saw that the vehicle was an expensive Jaguar rather than a Land Rover, I nudged the soldier next to me and whispered, "It's not him."

"So who is it?" he'd whispered back.

I shrugged and turned back to the car, whose driver was just climbing out of it. He was tall and lean, dressed in a tight-fitting black suit that differed from the traditional Afghani *perahan tunban,* which consisted of a tunic shirt, pants, and head covering. The door to the house opened and a woman in a colorful, flowing dress ran out with her arms open wide. The two embraced and kissed passionately.

My captain whistled under his breath. "That's Ghulam's wife," he said in answer to our questioning looks.

The couple, arm in arm, walked back into the house and I looked to the captain. "What do we do now?"

He'd opened his mouth to answer when another flash of headlights illuminated the night, causing us to crouch down again. The Land Rover was back.

"Oh shit," I muttered under my breath. Even now, years later, I can still remember the feel of the adrenaline thrumming through my arms and legs. Muslims have very strict rules about fidelity and chastity, especially when it comes to women, and Ahmad Ghulam was fanatically religious. This was not going to end well.

We watched, helpless, as Ghulam strode into the house, only pausing long enough to stare at the Jaguar with an expressionless look on his face. It wasn't long before we heard shots fired, saw the illumination of muzzle flashes light up the windows.

I rose, still crouched down but now on my feet and ready to assist.

"What are you doing, Hartwell? Get back down."

"We have to go help her, sir," I said, gesturing toward the house.

My captain shook his head. "She's already dead. Let's go." He turned and started low-walking away, using the stone wall as cover.

I didn't want to go, didn't want to leave her to her fate, but knew there was nothing I could do to help her that wouldn't put me and my fellow soldiers in harm's way. Later, we learned that both Ghulam's wife and her lover had been found dead and mutilated in a ravine. Their secret love affair had turned deadly—and then and there I'd vowed that love would never force me to make the same stupid mistakes as it'd made that beautiful woman in the colorful dress make.

My office phone rang, pulling me back into the present. I reached out and answered it.

"Maya, I heard some disturbing news today about you asking for a continuance on the AME trial. I think you should come to my office and explain yourself."

I gulped, blinking. It was my boss and he did not sound happy. In fact, he was using the same tone of voice he'd employed when firing the co-worker who'd initially won the promotion to senior partner that I'd been eyeing for years. When it turned out that he'd been taking bribes and purposefully losing cases, he'd been fired and I'd ended up getting the promotion that I'd deserved all along. But right now, it sounded as though my boss was regretting the decision to promote me. *Thanks a lot, Nancy and Tim.* I knew it had been one of them who'd spilled the beans.

"Yes, sir," I said, the echo of reporting to the senior officer from my earlier trip down memory lane not lost on me. When would I stop having to kowtow to men? "I'll be right up, sir."

I hung up the phone and stood, mentally gathering myself. I couldn't tell my boss about the blackmail; he'd take me off the case so fast it would make my head spin. I'd have to think of something—and quick.

Chapter 4

When I walked into my apartment on Wednesday evening, after two grueling days of forcing myself to work on the AME case when all I wanted to do was wait by my computer, I was greeted with an ebullient Wren.

"We've got him, Maya! TJ worked!" He grabbed me by my upper arms and danced me around in a circle. "It worked! I'm a genius!"

The leather satchel slung over my shoulders was banging painfully against my thigh and Wren kept stepping on my toes but I didn't care. I was one step closer to finding out what'd happened to my father. "You are a genius!" I agreed enthusiastically.

Letting me go only long enough to pull me in for a hug, Wren spoke into my hair. "I mean, I wasn't sure that it would work but I was pretty sure that I'd done everything right even though it's been a long time since I've done something like that but I—"

Laughing, I pulled back. "Whoa, slow down for a second. You're starting to babble."

Red-faced, he took a step back and ducked his head. "Sorry. It's just that the waiting has been killing me."

"Me too," I said with a nod. "So, what do you know?"

He led me into the living room, our makeshift office, and sat me down on the couch. Settling in beside me, he walked me through the events of the afternoon.

"I was in the kitchen getting a glass of water when I heard a *ping* coming from my laptop. When I checked it, I saw that Citizen had opened the email and TJ had granted me access to his computer. In minutes, I had everything." He ticked items off with his fingers. "His webcam, his contacts, his passwords, everything. The best part is..." He paused for dramatic effect. "...I got Citizen's name and address."

My mouth dropped open. In theory, I had known what TJ was capable of, but actually coming face to face with all of the information we'd been hoping for was such an astonishing surprise. "You are a genius," I repeated, this time with quiet reverence.

He nodded. "I know." Wren turned his computer screen so I could see it and pointed at a screenshot photo of Concerned Citizen. We'd been right: the blackmailer was a man.

"What's his name?" I asked, bending at the waist to peer at the man's picture. He was overweight, the excess fat on his face puddling around his chin and neck. His dark hair was unkempt, as though he continually ran his fingers through it, and he squinted through the thick lens of black-framed glasses.

"Peter Gilmore."

I shook my head. "Hmm, I've never heard of him. I thought that maybe the blackmailer would be someone I knew but I guess not."

"In about two minutes we're going to know everything about Peter there is to know. I was in the process of hacking into the CIAs mainframe when you came home and—"

"The CIA?" I interrupted, choking in shock. When I finally caught my breath, I said, "You're not a genius, you're crazy! What were you thinking, hacking into the Central Intelligence Agency?" I looked wildly around the room. "Oh my god. They're going to bust the door down any second now. We're going to prison."

Wren patted the air to calm me down. "Easy does it. No one is going to prison. I'm so deep behind a smoke screen of fake servers and ghost mainframes that they'll never be able to pinpoint our location. Take a deep breath."

Jumping to my feet, I excused myself. "I'll be right back."

When I returned, I carried two wine glasses brimming with a white I'd been saving for a special occasion. I figured if I was going to be put away, I'd better drink it while I had the chance. "Okay," I said, after setting his glass down on the coffee table and cradling mine with both hands. I took a desperate gulp, figuring that I'd savor the bouquet of the second glass, and exhaled loudly. "I'm ready. So, you're hacking into the CIA to find out who Peter Gilmore is and I'm aiding and abetting you. Now that we've got that straight...are you in yet?"

Wren looked away from his computer screen long enough to wink at me. "You bet I am. While you were fortifying yourself in the kitchen—thanks for this, by the way." He sipped from his glass. "Wow. That's the best wine I've ever tasted. What is it and where does it come from?"

"It's a 2012 chardonnay Cuvee Cathleen from the Kistler Vineyard." I waved away the wine commentary. "Let's focus. Who the hell is Peter Gilmore?"

Squinting at the screen, Wren said, "He's been arrested for white-collar fraud and extortion but there's never been enough evidence for any long-term prison sentences. It looks like," he scrolled through the data, "this guy will do anything and everything for money."

I bit my lower lip. As senior partner, I made a decent salary but nothing that would attract the attention of an extortionist. On the other hand, when my father had died, he'd left me a substantial inheritance of stocks and bonds, a collection of rare and exotic wine, and a high-yield account he'd opened in my name when I was born. I was, for all intents and purposes, a well-to-do woman. Like Superman, though I might appear to be a "normal" working girl, I had an ace in my pocket—the last paragraph in my father's will.

Wren's computer *pinged* and we looked at each other for a brief moment before he turned back to the screen.

"Concerned Citi—I mean, Peter, just sent us an email. It says, 'I guess the truth doesn't matter to you, Ms. Hartwell. If it did, you wouldn't have asked for a continuance. Are you playing games with me? Trying to buy time? Don't. Lose the case or lose the evidence. You decide.'" Wren's hands clenched into fists. "What an asshole."

Knowing who I was dealing with, being able to put a face and name to the mysterious designation he'd given himself, made all the fear I'd been harboring toward Concerned Citizen disappear.

"Tell Peter that the evidence I've gathered is so compelling that I needed time to think about how to throw the case without getting fired. That will keep him from doing anything stupid like destroy the video while we try to figure out what we're going to do. But make sure you ask about the validity of the video. We saw the clip but that doesn't prove anything."

Wren nodded and tapped at his keyboard. When the telltale *woosh* of the reply echoed through the room, I sat back into the couch and took another swallow of wine. It was hard to believe what some people would do for money. What kind of person would extort a bereaved daughter? As I put the pieces together,

I realized Peter's take had the potential of being twofold. One, he'd get whatever AME had offered to pay him—they had to be the ones who put him up to this. Nothing else made sense. And two, he could just as easily demand more money from me even after I threw the case, seeing that since I wanted the video enough to lose such a high-profile lawsuit, I was the perfect target.

Wren's computer *pinged* again and I straightened. "That was quick."

"Yeah, he's got a lot invested into this scam," Wren said as he opened the email. I watched his eyes as they scanned the print, trying to guess from his expression what Peter had written. "He says, 'Don't trust me, Ms. Hartwell? What a shame. Well, I guess it wouldn't hurt to share some of my methods with you. I often scroll though the dark web, looking for opportunities, and one night, while trolling a video-based auction site, I saw a film on offer that caught my attention. It was being sold for an enormous sum, a number so big that I did some digging and found some loose-lipped sucker on an encrypted chat who was willing to part with some information for the right price.'"

"What is the dark web?" I interrupted, figuring that if Wren knew how to hack into the CIA, he'd know about that too.

"It's a part of the internet that can't be found on search engines like Google. It requires the use of an anonymous browser called Tor that keeps everything completely incognito, nameless. It's used for a lot of nefarious activities, where anonymity is of the utmost importance."

Nodding, I motioned for him to continue reading. I still didn't understand the concept of an internet that was separate from the one I used to look up legal briefs and movie trivia, but let it go as unimportant.

Wren continued. "He says that he was able to watch the same clip he showed us and saw the license plate on your dad's car. Hmm, did you catch that?"

I shook my head. "No, I was too concentrated on my dad. I guess I missed it."

"'When I checked to see who the car belonged to,'" Wren read, "'I found out that he was a rich lawyer and I got excited—then realized the guy was dead. I almost gave up on the whole thing but decided to do a little more snooping. When I discovered not only that he had a daughter who was a lawyer too, but a lawyer who was working on a case against one of the biggest pharmaceutical companies in the United States, well, I figured there was something there I could work with.' Jeez, this guy is such a parasite," Wren said with a disgusted sneer.

"Finish it," I said through gritted teeth. My stomach ached with tension and I set the wine glass down, unable to keep drinking it.

"'As usual, I was right. After contacting them and explaining what I'd found and what it might mean to you, the company agreed to give me a lot of money if I could find a way to make you drop the case against them. So you can imagine my frustration when I learned that, instead of bowing out, you merely asked for a continuance. Let me remind you of what's at stake: if you don't find a way to lose the case against AME, I'll destroy the video—bought with the nice bonus they gave me—and you'll never know what *really* happened to your father.

"'With warmest regards, Concerned Citizen.'"

I let out a long exhale as I closed my eyes, trying to ease the tautness in my neck and shoulders. After learning more about the origins of the video and AME's offer of a payout should I lose the case against them, I felt a mixture of emotions that was hard to describe. There was anger, lots of it, but also a certain amount of relief that the clip we'd seen was legitimate and could offer the closure I'd been missing ever since Concerned Citizen had first emailed me.

"How do you want to reply, Maya?" Wren asked, his voice soft.

Opening my mouth to say that I wanted to tell Peter Gilmore he could go to hell, I held back and forced myself to take a calming sip of wine before answering. "Well, we have his criminal record, right?"

"Yep."

"And we have proof that he's involved in extortion and blackmail, right?"

Wren cut his eyes from me to his computer. "Yep."

"I'm guessing, considering his record added to the evidence we have in the emails he's sent, that Peter Gilmore is looking at some substantial jail time."

Smiling at me, Wren nodded. "I see where you're going with this. It's time to turn the tables."

"Exactly. Violating the Hobbs Act can result in up to twenty years in federal prison and what with his record of near misses, the authorities would love the chance to get this guy behind bars."

"The Hobbs what?"

I waved a hand through the air. "It prohibits actual or attempted extortion but that's not important. What is important is that we have everything we need to give him an ultimatum. Give us the video or we go to the police."

Wren scooted to the end of the couch and placed his fingers on the keyboard of his laptop. Tilting his head from side to side, the cartilage in his neck popped and he let out a satisfied sigh. "I'm looking forward to this. Do you mind if I write it?"

"Go ahead. I'm probably a little too amped up to do it without scaring him so bad he'll disappear forever."

I sat back and watched Wren type. I was lucky to have him on my side. He was cool under pressure and smart and had a sense of humor that didn't evaporate in stressful situations. He reminded me of some of my close friends from the Marines; there was a toughness that underlaid his geeky exterior. Not for the first time, I wondered about his background. Iowa farmboy? I just couldn't picture him with cow manure on his boots and hay in his hair.

"Here's what I've got so far," he said, his words cutting through the improbable mental image of Wren perched on a big green tractor with miles of corn in the backdrop. "'Dear Concerned Citizen—or should I say Peter Gilmore of 165 Brighton Avenue in Cheshire, Virginia? Are you the Peter Gilmore who owns a silver Audi that recently got an oil change at the dealership by the freeway? The Peter Gilmore with four credit cards and three bank accounts, one of which is in Switzerland? I guess it doesn't matter either way because if you're not him you don't have anything to worry about and if you *are* him you don't have anything to worry about—as long as you send over the master copy of the video. If you don't send the video...well, I'm sure the FBI would love to know you're back to your old ways of extortion and blackmail. I have all the evidence they'd need to send you away for a very long time. Those glasses don't hide the fact that you've got very pretty eyes and I'm sure your fellow inmates would *really* appreciate those full lips—'"

I held up a hand. "Whoa, there. Too far."

Wren smiled at me and winked. "Just joking. I just made up that part about the eyes and lips, it's not in the email."

Laughing, I bumped his shoulder with mine. "You're a funny man, Wren. How did you really end it?"

"Let's see, I wrote, 'I have all the evidence they'd need to send you away for a very long time. I'm willing to keep it a secret that'll stay just between us if you send the video within the next twenty-four hours. I'll be waiting.'"

"That's perfect. You let him know we mean business by hinting at all of the personal information we have on him but didn't play hard ball to the point that he'd try to disappear."

Wren shrugged. "He'd have to know that it didn't matter if he did try to disappear. I'm in his system now and I'd see any moves he made. Checkmate."

"Send it." Unable to stay still, I jumped to my feet and paced the room, stepping over the various power cords and cables that spanned the space between the coffee table and the far wall. I heard the *woosh* of the email being sent and gnawed on my lower lip as I thought about how interminable the wait for his reply was going to be. What if he refused our offer? I would have to hand over the evidence to the FBI and he would go to jail but where would that leave me? The implications spread wider the more I thought about it. If Peter was stupid enough to leave evidence of his deal with AME on his computer or in his personal files, the pharmaceutical giant would be facing more than a civil suit—they'd be facing criminal charges that would supersede my firm's claims and put my trial on hold. My clients wouldn't get the restitution they deserved. I clasped my hands behind my back as my thoughts turned from them to myself. I might never find out what happened to my father. The video files, along with everything else in Peter's house, would be evidence and wrapped in red tape for the foreseeable future; the truth might get buried beneath justice.

I turned to Wren. "Do you think—"

An incoming *ping* sounded and Wren held up a finger as he bent over his computer. His face went through a series of changes, from curious to surprised to pleased and finally to somber. The skin around his eyes tightened as he looked from his screen to me.

"We got the video."

The next few days flashed by in a whirlwind of legalities and emotional strain. The day after email messaging with Peter Gilmore, a representative of AME contacted me with news that the company wished to settle the case outside of court. My bosses were delirious with happiness—taking a lawsuit to court required the logging of a lot of payable hours that they were delighted not to have to reimburse—and proverbially slapped me on the back with compliments on my use of the continuance tactic I'd employed, convinced that the move had been a purposeful ploy to put pressure on the defendants.

Feeling blurry and out of focus, I accepted the congratulations with a kind of numb tolerance. I hadn't won the case but I hadn't lost it, either. It wasn't until I met with AME and settled the suit for millions of dollars that reality sunk in. My clients were going to get the restitution they deserved. That was all that mattered. I'd wanted to take AME to court, to publicly put them to shame and drive home the idea that big pharmaceutical companies, no matter how big, had a responsibility to ensure that their products did exactly what they claimed to do and nothing more. But while the lawsuit hadn't seen the light of day, news of the settlement would spread and others who had been taken advantage of by big corporations would come forward. I'd been a part of something that mattered. It was all a lawyer could ever ask for.

So why was I so nonplussed? Why did the settlement make me feel nothing but a sense of anesthetized immobilization? I knew why but wasn't able to articulate it to myself until the dust had settled and I was able to turn my attention from my work at the firm back to my personal life. The four words Wren had told me that night, sitting on the couch after blackmailing the ultimate blackmailer, were the impetus behind my emotional deprivation.

We got the video.

It wasn't until three days later that we watched it.

Chapter 5

"Are you sure you want to do this?" Wren asked, reaching out to grab my hand. "I know you need closure but—"

"You don't understand, Wren. This isn't about closure. This is about finding out what happened to my father. Nothing else matters."

We were in my living room. Wren was seated on the couch and I was standing next to the coffee table that held our computers, our hands connected but our perspectives leagues apart. The fact that Wren thought this was all about a conclusion, about the end of something, proved that; watching the video was only the beginning.

I took a deep breath and closed my eyes. When I opened them again, I glanced apologetically at Wren before turning my gaze to one of the laptops that lay on the table in front of us. Its silver surface gleamed dully in the soft, late-afternoon light issuing from behind the closed curtains of the living room. "I'm sorry. I didn't mean to snap at you. It's just—"

"You don't have to explain or apologize, Maya." Wren gently squeezed my hand. "I'm here for you."

I felt my lips curve into a faint smile and some of the tightness in my body ease. "I know." Inhaling through my nose, I released his hand and sat next to him, scooting toward the edge of the dark leather couch to pull the laptop closer. Switching it on with the tap of a finger, I tried to hide the fact that my hands were shaking uncontrollably. I cleared my throat and said, "I received the video file too, right?"

Wren nodded. "Yes. Peter sent it to your email address. The only reason I got it was because I had your inbox open at the time. You should have it on your computer too."

Leaning forward at the waist, I squinted my eyes at the screen, having to scroll down through other personal and work emails before finding the one from Concerned Citizen. Waiting three days to watch the file had been a necessity as the scramble to organize meetings with AME and gather all the documentation needed to facilitate the settlement had taken over my life. It wasn't only work obligations that had caused me to postpone the watching of it, though. The video represented the start of something new, the commencement of a chapter in my life in which my dad hadn't died of an accident but by the hand of a murderer—I hadn't been ready for it right away. But I was now.

Tapping on the email, I double clicked on the video file and watched anxiously as a separate window opened and the small icon of an hourglass appeared.

"It's thinking," I said unnecessarily, taking my hair out of its work-chignon and letting it fall loose around my shoulders. It was silly, but I felt that the weight of my hair covering my neck acted like an anchor, something secure against the emotional whirlwind to come. I started tapping my feet against the marbled floor, my knees bouncing up and down. The motion must have annoyed Wren because he reached out with both hands and pressed down on the tops of my thighs until my legs stilled.

"It's ready," Wren said, lifting one hand to point at the screen. "Are you?"

I didn't reply. I simply tapped the play icon that had replaced the hourglass and stared at the screen as it changed from black to showing dimly colored images. The lighting was low; it looked to be the late evening. In the center of the screen was a car canted crazily on the shoulder of a road that looked darkly wet in the dim light. I recognized some of the features on the image from the clip Peter had sent; the setting dark and cold, Dad's BMW smashed and mangled.

My shoulders instinctively hunched around my ears when I spotted the outline of my father's head through the rear windshield of the car. The headlights from the vehicle sporting the camera illuminated the interior of my father's car, and I could see that the airbag had been deployed, the light-colored safety device hanging limply from the steering wheel.

The video didn't feature sound, but when the image rocked gently side to side, I imagined that whoever was inside the car had exited, the displacement of weight causing the camera to sway. Leaning forward until my face was only inches from the screen, I squinted at the figure who appeared in the video, trying to make out some distinguishing characteristics.

"Who's that?" Wren muttered. His voice was so low I wasn't sure if he was talking to me or to himself, so I didn't reply.

The figure—I thought it looked like a man—approached my father's car and I felt my heartrate increase. What followed had been featured on the video clip we'd already watched and even though I knew what was to come, the *how* of it all still felt...unknown. Vague. And as the figure leaned down and reached in through dad's smashed and broken window, I could feel my accelerated heartbeat knock against the tops of my thighs. I swallowed past the lump of anxiety lodged in my throat.

"Let's see if we can make out any identifying characteristics this time around," Wren said softly. "I wasn't paying close enough attention when we watched the clip but we should have an opportunity to see something in the full video."

I nodded silently as the figure, who I could now clearly see was a man wearing a long trench coat and leather gloves to ward off the cold, reached inside the interior of dad's car. That's where the footage we'd already seen in the clip ended and new material played out before our eyes. The man's hand seemed to cup the back of my father's head, as though to assess it for injuries, but then violently shoved it forward against the steering wheel.

One hand flew to cover my open mouth as I blindly reached out with the other and gripped Wren's leg. "Oh my god," I said, my voice hoarse with shock as the man leaned farther into the car. The headlights from the car the camera was attached to reflected against the seatbelt buckle and a bright flash of light winked in the gathering darkness. It looked as though the man had unbuckled my father's seat belt for some reason. Even though I'd witnessed his aggressive shove, I still couldn't help but think that maybe the man was unbuckling my father to help him out of the car—it was the last moment of denial I'd be able to enjoy.

My last futile hope was dashed when the mysterious man thrust my father's head forward again, this impact twice as violent as the first one. As my dad slumped to one side, his head lolling bonelessly on his neck, I half-screamed, half-growled into my palm. Awkwardly, I stood and stumbled away from the video, the laptop, the table, the couch we'd been sitting on. Away from it all. I didn't stop until I entered the kitchen and had nowhere else to go. Turning, I leaned against the counter, next to the sink, and dropped my head into my hands.

I'd seen death. A lot of it. But seeing my father, the man who'd pushed me on the swing that hung from my favorite tree, who'd made me crepes every Sunday morning, seeing him treated so brutally jerked on a nerve deep in my stomach. I wanted to retch and lash out and weep and draw blood. The confusing rush of emotions made me dizzy.

Wren followed me into the kitchen, coming to a stop next to me and propping one hip against the counter. Pulling me close, he tucked my face into his shoulder as he offered calming, repetitive sentiments. "It's okay. It's okay, Maya. I'm here. You'll be okay."

Letting out a wordless moan, I shook my head. When I finally felt able to speak, I said, "My father didn't die in a car accident. He was murdered." My chest heaved with a smothered sob. "Nothing is okay, Wren. Nothing will ever be okay again."

There was nothing to say, after that. Not for a long while.

It was me who broke the somber silence. "I need to find out who did this. Who killed my father." I pulled back from Wren's shoulder to look him in the eye. "Will you—" my voice caught in my throat and I had to clear it noisily before I could continue, "will you watch it again? Look for some clue as to who that guy is?" I shook my head. "I don't think I can. Watch it again, I mean. Not right now." I couldn't think coolly and rationally, not yet, and I didn't want to miss any important pieces of information.

"Of course, I will," Wren said, straightening his shoulders and nodding as though I'd asked him to go to battle for me. "Stay here. I'll call you back into the room when I'm done."

Wren must have watched the video several times because it was almost half an hour before he called me back into the living room. I brought the glass of wine I'd been nursing, as well as one for him, with me and sat on the couch beside him.

"Did you see anything?" I asked.

Nodding, Wren took the proffered wine and took a hearty swig before answering. "This is all so strange. I've been trying to piece things together into something recognizable but it's been hard because I keep getting distracted by the fact that your father was a lawyer, not some mafia don."

I frowned. "What do you mean?"

"Well," Wren exhaled, running a hand through his thin hair, "I think the man in the video, the guy who killed your dad, is a professional. As in, a hired assassin. Why in the world would your dad be mixed up in something involving a hitman?"

"What makes you think he's a professional? I've seen kids fresh out of high school kill people with all the concern of swatting at a fly."

Wren shook his head. "No. This guy's good. Really good. You see, he switched out your dad's seatbelt. That's the flash we saw, he unbuckled your dad's belt and replaced it with another."

My brows drew together in confusion. "Replaced it? How? Why?"

"Well, when you get in an accident, your seatbelt locks from the sudden application of g-forces and needs to be unlocked by a specialist. The guy," he motioned at the computer, "unbolted the old seatbelt from the frame of the car and replaced it with one that wasn't locked." By doing so—"

"He made it look like my dad hadn't been wearing his belt when he got in the accident," I finished for him. "Wow, I never knew that stuff about seatbelts." Squinting, I stared suspiciously at Wren. "Read that in a book, did you?"

He pressed his lips together and nodded, looking away from me as he continued. "This means that someone hired a hitman to kill your father. It's the only scenario that makes sense. No regular citizen would know that about the belts," he ducked his head into his shoulders, as though he could see my raised eyebrows without even looking at me, "so it must have been a professional. Which means we'll never find him."

I straightened, replacing the interest his *regular citizen* comment had produced with outrage. "Why not?"

"Maya, the level of planning that went into it and what with this happening six years ago, that guy is long gone. He's probably got passports from ten different countries and—"

I banged my fist down on the coffee table. "That doesn't matter. If it's the last thing I do, I will find that asshole and bring him and whoever hired him to justice." The ferocity in my voice lessened as I continued. "It's what my father would do."

***

As I drove down the winding road that cut through the hills to the east of San Francisco, I thought about how to tell my mother about dad's murder. Should I ease into it and torture myself or just blurt it out and hope for the best? Maybe I'd—my musing was cut short when I saw the lonely stretch of road on which my father's car had been found.

I'd driven past it before, many times since his death, but knowing that he'd been murdered made the leaf-filled trees seem somehow macabre, the evening sun shining through their lacy branches ominous. I wasn't sure if I'd ever be able to drive this path again without envisioning my father's bloody face or the flash of his seatbelt being removed or the expression on his face before it was thrust into the steering wheel. Thinking of it now made my throat and fists clench shut.

It wasn't until Wren tapped gently on my white-knuckled fingers that I took a deep breath and eased my grip on the wheel. No need to add other casualties to this stretch of pavement.

When we pulled up to my mother's house, I felt the muscles in my neck and shoulders relax. The view was as familiar as it was calming. My mother's late summer garden was abuzz with life. Bees darted from rose to lavender to helenium, gluttons intent on completing their last harvests before fall set in. Birds chirped and flitted around the garden's edge, where stately trees delineated the boundary between grasses left to grow wild and the carefully cultivated growing spaces my mother loved so much.

"I've never seen a garden like this before," Wren said as we got out of my car. "Your mother must have a green thumb the size of Mount Rushmore."

"The size of the Eiffel Tower," I corrected as they walked up a paved pathway lined with a small white fence. The garden, showcasing different hues of green and red and purple, stretched out to either side of the walkway, even reaching out atop it from an arbor covered with delicate vines of peas dropping curling tendrils and pale, bifurcated flowers. Brushing a light green shoot away from my face, I warned, "Watch out for American references around *Maman.* She is very proud of her heritage and uses every opportunity to remind you of it."

"Right," Wren said with a nod. "I'll be careful to only talk about French fries and French braids and—"

"Okay, okay," I cut him off with a soft chuckle. "Oh, and watch out for Choupie. He's my mother's French bulldog."

I looked around the garden, searching for tan, pointed ears amidst the greenery. "He loves her but hates everyone else."

"I'm pretty good with dogs," Wren said.

"That won't help you with Choupie," I muttered under my breath. We were at my mother's house because I'd known the moment that Wren told me the murderer was a professional that I would have to tell her. Since I didn't know about anything that my father had been involved in that would necessitate a hitman, I had to warn her, in case it was some kind of personal vendetta that might embroil her even after all this time. The killing had taken place six years ago so I didn't think my mother was in any immediate danger, but what with Wren and me unearthing the video, I had to be careful. I didn't want to lose the only parent I had left.

I knocked on the front door as I opened it. No matter how many times I warned her about the dangers of living alone, she never locked her doors. "*Maman?*" I called. "*C'est moi.*"

"Maya?" came a call from the interior of the house. "Is that you?"

The question was heavy with the letter z, *"Iz zat you?"* and I imagined that to Wren's American ear, my mother sounded exotic and foreign.

"*Oui.*"

We entered the house and I instantly noted the smell. It was wonderful. Intoxicating.

"Oh my god," Wren intoned, sniffing the floral, yeasty air. "It reminds me of a patisserie I went to in New York City." His nose was in the air and a beatific smile was on his face. "Espresso and flowers and freshly baked bread." Sighing blissfully, Wren followed me into the foyer, where a tasteful bouquet of flowers took center stage atop an intricately carved round-topped table.

When my mother swept into the foyer, she was alternately patting her hair as though to put it aright and swiping her hands over the front of her apron. White puffs of flour accompanied the swipes and reinforced what the aroma wafting through the air inferred.

"Oh, *ma chérie.* It is so good to see you." We bussed on both cheeks in the traditional way and my mother whispered into my ear, "He's cute, Maya. *J'adore* freckles." I rolled my eyes as my mother turned from me to look expectantly at Wren. "And who is this?"

"Wren, this is my mother, Sophie. *Maman,* this is my friend Wren."

"En-enchanté," Wren stuttered.

I could understand his trepidation. My mother was the pinnacle of French sophistication, from the top of her perfectly coiffed head to the tip of her ballet flats—a stark contrast to his rumpled jeans and wrinkled shirt. The poor guy hadn't even had a chance to grab a bite to eat or change his clothes before we'd left my apartment.

"*Bonjour*, Wren," Sophie replied. "It's so nice to meet one of Maya's friends." She looked pointedly at me. "She works so much that she never finds time to have fun."

I glanced at Wren over my mother's shoulder and rolled my eyes again. "I know, *Maman*. I'll try not to work so much."

"I agree with you, Sophie. Your daughter works too hard. Have you seen the inside of her fridge? She doesn't have fruit or vegetables, any trace of a healthy protein or complex carbohydrate. She's too busy to buy groceries."

I glared at him but before I could change the subject, my mother jumped on the chance to chastise me for my eating habits.

"*Je sais*! I know," she translated, seeing his confusion. "I've been trying to get her to come with me to the market for years." My mother shook her head sorrowfully. "It's a shame. I raised her better. But come with me and I will feed you, *mon petit*."

She led us to the back porch, where a large deck was surrounded by a manicured backyard brimming with fruit trees and flowering plants. The patio was shaded by a stately walnut tree that branched out over the wicker chairs she ushered us into.

"I'll be right back," she said before gliding away in a measured stride that both covered ground and looked absolutely effortless at the same time.

"Too busy to buy groceries?" I growled at Wren once my mother had disappeared into the house. "Really?"

He shrugged. "She makes me nervous. I didn't know what to say."

I opened my mouth to reply but a strident bark rang out before I could. I jerked my feet off the ground, scooting back and tucking my heels onto the seat of my chair as I looked around for Choupie. I was about to tell Wren to watch his ankles, Choupie loved a good Achilles heel, but narrowed my eyes and thought again. He could figure that out firsthand. *Complex carbohydrate, my ass.*

My mother reappeared carrying a charcuterie tray with one hand and a bottle of champagne in the other. Behind her trotted Choupie, who froze in place when he noticed me. Baring his teeth, his beady eyes swung to Wren and the hair on the back of his neck rose. I held back a grin, waiting for the little bulldog to attack—and almost toppled out of my chair when Choupie trotted over and licked Wren's proffered hand.

Seeing my expression, Wren said, "I told you I was good with dogs."

My mother set the tray, complete with cured meats, cheese, nuts, and empty champagne glasses, down and proceeded to open the bottle. After pouring us each a glass, she gestured at the tray with a nod, "*Bon appétit*," and sat down in a chair near Wren.

"Her father worked too much too," she said, continuing our previous conversation as she nibbled on a piece of cheese. "I missed him dearly even before his accident."

I saw Wren's throat convulse as he almost choked on the swallow of champagne he'd just taken. If there was ever a perfect opening for what we'd come here to say, that had been it.

I cleared my throat. "That's why we came, actually. *Maman*, I have something to tell you about *père*."

As she looked at me with a curious expression, I struggled to find the right words. Words that would cushion the blow I was about to give her and deliver the news of her husband's murder without causing her to break down.

"*Maman*," I had to clear my throat once more before forcing the words out. "*Père* didn't die in an accident. He was murdered."

She didn't respond. Her expression didn't change. A stoic silence settled over our small gathering and continued for so long that I wondered if she'd understood what I had said. Should I repeat it in French?

When fine lines appeared between the arches of my mother's brow, when her pale pink lips compressed into a faint grimace and the corners of her blue eyes glistened with unshed tears, I knew she'd heard and understood. Wren took his hand out of reach of Choupie's slavering tongue and leaned forward, placing it on my mother's knee.

"I'm sorry," he said.

"*C'est vrai?* Justin was murdered?" she asked, her voice trembling. "But, why?"

Feeling my own eyes tingle with unshed tears, I shook my head. "I don't know, *Maman.* But I'm going to find out. I promise you."

My mother's shoulders drooped as she raised quaking hands to her face. "*Mon Dieu,*" she whispered before bursting into tears.

I got out of the chair and stood by her side, hugging her to me as I rocked gently from side to side. Wren turned his head away, giving us some emotional, if not physical, space. Murmuring the same French sentiments that she'd offered me six years ago, when she'd called and told me about my father's death on a lonely, icy road, I let her weep. We'd both have to grieve again now, relive his death as the knowledge that it was at the hand of a killer rather than an accident forced itself into us and tainted what little closure we'd managed to obtain.

When she pulled away, patting her tears dry, I took her hands and caught her eyes with my own. "You can't tell anyone about this, *Maman.* Do you understand? The chain of evidence has to be clear and incontrovertible, and involving anyone else might jeopardize that. *Comprenez-vous?*"

Sophie nodded, her lips still tremulous but now pressed into a determined line. "*Oui, je comprends.*" That line softened as her brows drew together. "But, Maya, are you putting yourself in danger? Can't you let the police handle this?"

"Their procedures are laborious, *Maman.* Anyway, I have resources that supersede those of the police." I glanced at Wren with an acknowledging nod. "And what little actual evidence we have wouldn't be enough to prosecute. But the man responsible for *père's* death will be brought to justice. You can count on it." I lowered my voice, making a vow to both of us. "I'll make it right. I promise to make it right."

Chapter 6

I made sure that my mother was okay before leaving and even though she assured me that she was alright, I still felt awful as I walked out the front door. Here I was, having just dropped an emotional bomb on her, going back home and leaving her to deal with the aftermath alone. I didn't see any other options, though. I couldn't leave Wren to find his own way back to the apartment while I stayed with her and, even more importantly, I couldn't wait to get back and start on our investigation.

We drove back in darkness, the summer evening warm as we left the rural area my mother called home and reentered the city, artificial lighting and tall buildings replacing the shadowed expanses of rolling hills and trees. Both of us deep in thought, it wasn't until I pulled up to my apartment that the silence between Wren and me was broken.

"She'll be okay, won't she? Does she have friends she can call who will stay with her? I hate the thought of Sophie being in that house all alone."

Hearing the concern in Wren's voice, I put the car in park and turned to him. "She'll be fine. She's tougher than she looks." I wanted to put him at ease but it also served as a reminder to myself. My mother *was* tough and had weathered heartbreak and hard times before with a Gallic durability that belied her polished exterior.

He shook his head. "I just can't stand the idea that she has no one to comfort her. Sophie needs someone else besides Choupie to rely on."

The repeated use of her name caused me to look at Wren closely. "She'll be fine," I repeated. Narrowing my eyes, I examined his expression and my eyebrows shot up at what I saw there. "Do you have a crush on my mother?"

"No!" he practically shouted, jumping in his seat as though I'd goosed him. "She's just...I mean...it's..."

Laughing, I opened my door and climbed out. Wren got out of his side and I grinned at him over the roof of the car, his face illuminated by the streetlight above us. "Calm down. I'm not accusing you of anything." I ignored the little voice that said I was doing exactly that. "My mother is a beautiful woman in a vulnerable situation. I understand your concern."

He grunted noncommittally, not speaking again until we'd entered my building.

"I'm going to watch the video again. See if I can find anything we missed. It's all the evidence we've got right now so we need to be sure we get everything we can from it."

I nodded. "You're right." I checked the time on my phone. "Are you hungry?"

"No, I'm still full from the spread Soph—your mother put out for us."

Biting back a grin, I agreed. "Then I'll open a bottle of wine."

When we got into my apartment, Wren made a beeline for the living room while I detoured into the kitchen. I grabbed a bottle of red, a local favourite of mine, a Brazin Lodi Old-Vine Zinfandel, its bold, intense, dangerously good and just what we need. I brought it along with glasses out to where he sat

hunched in front of his computer screen. It was late and the
wine was an indulgence, but I needed to settle myself after
the emotional day I'd just had. Setting the wine on the table,
I walked over to the wooden tv console against the far war and
thumbed through the albums stacked against the record player
sitting atop the highest shelf. I didn't own a tv but thanks to my
father, had an extensive collection of vintage records. Not only
had he bequeathed me his large collection, he'd influenced me
to many different bands and musical genres I probably wouldn't
have heard through casual listening on the radio. Picking "The
Dark Side of the Moon," I placed it on the player and waited
until Roger Waters' thrumming bass filled the room before
pouring the wine and carrying the glasses to the coffee table
in front of Wren.

Humming along to "Any Colour You Like," I sat next to Wren
and checked my email. I sighed. The rest of this week was
going to be packed with meetings as my firm hammered out the
details of the settlement; when was I going to get the chance to
investigate my dad's murder? My work ethic had been instilled
by the man and throwing my job aside to find out who killed
him was out of the question. I glanced at Wren out of the
corner of my eye, thinking back and trying to remember if he'd
said exactly how long his vacation was. I didn't want to take
advantage of him but as long as he was here...

Two hours and two glasses of wine later, we had nothing
new to show for the time we'd spent hunched over in front of
our computers. I was exhausted and, even though he claimed
not to need sleep, Wren looked tired too.

"Let's call it a night," I said, pushing myself to my feet.

He nodded. "My eyes are starting to cross. I'll look over the
video again tomorrow."

Sighing, I dropped my chin to my chest. "Do you really think there's anything left to find in the video? We've watched it so many times and come up with nothing."

"It never hurts to be thorough," he said, running a hand over his face.

We said our goodnights and I stopped to turn off the music before walking down the hall to my bedroom. His quest to squeeze more information from the video felt hopeless but I was still grateful he was so interested. If there *was* anything to find, Wren was the man to do it.

***

The next morning, I left for work early. Wren was stretched out on the couch, a forearm draped over his eyes. His hair was tousled and his feet bare and I'd never seen a grown man look so...what was the right word?

Cute.

I smiled and quietly let myself out the front door, mentally promising Wren that I'd be home early—with the makings for a home-cooked dinner.

Work proved to be challenging. It was full of the legalities involved in hammering out the details of the settlement, going over documents provided by Nancy and Tim, and constantly checking my emails and texts for news from Wren. It was uncharacteristic of me to be so distracted but I couldn't help it. When the clock struck five, I made my excuses and left the office, leaving my paralegals huddled over textbooks and notepads. I didn't feel too guilty; they had to trudge through the trenches, the same as I had, to get what they wanted. Though I wondered if being a lawyer was something they'd still want, after all was said and done.

I stopped by the store and got the makings of spaghetti before going back to my apartment. "Honey, I'm home," I sang out as I entered. I'd watched *I Love Lucy* as a young girl and had been enraptured with Ricky. Those eyes. That thick dark hair. Lucille Ball was a lucky woman.

"I'm in here," Wren answered. His tone sounded distracted. "What do we have here?"

This last was said more to himself than to me, but I hurriedly dropped off the groceries in the kitchen and made my way to the living room.

"What is?" I asked, leaning over to look at his computer. An image of the video had been captured and was enlarged on the screen. Squinting, I saw what he was focused on. "What is that?"

"Looks like a watch, doesn't it?" he said, an index finger tapping his chin as his eyes flicked over the image. "Can't make out the model, too much of it is covered with the sleeve, but maybe if I..." His fingers tapped and enlarged and enhanced, the blurred image responding to his commands and coming into focus.

"What part of the video is this from?" I asked as he worked.

Wren cleared his throat. "This is from, um, when the killer reached out to, uh, unbuckle your dad's seatbelt, just before..." he trailed off.

Seeing and hearing his discomfort, I reached out and put a hand on his shoulder. "It's alright. You'd be amazed at my powers of compartmentalization."

"I keep forgetting you were a Marine. You must've seen and experienced things I can't even imagine. We don't see much combat in the aisles of the library."

"That's a good thing, Wren." My gaze moved from him to the middle distance, where lost comrades and bloodshed always waited. I hadn't been kidding about my ability to compart-mentalize, however, and pulled my eyes and mind back to the frozen image on the screen. "But how is knowing the killer wore a watch going to help us find him?"

"It's not the fact that he wore a watch that's important, it's the kind of watch. Look at that." He pointed at the image. "See that shape? Look at the size and placement of the buttons coming out the side. And the shine that you're seeing? Plastic or some kind of cheap composite material wouldn't be able to catch and reflect the dim lighting. I'd bet that's something extremely durable and expensive like titanium or some kind of similar alloy."

I stared at him. "You break things down like a lot of military analysts I knew back in the day. Who are you, Wren?" This last was asked with a joking undertone but I wasn't completely kidding. Sometimes I got the impression that I didn't know Wren at all.

"I'm just a guy who knows a little about a lot of things," Wren said, his voice distracted. He was leaning forward, his elbows on his knees and his chin supported in both hands; it was a posture that made him look young and innocent and vulnerable—I suspected he was probably only one of those things.

When he spoke again, it was with a growing excitement that was contagious. "I have a contact in the world of watches who might be the perfect guy to figure out more about that," he pointed at the image. "I'll email him right now."

He tapped away at the keyboard as I peppered him with questions.

"Who is this contact? How did you meet him? Where does he live?"

"His name is Hans Müller and he's from Germany but now lives in Landsfield Ridge. He comes into the library all the time and always borrows books about watches and different timekeeping methods throughout the ages." Wren paused his typing for a moment to sip from his wine glass before resuming both his email and our discussion. "He's an interesting-looking guy. I think he looks exactly like Albert Einstein, from his prominent nose to his crazy white hair, but it was his devotion to books about watches that made me strike up a conversation with him. I learned that he'd been in the horology business for over thirty years before he retired to Landsfield Ridge and opened a small repair shop just down the street from Lili's cafe. We got to talking and became pretty good friends. We had the whole immigrant thing in common."

I nodded in understanding. Wren wasn't referring to international immigration but the fact that everyone who wasn't born in Landsfield Ridge was considered an outsider. I would never forget the time I'd spent in the town Wren hailed from. It was small, about four and a half hours north of San Francisco, and was as tightly knit as they come. He and I had solved two murders during my short-lived vacation there; one decades old and the other painfully fresh. Outsiders were viewed with distrust at best and outright suspicions at worst, and no matter how long you lived there, if you hadn't been born within the city limits, you were considered a perpetual stranger.

"There," he said as the *woosh* of an outgoing email joining the strains of Pink Floyd. "Now all we have to do is wait for Hans to reply."

We sat in silence, listening to the music and sipping our wine. I was lost in thought, my mind preoccupied with the past and present. The murders in Landsfield Ridge had been tough cases but nothing like what I faced now; my personal investment in finding out who murdered my dad made this investigation feel like the most important thing I'd ever involved myself in. More important than the Landsfield Ridge murders or the more recent case I'd worked on clearing my best-friend's name of wanton revenge-killing of villagers in the Middle East. The weight of responsibility I bore was palpable, something that I wasn't sure I'd be able to handle without Wren's help.

"It's late," I said. "You must be tired."

Wren shrugged. "Not really. Like I said, I don't need much sleep."

My jaws cracked in a wide yawn. "I do. I'm gonna hit the sack." I stood and stretched. I could feel Wren's eyes on me and was suddenly aware of the hour, the wine, and a loneliness I hadn't realized I'd been harboring for some time now. Stilling, I hesitated. What would he say if I asked him to join me? Would it ruin the camaraderie between us? Was that a door I really wanted to open right now?

"Goodnight, Maya," he said softly, breaking into my internal conflict and replacing my unanswered questions with a sense of exhausted well-being. It was like he'd known what I was contemplating and understood both where I was coming from and why it wasn't a good idea right now. I was emotionally worn out and had had too much wine to make rational decisions and was glad that he'd made this one for me.

"Goodnight," I replied, smiling gratefully down at him before I walked over to the record player and turned it off, silence filling the room.

***

The next morning I was awoken by the sound of voices. Frowning, I rolled out of bed and wrapped myself in a robe before padding out to see who Wren was talking to. He was alone. A voice was coming from the cell phone laying on the coffee table, the strident, Germanic accent harsh against my newly roused ears.

"I've heard of zem but have never seen one in ze flesh before," said the voice. I guessed that it belonged to Hans Müller and hurried to the kitchen to get some coffee. I didn't want to miss anything the watch expert had to say.

As I poured half and half into my cup, I heard Wren ask, "Are they rare?"

"Och, yes. Zey are very rare. The Richard Mille RM50-01 Lotus is extremely expensive. Only the very wealthy can afford them. But the vatch you sent me is even more rare."

I had to listen hard to understand what Müller was saying. His German accent was very thick and it was very early but I mentally switched his use of 'z' with 'th' and 'v' with 'w'.

"Why? What makes it so rare?"

"It is a limited-edition model of the G-Sensor Tourbillion NTPT. The good news is that only thirty of them were made and only twelve were sold."

I felt a thrill run through me. Only twelve? That certainly narrowed down our list of suspects.

Müller continued. "There is a central register that is held on the owners that stops the watches from being stolen as no dealer would ever buy a watch that isn't properly registered."

My head spinning from all of the auto-translation I'd had to do on that sentence, I walked into the living room and sat on a side chair. Wren was stretched out on the couch with his head facing the other way and hadn't seen me come in. "How can we get out hands on that register?" he asked.

"Ah, my young friend. I have already acquired it and will email it to you straight away. When are you coming back to the library? The old woman they have put behind the desk is a harridan."

Wren laughed. "I'm not sure when I'll be back. I have some things to take care of down here and I don't know how long the situation will take to be resolved."

"And the young woman you talk so much about? Is she this 'situation' you speak of?"

I bit back a laugh, not wanting to embarrass Wren.

"She's a part of the situation, Hans, but not in the way you mean."

"Och, to be young and in love again. It feels like only yesterday that I—"

I must have made some kind of sound because Wren jerked against the couch and arched his neck, his face turning toward me. When his eyes caught mine, they opened wide and his cheeks instantly reddened.

"Sorry, Hans, I've got to go. Send the register and I'll talk to you soon. Thanks." He fumbled for the phone, tapping it wildly until the call was ended. "Uh, hey, Maya. D-did you sleep well? How long have you been sitting there?"

Unable to hold it in any longer, I laughed. "You should see the look on your face."

I hadn't thought it possible, but his cheeks and forehead blushed a deeper shade of red as he scrambled to a sitting position.

"You talk about me?" I asked him. "What do you say?"

He made a big show of arranging himself on the couch, placing a heel on the opposite knee and tugging down his pant leg, before answering. "Hans has a list of people who own the watch from the video and is sending it to me."

It wasn't an answer to my question but I figured it was all I was going to get so I let it go. "That's great."

Wren nodded. When his computer chimed with a new email, the transparent alacrity with which he turned his attention to it made me have to hide another smile in my coffee cup. He was so endearing when he was flustered.

His brow furrowing, he read the email, paraphrasing it for me. "Hans says that four of the twelve watch owners are famous sport celebrities and two are well-known actors. So that leaves us with six names to check out. He says it shouldn't be too hard to find them because the wealth and status needed to even be able to try one of those watches on narrows down the playing field immensely."

"Okay. So, we know that the killer is wildly affluent, which would make him either way overpriced or very skilled."

Rubbing his stubbled chin, Wren said, "I'm going to say he's very skilled because he's obviously practiced at making his kills look like accidents, which is harder than making them look like what they are: cold-blooded murder."

I sipped from my coffee cup, my mind working feverishly. "If he's managed to do this so often that he can afford a watch like that, there has to be some kind of profile on him somewhere."

Wren straightened. "Want me to hack into the CIA again and snoop around?"

"No." I shook my head. "I don't want to risk it. Let me contact a friend from college who works as a profiler for the Chicago PD. Lauren should be able to come up with something that will help us, especially since we have a list of six possible suspects."

As I stood to get my phone and send Lauren an email, I felt that distinctive jolt of investigative excitement that always hits me during my cases. It was the thrill of the hunt, the quiver of a predator nearing its prey. I was going to find this guy and make him pay for what he'd done to my father—and to me.

Chapter 7

I was looking forward to reaching out to Lauren. We'd been close in college, having met during an especially trying astronomy class. I took the class because I'd needed science credits and astronomy seemed the most interesting, while Lauren had taken the class because it was taught by a young, good-looking professor. And while her love life hadn't benefitted from the course—neither had my grade point average as the material proved impossible for a laymen like myself to learn or be interested in—Lauren and I had enjoyed a close friendship ever since.

After making dinner for Wren and myself that night, I got into a hot bath and soaked for a while before grabbing my phone, scrolling through my contacts until I found her name.

Hey! Long time! Can you give me a call tomorrow? I want to talk to you about something.

Immediately after sending the message, the blinking ellipses of her writing a reply appeared. Lauren must keep her phone close at hand.

Of course! I'm off duty at eleven. I think that's nine, your time. Working the night shift—ugh—but I'll give you a call!

I set my phone down and settled deeper into the water. My thoughts drifted from memories of Lauren to those of my dad, finally settling on current events. How was I ever going to be able to repay Wren for what he doing for me? He was going above and beyond the call of friendship and even though, in the back of my brain, I thought that he would be very happy should our relationship progress from friends to something more, I wondered how such a progression would work.

He lived almost five hours away and was almost as busy as I was. How would we ever find the time for each other? My parents had done it. My dad had met my mother while on a business trip in France and while he'd been something of a workaholic his whole life, they'd still been able to find happiness with each other, producing both me and my older brother before moving back to the U.S. and seeking the elusive American dream together.

Dunking my head under the warm, sudsy water, I resolved not to think about it right now. It was fun to idly consider what a relationship with Wren would be like but in reality, there was too much up in the air for me to even think about starting up something with him. *Deal with one thing at a time,* I counseled myself as I came up for air. *First up: Dad's murder.*

***

I decided to leave a little bit early and walk to work the next morning. I wanted extra time to collect my thoughts before Lauren called me at nine and needed the exercise; I generally ran or did yoga a couple of times a week but having a house-guest had thrown off my usual schedule, so I added sneakers to my work attire and set off down the street, the streetlamps just starting to turn off in acknowledgement of the rising sun.

Even though I waded through knee-deep fog, I enjoyed climbing up and down the hilly terrain, veering off to trot up stairs and picking my pace up to a light jog on the downhill slopes. I was breathing heavily but feeling good by the time I stopped in front of my law firm's building. Taking a moment to stretch, I checked the time on my phone and saw that I had an hour and a half before my call with Lauren. Perfect.

The morning was spent as the day before had been, languishing amid piles of paperwork and legal briefs, and I was grateful when the mental alarm I'd set went off and I excused myself to get ready for Lauren's call.

I entered my office and closed the door, making sure to pull the blinds over the large pane of glass that occupied the center of it, as it helped keep noise from coming in and—more importantly—going out. Sitting behind my desk, I arranged a pad full of bullet-pointed notes I'd taken in front of me and reviewed them until my phone vibrated with an incoming call.

Lauren's ebullient voice rang in my ear. "Maya! It was so good to hear from you!"

I smiled. "I can't tell you how nice it is to hear your voice. How are things with you?"

"Oh, they're how they always are. Hot child in the city, and all that."

Laughing, I finished the chorus line. "I haven't heard that song in forever! Who sang it again?"

"Nick Gilder. It figures that you wouldn't know seeing as you only ever listen to Pink Floyd."

I could hear sirens sound off in the background and pictured Lauren walking down the crowded, bustling streets of Chicago, doing a good imitation of the "running wild" part of the lyrics. "Hey, I listen to other stuff. Just not one-hit-wonders from the eighties."

"You're missing out," she said with a laugh. "So, what did you want to talk to me about?"

"Are you sure this is a good time?" The noise in the background made it hard to hear her and I didn't want to have to shout. "I can call you later if you need some time to get home—"

"No, I'm just walking to the coffee shop I always stop at after work. Here it is."

I could hear the tinkle of a door topped with a bell being opened, and a chorus of hailed greetings replaced the sounds of traffic. I waited while she ordered, a tall black coffee and bagel, and took a seat.

"Okay, now we can talk. Sorry about that. I need one last shot of caffeine before I go home and crash for eight hours. So, what's up?"

I told her everything. The video, the blackmail, finding out who Peter Gilmore was, and our latest intel of the expensive watch.

Lauren whistled. "He hacked into the CIA? Does he need a job? I would love to have him on hand here in Chicago."

"Wren's all mine," I replied. It wasn't until the words dropped from my mouth that I realized how they sounded but it was too late to take them back.

Lauren sucked in a deep breath. "Oh, it's like that, is it?"

Vehemently shaking my head, I said, "No, it isn't. I didn't mean to say it like that."

"Maya, I do this for a living. You have the hots for him. I can hear it in your voice." I started to protest but she overrode me. "But that doesn't matter right now. What does matter is that you're dealing with a professional hitman. Tell me more about the video. His posture and dress, how he moves. Anything you can think of."

I told her everything that came to mind, spending the next five minutes recounting every nuance of the video, adding that I had a list of six possible suspects.

"Give me the names."

I rattled them off, saying that we'd done an initial search on them but hadn't been able to come up with much.

"Hmm. That tells us something right there." Lauren's voice was thoughtful, and I could picture her thinking, her dark hair falling over one eye like it had always done during our study sessions.

"What do you mean?"

"Your man Wren can hack into the CIA and find out the boxer size of a complete stranger but can't find anything on these six people? That means something. We already know they're rich, because they own that watch, but now we know they are *exceedingly* rich. It's only the very very wealthy who are able to cover their tracks well enough that they leave no technological trail to follow. Which means that the man who killed your father is really good at his job."

I rubbed my forehead with the tips of my fingers. "Which is going to make him really hard to find."

"We'll see about that. Give me a couple of hours to come up with a profile. It will help us narrow down the suspects."

I immediately felt bad about taking up time Lauren needed to rest after her long night shift. "Don't worry about that today. Go home and rest."

"You kidding? How am I supposed to be able to sleep knowing that you've got a hitman on your hands? I'll get something to you in a few hours."

"Thank you, Lauren. This means a lot to me."

"Yeah, well, you did let me cheat off your astronomy homework. It's the least I can do."

"Cheating off my homework almost made you fail the class," I reminded her.

"Oh, yeah. Well, it's a good thing that I'm doing the homework this time then. Talk to you soon."

"Bye."

I ended the call and sat back in my office chair, feeling a strange mixture of relief and obligation. Knowing how good Lauren was at her job, I felt like the list of potential suspects was in good hands—but at the same time knowing how many other responsibilities those hands had to juggle made me feel like I was taking advantage of our friendship. I resolved to take some vacation days and go visit Lauren in Chicago the first chance I got. I'd assuage my guilt by forcing her to listen to Pink Floyd for hours on end and plying her with good wine. I smiled at the thought and stood, ready to join my colleagues and get back to work before my brain got too distracted with waiting to hear from Lauren.

The day passed slowly. I kept checking my phone, looking for texts or emails from her, but when there was no new correspondence by four o'clock, I decided she'd probably dropped from exhaustion and I might not hear back today.

I walked home, breathing in the Indian summer warmth—along with a healthy dose of car exhaust—and thinking about what to prepare for dinner. Feeling a little bit put upon, what with having to work and dealing with a professional assassin, I'd decided on left-over spaghetti when I felt my phone start vibrating. I checked the screen and saw that it was Lauren. Ducking into the nearest shop to escape the traffic noise, I answered the call.

"Maya, sorry about taking so long. I told you that it was going to be hard checking up on these people but I didn't think it'd be *that* hard."

"It's okay, Lauren. I didn't expect to hear from you until you had a chance to get some sleep anyway."

"Oh, there's been no sleep for me today. I went back to the office after we talked earlier so I could log into our search engine and use it to track these people down."

I opened my mouth to apologize for taking up so much of her time but she anticipated me.

"You know how much I love this kind of thing, Maya. Put me on the hunt and I'm a very happy woman. So don't apologize and don't go on about how much you appreciate everything I do for you. You can save that for later—believe me, I'll be expecting it after you learn what I found out today."

I moved through the store, which turned out to be an antique shop, and pretended to browse. "Tell me everything," I said, my voice low. The proprietor, who had been watching me suspiciously, seemed to be satisfied when I started eyeing overpriced chaise lounges appreciatively.

"Okay, so I'll start with how I profiled the hitman. I figure this guy is highly skilled, an experienced professional who's been doing this for a while. He can manipulate the environments and circumstances of his targets so as to create the perfect murder without raising suspicion, making the deaths look like accidents. He thinks a lot of himself, based upon his decision to buy a six-figure watch. He believes he can't be caught, which tells us that he thinks of himself as highly intelligent and above the law, which points toward a god complex. He has no close friends or relatives, no girlfriends, boyfriends, or spouses.

"He's technically gifted and has a high brain function. He can work meticulously, down to the most minacious of details. That's the profile I put together."

Here, Lauren paused, as though unsure of what to say next. When she continued, I felt a sinking feeling in my stomach as I fingered the price tag of a Tiffany's lamp.

"He's going to be extremely difficult to find, even harder to catch. He'll always have to live under a false identity. Based upon my profile, I was able to narrow the list down. One of the names was married with kids, one of them was recently incarcerated for drug charges, and two are high profile businessmen whose lives are so well documented on social media that there is no way they could be moonlighting as killers. That leaves us with two. And let me be clear, these were only *exterior* names, like the names actors assume when they take on a role. Finding out their real names is what took me so long."

"Lauren, you're amazing," I said, meaning every word. I was so lucky to have the brightest minds in their fields as friends.

"I know. So, the first name is a guy with a main address in L.A. who works in the tech industry but moves around erratically between the three different houses he owns in three different countries. He has no fixed schedule and a private jet." She snorted. "Must be nice. Anyway, the second guy was even more difficult to pin down. He has an address in Mexico and, from the looks of it, even more money than the L.A. guy. Now I didn't find out as much about him as I did the other one, as crossing international borders is not something that's easy to do from the offices of the Chicago PD, but I did get the picture from his U.S. passport and I'll send that to you after we get off the phone." Lauren sighed loudly. "So, that's what I've got for you, my friend. What's your plan?"

I shook my head. "I don't know. I guess I'm going to have to ask for time off of work, which won't be easy because I'm in the middle of a big case—"

Lauren interrupted me. "Why do you need time off work?"

"So I can chase these two guys down," I replied, in a tone that implied how obvious my answer was. "I can't do that while I'm working full time and—"

She cut me off again. "Chase these two guys down? Are you insane? By plan, I meant which law enforcement agency you were going to take this evidence to, not what you were going to do personally. Maya, you cannot go after these guys. They are incredibly dangerous."

I threw my free hand up into the air, exasperated. I heard the shopkeeper inhale sharply, as though worried I was going to knock something over, so I moderated my tone as I shot him a reassuring look. "You expect me to take this flimsy evidence to the police? To the FBI? And say what? That I'm working off hunches and a profile, though constructed by a professional, that's mostly based off conjecture and guesswork? It won't fly, Lauren, and you know it. They'll take one look at my theory and laugh in my face. My father's death was categorized as an accident and no one is going to be willing to say otherwise based on what I've managed to gather so far. I need concrete evidence. Incontrovertible facts." I took a deep breath, trying to slow my racing heartbeat.

"I know how much this means to you, Maya," Lauren said, her voice gentle. "And I'm not trying to downplay the importance of finding your father's killer. I'm not. The only thing I'm saying is that you can't—*shouldn't* do this yourself."

I looked at the floor. Lauren knew that telling me I couldn't do something was like waving a red flag at a bull, but I could hear the care and concern in her voice and knew she was only looking out for me. "I won't be doing this alone," I said. "And even if I was, I can look out for myself."

She sighed. "I know you can. You're a badass bitch and woe to anyone who stands in your way. It's just that...if anything happened to you based off information I gave you, I would never forgive myself. I wish I could fly out west and help you."

Nodding, I started moving toward the door, figuring I'd worn out my welcome in the antique store. The shopkeeper was watching me closely, his hands on his hips and a scowl on his face.

"I wish you could too," I said, stalling by the entrance, wanting to finish the conversation before going out to the street and its accompanying noise. "But, I've got Wren and he's pretty formidable." I blinked. I'd never thought of him that way before but having said it aloud, I suddenly knew it to be true. He was a force of nature wrapped in an unassuming package.

"He'd better be," Lauren said, defeat plain in her voice. "Just promise me you'll be careful, Maya."

"I promise," I said. "Talk to you soon, Lauren." I ended the call and pushed the shop door open, uncrossing my fingers as I stepped out onto the street.

Chapter 8

"So our list has been narrowed down to two?" Wren scratched his chin, his nails scraping against stubble. We were seated at our command center, boxes of Chinese takeout scattered over the coffee table.

"Did you bring a razor?" I asked. He'd always been clean shaven before and seeing the uneven growth of hair on his chin and jawline made me understand why.

Ducking his head into his shoulders, he assumed a sheepish expression. "No, I forgot. And I've been so wrapped up in our case that I haven't really thought about it."

Our case. I forced back a smile at hearing those words. I'd always been a bit of a loner, always keeping to myself so I could do things my way without having to worry about agreeing to a consensus for every decision. Maybe it was years of taking commands in the Marines, but the rest of my adult life had been spent making my own decisions, accepting the consequences of them, and being grateful for the ability to do both.

"I'll pick some up the next time I go out," I said. "I doubt you want to use my pink ones."

Wren shrugged. "I don't mind. I've been meaning to ask you if I can use one but keep forgetting."

I lifted one of my legal pads, scribbling notes covering the yellow surface. "Back to our case." I felt the thrill of being part of a team again. "How do you propose we figure out which of the two is our killer?"

"I think we should focus on the guy from L.A. first, since he's closer."

I bit my lower lip. "Yeah, but he's an international traveler. He could be anywhere."

"So, we'll start by researching his jet and the airport he keeps it in. From there, we find out who his pilot is and whether or not he's available. Officials keep registers about the different certified pilots who fly private planes in and out of their airports—that's mandatory. If the pilot is available for an immediate departure, then we'll know the guy is in L.A. If not, then he's elsewhere and maybe the flight plan the pilot turned in will include the final destination."

"That sounds good." It seemed like a lot of conjecture and luck would be needed for us to nail down the pilot and I hated relying on luck, but I didn't want to pile a lot of negative weight on Wren. Being helpful and supportive is one of the most important aspects of being a good member of a team—which is why I always tried to avoid them. Patience isn't a virtue I'm known for. I couldn't help but poke holes in Wren's plan—but they were tiny ones. "What if this guy has his own private airfield? Doesn't keep his plane at an airport willing to give out information?"

Digging his nails into his cheek, Wren pursed his lips in thought. "Well, there are other ways to get what we need. I could contact his landscape team. They usually know when owners are in residence and are willing to share that information for the right price."

"What if he doesn't live in a place that needs landscaping? He could live in a building like this one." I gestured at our surroundings.

"If he's rolling in money, he wouldn't be staying at a place like this."

I narrowed my eyes. "Oh, really? A place like this, huh?"

Wren snatched a chopstick out of the fried rice container and whirled it between his fingers, avoiding my gaze. "You know what I mean. This isn't exactly the Ritz."

"Would you prefer a luxury suit in the Plaza up the street?" I asked sweetly. "I'm sure room service and mints on your pillow would be available there."

His cheeks blazed red. "No, that's not what I meant. I'm just saying—"

Laughing, I interrupted him. "Calm down. I'm just joking. I know what you mean. Lauren gave me his address and it's a huge house in a pricey residential neighborhood outside the city, in the hills. Checking out landscape companies that service that area is a great idea."

"Thank you," he said on an exhale. "For a second there, I thought you were going to kick me out."

"And miss out on the pleasure of your company? No way." I bumped my shoulder against his. "We're a team. And I should be the one thanking you for everything you've been doing for me. I don't think I've done that often enough."

He smiled at me, dimples creasing into his furry cheeks. "No, you haven't. But I'm willing to let it slide. So," he held his hand out for my pad and I handed it over, "let's get started. I'll cross reference his name with the make and model of his jet and see if I can't find out where he keeps it. From there, I'll contact the airport and make some inquiries. Sound good?"

I nodded. "Yep. What do you want me to do?"

"You can start looking up the landscape companies that work in his area, just in case I don't come up with anything on my end."

We worked in silence, the living room slowly darkening as the evening wore on. I got up to turn the lights on and glanced at the clock on a nearby mantel.

"Oh my goodness! It's almost eleven. What do you say we call it a night?" Time had slipped away from me, as it always seemed to do when I worked in companionable silence next to Wren.

Stretching his arms over his head, Wren nodded in agreement. "Sounds good. I think I've found the airport where he keeps his jet but I won't be able to talk to anyone until tomorrow anyway. I didn't realize it was that late."

"Time flies when you're having fun," I said as I started toward my bedroom. "You're not going to crash on the couch again, are you? It makes me feel bad, like I'm working you so hard you just pass out wherever you happen to be."

He bounced up and down. "This is a comfy couch. And I stay up pretty late working and don't want to wake you walking down the hall and stumbling into the guest room. Don't worry about me."

I nodded. "Okay, then. Good night, Wren."

"Night, Maya."

Something hung unspoken in the air between us. I could feel it as I walked out of the living room and into the hallway toward the bedrooms. I felt as though I could make out what it was that wanted—needed—to be said if I concentrated hard enough, but shied away from doing so. Feeling like a broken record, I reminded myself that this was quite possibly the worst time in my entire life to start a new relationship. And besides, he wasn't even my type.

Entering my bedroom, I sat on the bed and thought about my track record so far, with guys who were "my type." It wasn't great. But before I could beat myself over the head with past lovers and the could've, would've, should'ves, that accompanied them, I slipped out of my clothes and into my pajamas.

"Go to sleep, Maya," I whispered to myself after turning out the lights and tucking into bed. Some time later, I did.

***

I did something I hated doing the next day: I took a personal day from work. It was a necessary evil—although Wren didn't see it that way.

"It's about time! I kind of expected you'd be taking more time off to work on our case." Wren was downing coffee like the world was running out, his couch-rumpled hair sticking out in every direction.

"That's the thing. I have two cases I'm working on, not just *our* case." I pulled my own hair, damp from the shower, back into a ponytail. "It would be really selfish and irresponsible of me to take more time off just because of what's going on in my personal life. My clients depend on me to see justice done in their name."

To my surprise, Wren rolled his eyes. "You sound like a self-righteous superhero, Maya. The world will keep turning without you spinning it on your finger and there are other lawyers who are just as eager to sue a big company for millions of dollars as you are."

I glowered at him. "Money has nothing to do with it."

"Really? I think that money has everything to do with it, in this case. After the company offered a settlement, that was it. Case closed. There was no jail time for the CEO or COO, they just got slapped on the wrist and told to pay up. How is that justice?"

While the emotional part of me wanted to yell at Wren, remind him that he wasn't a lawyer and had no idea how the legal system worked, the rational side of my brain agreed with him. Since when did paying out money equate to punishment? My clients, especially those who had loved ones die, would probably have preferred that the bigwigs from AME go to jail over a payout.

Sighing, I smoothed stray strands of hair back from my forehead and nodded. "You're right. I'm just a little cog in a big wheel that may or may not represent fair play or integrity. It's not a big deal if I take a few days off of work."

"Don't get me wrong," Wren said, offering me his coffee cup in an act of *mea culpa*. When I shook my head, he continued, "It's not that I don't think you're a vital member of your firm. It's just that I think you're taking on too much, concerning yourselves with other people when you should be focused on yourself—for once in your life."

"Have you been talking to my mother?" I asked, my eyes narrowed in suspicion. That last statement sounded exactly like something she would say.

He chuckled and shook his head. "So, what do we have planned for the day?"

Even though he evaded my question better than any expert witnessed I'd ever cross-examined, I played along. "You've got to call the airport and I've got to track down Los Angeles Landscaping, Inc." Yesterday I'd discovered the company that did all the landscaping for our suspect's neighborhood, so today I'd call the owners and see if they could give me some information about his travel habits and whether or not he was currently in residence. "After that, based on what we find, we should plan on being mobile today. Either going to the airport to follow up or doing a drive-by of his house. Then, we should think about next steps, what our plan is if he is in L.A. right now."

"Right," Wren said with an officious nod, straightening from his comfortable seated position on the couch. "Then we'll go back to the bat cave and see if we can't get Jeeves to work on our spidey suits." He caught my eye and leaned back against the couch, laughing and slapping his thigh. "I'm sorry. You're just so efficient and capable. If there *were* superheroes among us, you'd definitely be one of them."

"You got Spiderman and Batman mixed up," I said, playfully kicking out at him.

He dodged my kick and stood. "I could never keep them straight. They were both traumatized by creepy crawlies but never gained any cool powers, not like Superman or Flash."

Crossing my arms over my chest, I cocked my head at him. "Tell me the truth, how many Comic-Cons have you gone to?"

He shook his head. "If I told you, I'd have to kill you."

I snorted. "Okay. We've gone way off course here so why don't you call the airport and I'll call the landscapers." Still shaking my head, I walked toward the kitchen, where I'd left my phone when I'd toasted some bread after my shower. I could hear Wren chuckling as I walked away and ignored the warm feeling blossoming in my chest. *He's insufferable*, I told myself as I grabbed my phone. *Absolutely and totally...* my thoughts trailed off as I checked my messages.

Maya, call me ASAP

It was from Lauren.

When I called her, she was breathless, as though she'd just finished a run.

"Hey, Maya," this was followed by a series of deep breaths. "Sorry, the elevator in my building is out and I just finished climbing six flights of stairs. I need to work out more."

"Don't we all," I said, looking at the loaf of thick brioche bread I'd cut slices from this morning. "What's up?"

"The guy in L.A. isn't the guy."

I frowned in confusion. "Isn't the guy?" I repeated. What with her heavy breathing and her cryptic word choice, I wanted to confirm what I thought she was saying.

"No. I mean, yes. He isn't."

"Okay, you're going to have to explain that a little better."

"I did a little digging on him, figuring that since he was U.S. based I'd have a better chance of finding more information on him. And I found hospital records stating that he was diagnosed with cancer seven years ago."

"Seven years ago...so he would've gotten the diagnosis a year before my dad's death. But that doesn't mean that he couldn't have been the killer."

"The records kept track of his treatment schedule. He was deep into chemo at the time of your father's murder. It was all kept hush hush because he'd always been a fitness fanatic and didn't want anyone to know that Mr. Healthy had gotten cancer just like the rest of us do. I mean, his lifestyle must have meant something because his cancer has been in remission ever since, but I'm thinking that being able to throw tons of money at the problem certainly helped too."

I'd been leaning against the kitchen counter and pushed off with my hip upon hearing this latest news, intent on telling Wren he didn't have to call the airport after all. "Thanks, Lauren. Narrowing it down to one suspect is really going to—"

"Let the authorities handle it, Maya." Lauren's voice was heavy with intent, as well as breath. "Don't try and cowboy this thing."

I rolled my eyes. "Yes, mom."

"Don't give me that attitude. You know exactly what I'm talking about. Remember when we found out that girl down the hall from us had been date raped at a frat party? Remember what you did? If not, let me refresh your memory. Instead going through the proper channels, like telling the dean or the police, you found the guy and beat the living crap out of him."

I smiled at the memory. "It wasn't just me. Those guys from the football teamed helped."

"But you organized it, Maya. You have got to be careful. Please?"

"Yes. I'll be careful. Where in Mexico is our guy supposed to be living?"

Lauren sighed before saying, "Chetumal. Near the border, by Belize."

"Thanks, Lauren. I've got to go. I'll talk to you later." I was energized by the knowledge that we'd narrowed our suspects down from twelve to one and didn't want to talk or be chastised any longer.

I strode out to the living room, mentally starting a packing list. I'd have to look into what airline laws said about flying with guns in your checked luggage; I was a little rusty on my international law but I didn't think it was allowed, unfortunately. I wasn't planning on using a weapon—but it'd be nice to have on hand.

"Pack your bags," I stated upon entering the living room. "We're going to Mexico."

Wren, who had his phone next to his ear, held up a finger, asking me to wait while he listened to the voice on the other end of the line.

Shaking my head, I walked over and plucked his phone from his hand, ending the call with a decisive poke of my finger. "Sorry," I said, handing him his phone back, "but that was a dead-end. I'll explain later."

His mouth opening and closing, shock making it hard for him to form words, Wren sat on the couch, staring up at me. Unmoving.

I slapped my hands together. "What are you waiting for? You wanted a vacation, right? So let's go get one." My gaze left his, my eyes seeking the middle distance, the place where my violent past waited. "Let's go hunting."

Chapter 9

"What do you mean, go hunting? Like, for deer?"

I smiled to myself, thinking about Wren's response to my enigmatic statement concerning going after the assassin. Now, tucked into my first-class seat, a glass of champagne in my hand and an open tabloid magazine on my lap, the memory was humorous; however, during the hours it had taken to convince Wren that flying to Mexico in search of a hitman was something I should do, our conversation had been anything but funny.

He'd alternated between accusing me of being criminally reckless and dangerously irresponsible. "We don't even know for sure that he's the man who killed your father!" he'd shouted, raking his fingers through his hair. "This could be nothing but a wild goose chase."

"He's the last suspect on our list," I'd pointed out. "A list supplied by *your* informant, I might add."

"A list of people who own watches! That's it! *Your* friend in Chicago is the one who got you so hot and heavy to chase after these people who could be guilty of nothing but buying an expensive watch."

"And the fact that my father's killer was wearing one of those watches means nothing? Suddenly it's a piece of evidence that doesn't matter?" By this time, my hard outer shell had started to crack, the tension of the past few weeks getting to me. My voice had faltered as I said, "You're supposed to be on my side, Wren. We're supposed to be in this together."

Seeing the raw emotion on my face, Wren had dropped his own into his hands, rubbing his forehead with the tips of his fingers. "I just don't want you to get hurt, Maya. I don't know what I'd do if something happened to you." The pain in his voice and posture had been evident. And when he'd raised his head, saying, "I'd never forgive myself if you got hurt or...or killed," I felt the sincerity in his voice and knew that if we continued down this conversational path, things might be said that neither of us were ready to say yet.

"Then come with me," I'd said, pausing in my pacing the living room to sit beside him. "Come with me and keep me safe." Tilting my head, I tried to inject some playfulness into the moment. "Maybe on the way back we can stop at the nearest superhero convention and get some of your favorite comic books. My treat."

When he groaned and threw himself into the back cushion of the couch, I'd known the deal was done. Now, sitting beside him as we were whisked away to the southeastern coast of Mexico, I wondered at his relative willingness to be talked into this venture. He could've just as easily provided support from San Francisco; maybe been an even bigger asset from our command center than he would be with me on the ground. As far as I knew, he had no experience in the field. How would that affect the outcome of our mission? Because that's how I viewed this endeavor, as a mission to be executed with the utmost discretion and caution—and I was the perfect woman for the job. Wren...I was undecided.

"Hey, do you think the latest *Top Gun* is as good as the original?" Wren asked, gesturing at the large screen tucked into the back of the seat in front of him, where fighter jets were zipping around at breakneck speed. "I think it is. And Cruise barely looks like he's aged a day. I wonder if he's had work done."

I shook my head. Definitely undecided.

When we landed at the airport in Chetumal, I stepped off the plane and took a deep breath. You can always tell you're outside of the U.S. by the smells. Southeast Asia smells of rotting fruit and verdant vegetation, the Middle Eastern countries smells of exhaust and dry sand, and Mexico smells of spices and, sorry to say, garbage. The country has never really been able to get a handle on its sanitation; I'd visited several times and there was always a pervasive smell of overfull dumpsters baking in the sun. But that never stopped me from returning every chance I got; I loved the culture and the food, the history and the colorful people. I just wished I was visiting under different circumstances.

We got through customs and hailed a cab to the Airbnb I'd picked out as our headquarters. It was close to where the killer lived without being too close, and had fast Wi-Fi so I could keep in contact with Nancy and Tim, who hadn't been thrilled to hear I would be traveling for a few days. But, I'd used the time-honored "family emergency" excuse, which is universally understood as the polite way of saying "I'm going to be gone for a few days and I don't want to talk about why."

After dropping our bags off, we got into the small two-door car that was for guest use and drove to the remote beachside village outside Chetumal, where the hitman lived. His house was far removed from the main part of the rural town, down a muddy dirt road that weaved through thick jungle. Wren, using a satellite mapping app on his phone, guided me past grazing goats and random herds of free-range cattle, until we reached the end of the road—a razor-wire-topped gate that blocked the way.

"The pin is dropped about a mile away, right next to the ocean," Wren said, pointing ahead. "We're going to have to walk from here."

I nodded thoughtfully. This initial trip was purely for reconnaissance but now that we were so close, I wanted to continue, to get even closer. "Did you wear your hiking shoes?" I asked, still peering out the windshield at the ominous-looking gate. The barbed-wire fence on either side was overgrown with vines and wide-spreading bushes. We'd have to lay something over the top of the fence to climb over it without getting slashed to pieces from either the wire or the sharp-leafed vegetation.

Wren lifted a shod foot in response. "And I even brought bug spray. I was an Eagle Scout and we always come prepared."

"An Eagle Scout, huh?" I said, looking over at him appraisingly. "What else did you bring?"

He hauled a Camelbak backpack from the space behind our seats and unzipped it, listing the contents. "Flashlight, matches, water purification tablets, granola bars, first aid kit, and some rope."

My eyes widened. "I'm impressed. Got anything like a bazooka or sniper rifle tucked in there?"

Assuming an aggrieved expression, Wren shook his head. "They confiscated my rocket launcher at customs. Sorry."

"Bummer," I said with a laugh. "That would've come in handy."

"Are we really going to do this?" he asked, turning in his seat to face me. The hot sun beamed through his window and darkened the recessed of his face, making him look older and stern, as though he had miraculously aged twenty years in a single second.

I nodded. I thought about going into how surprise was our greatest weapon, how time was of the essence, how fate favored the bold, but decided he'd see through all that macho crap. So, I stuck with nodding.

He nodded back and turned from me to open his door. Once outside, the humid heat was palpable, a thick blanket of hot moisture that settled on my skin and instantly made me break out in a sweat.

"Holy cow. This is unreal," he said, wiping his forehead with the back of his wrist. "This must be what hell feels like."

"This is nothing," I said, softy closing my door and walking around to the front of the car. "You should feel what summer in Afghanistan is like. This is balmy compared to that." I inspected the gate, looking for electric wires or some kind of indication that the fence was electrified.

"What are you thinking?" Wren asked softly, looking from me to the fence.

"I'm thinking that this is *supposed* to look overgrown and decrepit." I pointed to the concrete pillars holding the gate up. "Look at those. Those are steel-enforced slabs of concrete. They wouldn't be left alone for the vegetation to slowly tear down." I shook my head, squinting. "And look at that spot where the wire connects to the pillar. You see that?"

Wren shook his head. "All I can see are steel wires." Rubbing his eyes, he looked away from them towards me. "The sun keeps glinting off them and making my eyes hurt."

"Exactly," I said with a nod. "There's no way that they wouldn't be just as covered as everything else—unless they're routinely cleaned off to ensure a good connection."

"Connection? Oh, you mean like an electrical connection?"

"We're going to have to follow the fence to the ocean and swim around it. There's no other way." I looked at Wren. "You can swim, right?"

"You're looking at a high school champion water polo star. I even did a little bit of competitive swimming in college. So, yeah," Wren shrugged into his backpack, "I can swim."

"Let's go then."

The trek through the jungle wasn't as bad as I'd feared it would be. Whoever kept the encroaching plants from covering the electrical connections also frequently cleared a path for the fence, with several feet of clearance on either side making for a decent trail to follow. The whine of mosquitoes and the caw of jungle birds was the only sound we heard as we made our way toward the ocean. Soon, I could smell the sea in the air, the tang of salt and the heavier smell of rotting seaweed telling me we were getting closer.

"Almost there," I said. From my position in the lead, I couldn't see how Wren was fairing but from his muttered curses and the occasional slap of hands hitting skin, I thought maybe he'd overexaggerated his Eagle Scout skills.

"You said that ten minutes ago," he replied, grumpily.

"Well, I mean it this time," I said, pushing aside errant branches and revealing a landscape of tawny sand and green water.

The fence stopped once it reached the sand, leaving the beach clear.

"He must be worried about storm tides taking the fence out to sea," I noted, peering past the edge of the thick vegetation, following the shoreline until I saw an imposing house in the distance. Our killer's house was staggering; at least three stories tall, each floor having a wrap-around porch that offered awe-inspiring views of the ocean. It reminded me of the classic architectural style once found in Florida, verandas wrapped by white railing and carved banisters leaning over aged wooden porches that offered breezy retreats from the sun.

"Wow," said Wren on an exhale.

"Yeah," I agreed.

I didn't see how we were going to get close without being spotted. The landscaping around the house consisted of carefully mowed grass that didn't allow for any covered ingress, spotted with bushes pruned into different geometric shapes. There was an Olympic-sized pool at the rear of the house that was lined with coconut trees, but the trunks were spindly and would offer no shelter or concealment. At the front of the mansion was a dock that jutted out into the ocean and broke the expanse of turquoise water with moored jet skis, a large white boat with two motors sticking out the back, and a majestic yacht that took up over half of the dock's length. *This guy likes his toys*, I thought, eyeing the collection.

"All of this he got from killing people?" Wren asked, mirroring my inner musings. "Do you think he kills a lot or gets paid a lot for the people he kills?"

"I don't know, but I hope to find out," I said resolutely. I was about to suggest that we go for a walk down the beach, two people just enjoying the beautiful weather and the sand beneath their feet, but I heard the sound of a motor approaching. I couldn't tell whether it came from air, land, or sea but it was definitely getting closer.

We ducked back into the cover of the vegetation, just inside the edge of the divide between jungle and beach, and searched for the source of the noise. Soon, we saw it. A helicopter cruised in from the north, coming from the same direction we had. It slowed, its rotors beating rhythmically as it hovered in place.

"What's it doing?" I mumbled, ducking down and craning my neck to look up at the helicopter through the trees.

"That's where we left the car," Wren whispered. "He must've spotted it from the air."

I cursed vehemently, causing Wren to look my way in surprise. Once he'd shaken off his shock, he grabbed my arm and started pulling me in the direction of our waiting car. "Come on. We've got to get out of here."

"No, we have to wait." I jerked my arm out of his grip.

"Wait for what?"

"Wait for the helicopter to land so we can see what this guy looks like."

The chopper continued on its journey, nose down as it proceeded toward the house.

"Are you crazy? We can't wait here. Once the chopper lands and the killer gets out, the first thing he's going to do is send someone out to check on the mysterious car parked outside of his gate." Wren was almost shouting to be heard over the rotor beats of the helicopter.

I shook my head. "It's the end of a road that parallels a beach. I'm sure people are always coming down here hoping to get beach access and I'm sure those same people get out of their cars and search for it when they realize it's a dead end. This is Mexico, Wren, not the Hamptons."

He opened his mouth to reply, the scowl on his face letting me know what he was about to say wasn't going to be pleasant, but I shushed him before he could. The chopper had landed and a man was stepping from it, his clothes whipping around his slim body in the downwash.

There he is. I memorized everything about him, knowing that this glimpse was going to be brief and probably the only one I'd get on this trip, unless something miraculous happened. He was tall and fit; I could see the definition in his arms through his lightweight linen sleeves and the unpredictable air currents caught the hem of his shirt, lifting it and showing the rigid lines of his abdominal muscles. The sunglasses on his face were stylish and large, covering most of the upper portion of his face but I memorized the cut of his jawline and how his dark hair fell against his high forehead. On his wrist was the expensive watch that had led us to him; I silently thanked it for being the giveaway that had brought me face-to-face with my father's killer. Without it, and the help of Wren and his contact, I wouldn't be here, staring this man, this assassin, in the face.

Wren's hand close around my arm and I looked over at him. It wasn't until I saw the concerned look on his face that I realized I had risen into a crouch, as though ready to sprint away and tackle the hitman. I nodded reassuringly, dropping back down into a resting position as I faced forward again.

The helicopter was lifting off, the man who'd disembarked walking casually toward his house. Too casually, I thought. He was walking slowly, his head moving side to side as though he were listening to music. Suddenly, he jerked his head toward us and Wren and I flinched back in unison. He didn't pause, didn't let on that he'd seen us, just turned away and kept walking until he had stepped onto the veranda and entered a side door.

"Do you think he saw us?" Wren whispered, his breathing fast.

"I don't know. He was obviously looking for something." He was looking for the people who belonged to the car outside his property. For us. "Time to go," I said reluctantly. Part of me wanted to storm troop the house and let fate decide what happened next, but I couldn't let Wren follow me into harm's way and I knew he wouldn't stay behind if I decided to ambush the assassin. Not that it would be much of an ambush; the guy was obviously on alert.

We crabbed backward, staying under cover of the vegetation until we were well away from the beach and the open area surrounding the beachside mansion. As we walked, I followed Wren but my mind was far away, tracing every line of the hitman's face, every movement, his posture and bearing. I wanted to be able to find him again, should he change names and change locations.

"What do we do now?" Wren asked, slapping the back of his neck.

I reached out and wiped away the smear of blood his hand had left. "I was just thinking about that."

"And?"

I shrugged, though Wren was in front of me and couldn't see the motion. "I have no idea."

Wren was silent for a long moment before he said, "Your dad was a lawyer too, right?"

"Yes."

"Well, was he working on a case when he was murdered?"

I pursed my lips in thought. "It's been a long time...yes, I think he was working on a case that had to do with the mob." I slapped my forehead. "The mob! Why didn't I think about that before? Maybe they ordered the hit on my dad to stop the proceedings."

"The mob? They have the mob in California? I thought that was only a Chicago, New York type thing."

"Organized crime is everywhere, Wren." I snapped my fingers, feeling purpose and direction fill me with excitement. "I know exactly what we'll do next."

"Let me guess," Wren said, in a resigned tone. "We're going to talk to mobsters."

"Exactly," I said, mentally rubbing my hands together in anticipation.

Chapter 10

Our short trip to Mexico felt eerily like it had never happened when Wren and I stepped into my apartment, our carry-on bags hanging from our shoulders like dead weights. We had been on such a tight schedule, thanks to my work obligations, that the two days we had spent there had been mostly taken up with traveling, and I felt a certain nonplussed ennui come over me as I unpacked and put my clothes in the washing machine.

Maybe I'm just coming down with a bug, I thought as I dragged myself from my tiny laundry room back to my bedroom. I sat on my bed and stretched, working out kinks in my neck and shoulders as I wondered at my listlessness. I had been so full of enthusiasm after my mobster epiphany that even arguing for hours on end with Wren hadn't dampened it. Thinking of Wren and my duties as hostess made me feel guilty for hiding away in my bedroom but I wasn't quite feeling up to playing the part. Mostly, I just wanted to crawl under the covers and hide from all of the responsibilities and obligations that were always there, waiting for me.

So that's what I did. I put on a loose shirt and the softest, most worn pair of shorts I owned and tucked myself into bed.

Just a quick nap, I told myself. *That's all I need. Then, I'll be ready to...* sleep overtook me before I could finish the thought.

***

The man poured himself a finger of scotch, the Scottish blend he'd handpicked during his last trip to Edinburgh swirling in the cut crystal and filling his nose with notes of heather and barley. Christopher—as he now called himself—lifted the glass and held it to his nose before taking an appreciative sip, rolling the scotch over his tongue as his eyes drifted close. The job that had brought him to Edinburgh was still fresh in his mind; the brisk yet temperate breeze of the Scottish summer had made capsizing the mark's yacht ridiculously easy, child's play, even.

When the authorities found the drug lord's yacht overturned on the craggy shores of Loch Ness, they would see evidence of the craft having run up on submerged rocks and the inhabitants—those who hadn't been lost overboard in the "collision" that had been carefully planned and executed by Christopher using marine-capable power tools and waterproof explosives—the victims of the very same drugs they peddled.

"Play Alyth," he called out, agitating his scotch as he carried it to his office. He'd first heard the Scottish singer crooning folk music while in an Uber on his way to his temporary headquarters on the shores of Loch Ness and had instantly fallen in love with the way her voice had caressed the lyrics, ringing out even over the bagpipes that occasionally accompanied her.

Sitting in his desk chair, Christopher set down his drink and flipped through the new birth certificate and passport he'd just been issued. His trip to Scotland had been dual-purpose; he'd taken care of the drug dealer, as he'd been contracted to, and also had visited a cemetery filled with new identities just waiting to be assumed. The birth date of Christopher McLaughlin had been close enough to his own to suit his purposes—and he even liked the name. It had a certain sense of prideful nationalism that was always useful when it came to fictitious identification. Most would be instantly lulled into ease when they heard the name presented in a soft Scottish brogue.

The thought of being lulled brought to mind those two people he'd seen snooping around his property line earlier. The man had seemed nondescript, wearing a working-class backpack favored by hikers and reddened skin particular to tourists new to Mexico's climate. It was the woman who'd caught his attention; it had been impossible to feel at ease with her piercing, resolute stare focused on him. He was used to finding vehicles at the terminus of the main road to his home, even familiar with finding people using his private beach as their own secluded vacation spot, but he'd known from the first second he'd laid eyes on her that she was no casual tourist. Her intense observation had aroused his innate sense of self-preservation; he would have to be on alert for the foreseeable future, just in case she was intent on causing trouble.

What kind of trouble, he had no idea. Christopher McLaughlin would be ready for anything, as he always was, as he'd trained himself to be, no matter his name or nationality.

***

When I woke up it was dark. I blinked several times, confused as to where I was. When I saw the familiar outlines of my dresser and nightstand, I exhaled and turned over onto my back, laying a forearm over my eyes as I mentally went over all that had happened recently. I was home. We had just gotten back from our whirlwind trip to Mexico, where we'd found the assassin. The jolt of adrenaline that shot through me at the memory of the man's face, the self-assurance in his posture, swept away the last vestiges of tiredness and renewed my sense of purpose.

During my nap, I'd come up with the name of the mobster informant my father had been dealing with at the time of his death. Pushing the covers off, I swung my legs over the side of the bed and sat up, taking a moment to send a prayer of thanks to my dad for helping me remember Little John Esposito before standing.

A small cog in the mob machine, Little John was anything but. The stereotypical overweight, beady-eyed bad gangster who'd ingested too much chianti and pasta, Little John had been charged with second-degree manslaughter and greedily taken a plea-bargain deal that entailed him ratting on his confederates. My dad had been in charge of the case against the big wig Little John had said was the leader of the San Francisco chapter of the mob: Luca Rossi. When he'd died before the case could come to trial, Rossi had gone free and Little John had been sentenced to a prison term that, though shortened due to his cooperation, had still felt like an injustice to the corpulent gangster, and his hatred of the judicial system had blossomed into something feral.

Since my father's death had been deemed accidental, Rossi hadn't been under suspicion as having anything to do with it—even though he'd directly profited from my dad's demise as the case against him had been dropped shortly afterward. I only hoped that I would be able to sweet talk Little John into telling me something, anything, about Rossi's involvement; specifically, how—if—he'd hired a contract killer who liked expensive watches and private Mexican hideouts.

Now all I had to do was tell Wren about my plans. I tapped my phone and saw that it was after midnight. Growling deep in my throat, my excitement thwarted by the time, I flopped back on the bed. Little John would have to wait until morning.

When I woke up, my mouth tasted like iron and my eyes were gritty. Rubbing them clear, I swung my legs over the side of the bed and yawned. When I remembered my objective for the day, I felt an influx of energy course through my arms and legs; it was time to get some answers.

Since Wren was already aware of my intention to question a gangster, he didn't put up much of a fight when I told him that Little John Esposito was the man we were going to see. He hadn't heard of him—I guess the activities of the San Francisco mob didn't reach up far enough to make the newspapers in Landsfield Ridge—which I was relieved to know. The second-degree manslaughter charge Little John had been incarcerated for had been an especially nasty; it had involved a baseball bat and an insolvent businessman who hadn't wanted to pay his debts.

Glossing over the details, I hustled Wren into my car and drove to Baradra Correctional Facility, where Little John was incarcerated. The last thing I'd done before falling asleep the night before was to take a quick check of the prisoner rosters in San Francisco, which had revealed his location and the length of his sentence. The poor guy still had fifteen years to go...I tapped the steering wheel with my fingers as I waited for a traffic light to turn green. *If I could offer Little John a reduced sentence, I bet he would jump at the chance to tell me if his old boss had ordered the hit on my dad.* Whether or not I could actually produce that reduced sentence...well, one thing at a time.

"Are you nervous?" Wren asked, gesturing at my drumming fingers and pulling me from my thoughts of promises made and promises broken—and what had happened to the last person who had owed Little John something and hadn't delivered.

"Not really," I said. "Just ironing some things out in my head before we talk to Little John."

"I'm nervous," he said. "Do you need help with the ironing? It would help keep my mind off what we're about to do."

I shook my head. "There's nothing to worry about. All we're going to do is go and visit with a mobster informant who was imprisoned for murder. What's so scary about that?"

We looked at each other and burst out laughing. It sounded more than scary; it sounded insane.

Before long, we pulled into Baradra and went through the laborious security checks that started with checking underneath our vehicle for explosive devices and ended with being wanded and frisked for concealed weapons. My lawyer credentials kept me from getting questioned too closely, as those of my ilk were regular visitors at the jail, but Wren had to go into detail about his intentions and desire to speak with one of the inmates.

By the time we were seated at a round-cornered metal table that was bolted to the ground, I was feeling dangerously impatient, my jaws aching from having clenched them for the past forty-five minutes it had taken us to get here.

Wren turned his head to look at me, a self-possessed expression on his face. "So, do you have a plan of attack?"

I squinted at him. He seemed strangely at ease, as though he regularly spent his days reposing in prisoner visiting rooms. Before I could reply, a heavy door opened and Little John trudged into the room. It looked as though he'd lost weight during the time since his arraignment; folds of flesh hung around his neck and waist, flashes of white, sagging skin peeking out from beneath his loose-fitting, prison-issued blue shirt.

The guard escorting him secured him to the floor and table, the handcuffs on his wrists and ankles clinking against the metal enclosures as they were locked. We were yet again informed as to the rules before the guard left us to stand near the door, a bored expression on his face.

Little John sat, looking back and forth between Wren and me, his chapped lips pursed and his brows hanging low over his blood-shot brown eyes. "Well?" he asked, after a long silence. "What do you want?"

"I'm Maya Hartwell and Justin Thomas Hartwell was my father. Do you remember him?"

Little John shook his head, the flesh hanging from his chin swinging. "Nope."

"Try again," Wren suggested. His face and demeanor were non-committal but there was a threatening undertone in his voice that hinted at a violent ferocity and widened Little John's eyes.

"Let me think. What'd you say that name was again?"

I repeated my father's name and this time saw a flicker of recognition in Little John's expression. I pushed harder. "Your boss, Rossi, he ordered a hit on my dad, didn't he?" I didn't phrase this last as a question. "He hired a professional to make his death look like an accident so the charges against him would be dropped." When I saw Little John hesitate, the muscles around his mouth making miniscule movements, I dropped the bait. "If you cooperate, I'm willing to draft an appeal for a shortened prison sentence. I can't make any promises but I'd do my very best to push for an appeal, at the very least get you a probationary interview that might hasten your availability for parole." I'd resolved not to make any offers I couldn't back with results; putting a target on my back wouldn't help me bring my father's killer to justice.

"Parole, huh? I don't know. I've started working out, lost some weight. Maybe I don't want to get out early." Little John was eyeing me appraisingly. "Besides, Rossi isn't the kind who forgives or forgets. If I ratted on him, he'd come after me. I'd be safer here than on the outside."

Shaking my head, I said, "He would never know. I'm not using this information to go after him. I want the assassin." I waved a dismissive hand through the air. "Rossi isn't even on my radar."

Wren spoke into the silence that followed my statement. "You might be eligible for a witness protection program, you know. If you help the authorities out, give them information they can use to catch some of the bigger fish out there, they would probably agree to hook you up with a new identity, a new life somewhere far away from here. Think about it."

My eyes flicked to Wren before fastening on Little John again. Where did he learn this stuff?

Little John's reply wiped any thought of Wren's suspicious proficiencies aside. "Tell me again who you want to know about?"

"Justin Thomas Hartwell," I said through gritted teeth.

His thin, wet lips pursed in thought, Little John shifted in his chair. "I don't know the name off the top of my head. I've been in here for five years now and we, uh, dealt with a lot of people, you know."

"He was a lawyer who was prosecuting your boss for extortion and murder about six years ago." I watched his eyes closely, looking for signs that he recognized who I was speaking of—and saw them.

"Ah, yeah. That guy."

I leaned forward in my chair. "And?"

Little John cleared his throat. "I don't know..." he trailed off as his eyes unfocused and stared into the middle distance. Suddenly, he nodded to himself, looking at me.

"I'm trying to be a better person, you know, because I found Jesus last year and now I'm asking myself all the time, 'What would Jesus do' and all that. And I think He'd want me to help you out." He took a deep breath and his eyes darted to the ceiling, as though asking the Big Guy for permission, before continuing. "It's all in the *Washington Post*."

Pressing my lips together, I nodded encouragingly. *They all find religion here.*

"What is?" I asked, confused at the apparent topic change.

"The guy places an advertisement in the *Post*, advertising a piece of gardening equipment, like a rake or a mower".

Whatever the tool is, it's spelled wrong, and the asking price always includes the numbers one, two, three, and seven."

I repeated the numbers, and Little John nodded.

"Yeah, for example, he'll be selling a used shovel, spelled s-h-u-v-e-l, and ask $1,237.00 for it. At the end of the ad, he always wrote that interested parties needed to contact the seller using the email address posted below. So," Little John shrugged, "we did. We sent the details of the hit to the email address, after using one of our IT guys to check everything out and make sure it was legit, and he emailed us back asking for a fifty-percent payment upfront using bitcoin, with the rest due upon completion of the job. Once the hit gets labeled an accident and all parties are in the clear, he gets the last half of the money and disappears. That's all I know."

Leaning forward over the desk between us, I asked, "How much money did you pay him to kill my father?" My voice was hoarse, my words clipped. It was possibly the hardest sentence I had ever spoken aloud.

"I don't know exactly but someone of that caliber, I'd think it would be in the millions."

I sat back in my chair. My father's life had been worth so much more than any monetary value, it was hard to reconcile the number, as big as it was, with the fact that my dad was no longer a living, breathing part of my life.

"You're scum," I said on an exhale, unable to control myself.

Little John merely shrugged, as though he were used to hearing that and worse. "You gotta do what you gotta do. Rossi had to get your dad off his back so hiring a hitman was what he had to do. It was just business, nothing personal."

That's what made it feel so awful. I opened my mouth, to say what exactly, I wasn't sure, but I knew it wasn't going to be complimentary, but Wren stood, pulling me up to stand beside him before I could speak.

"Let's go, Maya. We got what we came here for."

I shot a last, hateful look at Little John before I turned away.

"Hey, lady, what about my parole?"

Looking at him over my shoulder, I shook my head. "Over my dead body." When he made an affronted noise, I shrugged. "It's just business, nothing personal." Taking ahold of Wren's hand, I kept my shoulders straight until we exited the visiting room. When the door closed behind me, I allowed Wren to pull me close, tucking my face into his shoulder.

"It's okay, Maya. It's okay."

I let his soothing words wash over me, hoping they would cleanse me of the deal I had been prepared to make, wipe away the stain my father's death had left on my soul, and leave me see this through all the way to the end.

Chapter 11

"I hate to say it but...what now?"

I dropped my head against the steering wheel. We were sitting in the parking lot outside Baradra, the sun beating in through the windshield and making my skin itch with heat. "I don't know," I replied miserably. Listening to Little John's confession had made me feel so many things that I was having a hard time dealing with all of the emotions coursing through me. Anger and sadness were being buffeted by eagerness and a fervent longing to bring the killer to justice.

"Where's the nearest newspaper stand?" Wren asked decisively.

"I don't know. I don't spend a lot of time in this area."

He whacked himself on the forehead. "What am I saying?" Before I could question him, Wren pulled his phone from the back pocket of his jeans and started tapping on it feverishly. "Pretty hefty paywall for the *Post*, but it's worth it. Let's go back to your place and get to work."

Nodding, I started the car and drove back to my apartment, my mind a revolving collage of images featuring Little John, the man from Chetumal, and my father. I parked and we entered my building, Wren still busy on his phone and me still wrapped up in a confusing tangle of thoughts.

Once inside my apartment, he hurried to the command center, dropping down onto the couch and alternatively glancing from the screen of his phone to that of his computer. I sat next to him, feeling numb and useless.

Finally, Wren sat back and laced his hands over his stomach, the expression on his face redolent of a cat with cream on his whiskers. "Here's the plan," he began, leaning his head against the back of the couch and gazing up at the ceiling, "I got an online subscription to *The Washington Post* and set up alerts in the classified section, so that whenever our guy posts an ad about shovels and rakes or whatever, I'll get a text. How does that sound?" He turned his head to look at me when I uttered a noncommittal noise. "I'm sorry, Maya. I didn't mean to take over and sound like a dictator. I just figured that you've been dealing with so much that I could help by getting things set up so we could catch the guy in the act."

"No," I shook my head. "It's a great idea. It's the only way forward. Can you set up the same Trojan horse program that we used to find Concerned Citizen?"

"Yes, but it will be a modified version. All we have to do is reply to his advertisement and wait for his response. That way, it won't matter if he changes names because I'll be in his computer."

I tapped my chin thoughtfully. "What if he changes computers?"

Wren shrugged his shoulders. "That doesn't matter. I've modified TJ so that it will sit on the email server shared by the computers he's using and the computer the person sending or receiving emails is using. We'll get a copy of anything sent to him or sent by him. It won't matter if he uses his own computer or one at an internet café."

I nodded. "That makes sense. All we can do is hope he's not as good as you, then."

Looking at me with a pleased expression, Wren said, "Few people are." He grew somber. "If it takes too long for him to post, I'll have to go back to Landsfield Ridge and wait there."

It pained me to do it, but I agreed with him; there was no use waiting around for something that make take months to happen—but I really *really* hoped it would happen soon. I didn't want to lose him.

It was almost a week later and Wren and I were seated at my dining room table eating soup when his phone *pinged* with a new message. In the days since he'd set the alert, we'd experienced quite a few false alarms but my pulse still quickened as he picked up his phone from the table next to him and checked the screen.

"It's him," he said breathlessly. "He's posted an ad."

"What's it say?" I leaned forward, planting my elbows on the table.

"Give me one second..." he tapped on the screen until he had the ad pulled up. "It says, 'For sale, a garden hose that's never been used. The price is firm at $2, 317. For inquiries, email etiller@hotmail.com.' Wren looked pointedly at me. "The word hose is spelled h-o-s-s-e."

"That's it," I said on an exhale.

He nodded. "That's it. Let's get to my computer and I'll send a reply. I don't have the TJ program on my phone."

We hurried to the command center and sat on the couch. Wren pulled his laptop towards himself and tapped in his password before opening up his email app. "What do you want me to say?"

I thought for a moment before saying, "How about this. 'Interested in the hose but the price seems too high. Is it a misprint?'"

Wren tapped out the message. "That's perfect." He looked at me with a questioning expression, a finger hovering over the return button on his keyboard. "Send it?"

"Send it," I replied, feeling my stomach turn over. We were actually responding to a hitman's message. I tried not to think about the implications of what we were doing. What if this was used against us later, during the killer's trial? Would any evidence we acquired through false pretenses even be applicable in a courtroom setting? The lawyer in me balked at the path we'd decided to take, but the daughter in me didn't care. We'd use this initial interaction as an avenue for more, irrefutable evidence that would hold up in court. As we sat there and waited for a reply, I repeated this thought every time niggling doubts entered my mind—which they did with annoying repetition.

Are you crazy? Emailing a hitman is no way to bring him to justice—but it's a surefire way to land yourself in jail.

My alter ego was about to offer my rehearsed rebuttable when Wren's computer *dinged.*

Before I could ask, Wren squinted near-sightedly at his computer screen and said, "It's him."

"What did he say?" I gripped the tops of my thighs, my knuckles white with tension.

"He says the cost depends on the method of shipment and he wants to know where we want the hose sent. Shipping internationally will cost more. He wants to know the details of the job, too." Wren chuckled as he pointed at the screen.

"He's actually pretty clever. He says that smaller gardens are outside the purview of the equipment on offer and that only jobs big enough to warrant the quality his hose provides will be considered."

"He'd have to be clever, trying to set up jobs through the classifieds section of a newspaper. You'd think there would be a better way."

Wren lifted one shoulder. "Think about it. I'm sure there are places on the dark web you could advertise services like his but even that wouldn't guarantee that you were dealing with people who were aboveboard. The way he has this set up is pretty ingenious. He's in complete control and can take or leave jobs without ever showing his face or offering up an identity."

I squinted at Wren. "You sound as if you admire the guy."

He shook his head. "Admire is too strong a word. I...appreciate the way he's thought this out."

I let that slide. I didn't share Wren's appreciation but could see where he was coming from. "So, what now? Should we email him back?" I couldn't help the subordinate role I was taking in this part of the mission; I was still reeling from our meeting with Little John and what with work obligations and the anniversary of my father's death approaching, I was a wreck. I was seriously contemplating taking time from work to see this out but doing so was against every bit of work ethic I'd instilled in myself. People were counting on me; how could I just drop my responsibility to them and selfishly focus on events in my own life?

"We don't have to do anything now," Wren answered, putting a hand on my leg. I think he could feel the inner turmoil I was struggling with. "TJ is in and all we have to do is wait for the killer to get another response to his hose ad. Once he does, we'll have all the evidence we need to put him away for a very long time."

If the illegal hacking of the killer's computer doesn't land us in jail first, I thought wryly. I would have to put my faith in the justice system and hope that it favored putting away a killer over worrying about a little technological lawbreaking. "So, we wait?" I asked, leaning back against the couch and trying to adopt Wren's nonchalant pose.

"We wait," he confirmed.

A week passed. Then two. My emotional rollercoaster evened out as time passed and I started to feel like myself again. I went for runs in the morning before work and came home to Wren every night; the routine felt nice and having someone in my apartment who greeted me when I entered was surprisingly pleasant. I thought that Wren would eventually overstay his welcome, that I would get tired of someone always being there—especially since I'd tried to live with boyfriends before and our personality clashes had always driven one of us out before too long. Not that Wren was a boyfriend. This was something I had to continually remind myself, especially during the weeks of waiting. When I came home bearing dinner and he opened a bottle of wine, Pink Floyd on the record player, I forgot that we were partners in crime rather than in a relationship and found myself pausing in front of lingerie storefronts on my morning runs, wondering about how I would look in a lacey nightgown or a sheer thong.

I told myself it was just the continued proximity we shared, that once he went back to Landsfield Ridge, these yearnings for domesticity would disappear, but the longer we waited the harder it was to remember we weren't a couple. During the second week, I asked Wren about his continued absence from work.

"Aren't they wondering when you're going to come back to work?"

Wren shrugged. "I've worked there without taking a single personal or vacation day for five years. They can deal with me being gone for a little bit."

"Are you sure? I don't want you to lose your job over this."

"I'm sure."

He never elaborated on why he was so sure, where his confidence came from, but he seemed completely unphased by missing so much work so I stopped bringing the subject up. I just hoped that he wasn't jeopardizing his career in order to help me. The pressure of that thought was too much on top of everything else I had to worry about.

Finally, just before we hit the third week mark, the killer got a reply to his ad. I was in the kitchen, stirring some chili while waiting for the cornbread to finish baking, when I heard Wren shout excitedly.

"We've got a hit!"

I dropped the spoon into the pot and ran into the living room. "What is it? What's the job?"

"Listen to this, 'The garden I have to till is a big one. I hope your tiller is up for the job. I want to plant some Senator Sunflowers and need the rows dug deep. Upon confirmation, I'll be happy to give you more information.' Then the buyer gives out a personal email account that I'm sure is encrypted. Not that it matters to TJ."

"Senator Sunflowers?" I repeated. "Does that mean what I think that means?"

"We won't know for sure until they get into a private conversation and drop all the pretense but yes, I think so. This person wants the hitman to go after a senator."

I bit my lower lip. This was big. Really big. I was starting to feel a little out of my depth. I shook off my uncertainty. "We need more information. I can't take that to the authorities and expect them to believe me. For all we know, they really could be talking about tillers and sunflowers."

"Do you think Little John would corroborate this evidence? It would put more of a target on his back with Rossi but if he's put his faith in God then maybe he won't find his old mob boss so scary."

"I don't know. Faith in God is one thing but I'm sure Rossi has people on the inside and Little John has to know that if he steps too far out of line Rossi will make sure a shank with Little John's name on it finds its way into the prison showers or the gym. No, I think we're on our own."

"Then, we're going to have to wa—"

"If you say wait, I'm pretty sure I'm going to scream. We've *been* waiting." I was practically jumping up and down with impatience. I wanted, no, *needed* some action. I needed to do something, not just sit around and wait by the computer. I was a soldier. We thrived on doing things, not waiting for things to be done.

Wrens computer sounded off and he leaned forward, tapping at the keyboard. "You won't have to wait long. The killer just emailed the buyer's private account. He's asking for more information."

I paced the room in frustration. Who communicates by email anymore? There were so many avenues of instant conversation that email seemed as old fashioned as snail mail. Five minutes later, the buyer responded.

"Okay, the buyer included details. Lots of details." Wren leaned in closer until his nose was only a foot away from his screen. I sat next to him, gently pulling on his shoulder until the screen was unblocked and I could see it too.

He scrolled through the email, which included picture and dossier files. I recognized the senator, he was a prominent figure in recent gun control lobbying and had been pushing hard for the illegalization of automatic rifles. "Senator Tim Collins," I said softly, reading a document that provided his up-coming political schedule and private calendar. I didn't follow politics but I knew enough that I could easily picture a National Rifle Association fanatic with too much money wanting Collins dead.

We scrolled to the end of the long email and Wren whistled. "Wow. One and a half million. That's quite a payday."

"And that's just the first installment," I said, pointing at the screen. "The total offer for the job is three million. Who has that kind of money that they can just throw it away like that?"

"Right wing enthusiasts in the oil and gas business spend that much on weekends in Vegas," Wren said. "And some of them would definitely be interested in getting rid of someone who's a proponent of gun control."

"There's some democrats who would be just as eager to silence Collins. He's a bit of a standout because his politics always ride the line between both parties. But, we still don't know if the killer's going to take the job," I pointed out.

"Oh, he took it alright," Wren said, gesturing toward his computer screen. "He wants the initial payment into a Bitcoin account. He says the tiller will be shipped within the next three months."

I nodded. "That makes sense. It would take time for him to set up a scenario for the senator that would make his death look like an accident."

"Yeah, and even more importantly, him agreeing to take the job implicates him. I think we have enough to bring to the authorities now."

I stood. "Let's go."

He looked up at me. "Right now? Can't we eat dinner first?"

My eyes shot open. "Oh my god! The cornbread! I forgot all about it!"

As I ran back toward the kitchen, Wren shouted, "Should I call for some Thai takeout then?"

Chapter 12

The cornbread was still edible and since it's impossible to mess up chili—one of the reasons it's a staple in my kitchen—we ate a satisfying meal at the kitchen table as we talked about how to spring the trap we'd set for the assassin.

I noticed that Wren was acting strangely during dinner, squirming in his chair as though unable to get comfortable, avoiding eye contact with me, and toying with his food rather than eating it. Finally, I decided to ask him what was going on.

"Have you ever heard the expression 'you've got ants in your pants'?"

Wren nodded, his eyes focused on the chili in the bowl in front of him. "Of course, I have."

"Well?" I prompted, lifting my eyebrows. "Do we need to call an exterminator or something? What's wrong with you?"

Leaning back in his chair, Wren shook his head as though saying "Nothing," but the expression on his face was impossible to decipher. I'd found it easy up to this point to figure out what he was thinking as he generally wore his feelings on his face but tonight it was as though Wren was struggling with an alter ego; a person I'd never met before and one I wasn't sure I liked. I'd come to rely on Wren's openness and lack of secrecy but it felt like he was gathering a shroud of concealment around himself that I would be unable to penetrate once it was securely in place.

"Wren," I said, reaching over the table to put my hand on his, "what's wrong? You can tell me anything, you know. We've been through too much together to keep secrets from each other."

He let out a pained sigh and ran his fingers through his fine hair, setting it up on end. "Really, nothing's wrong, Maya. It's just that..." He sighed again. "It's nothing. I'm just dealing with some personal stuff." For the first time since we sat down, he looked at me and the eye contact seemed to pull back the mysterious veil he'd been drawing around himself. "It's nothing," he repeated, offering me a tight smile.

"It's not nothing, but if you don't want to tell me that's fine. I won't push it. So, you've got us this far, I hope you have ideas on what to do next because I've got nothing." I squeezed his hand before sitting back in my chair. "Which is surprising because my ideas are usually plentiful, not to mention genius."

This got Wren to smile at me with more sincerity. "You mean *my* ideas are genius and plentiful. I'm pretty much carrying this operation."

"I know and I'm really grateful. But if there's anything that you have to go and take care of back home, you know that's okay with me, right? You don't have to stay here and keep helping me out." I had my fingers crossed beneath the table; I don't know what I'd do if Wren decided to take me up on that offer.

"No, it's not like that. Forget I said anything." Wren sat up straight. "I know what we should do next."

"Really? What?"

"I think we have enough to take to the FBI. Where's the nearest office?"

I pursed my lips. "Are you sure? I wouldn't prosecute on the evidence we've managed to gather so far. We need something concrete, to catch him in the act. All we have so far is conspiracy to commit murder, at the most." I shook my head. "It's not enough."

Wren sighed. "I know some people who would be willing to help us. I'll contact them and have them meet us at the San Francisco office. There is one, isn't there?

"Yeah, it's over on Golden Gate Avenue, I think. I've driven past it a few times but I've never had reason to stop in there before." I gazed questioningly at Wren. "How do you have friends at the FBI?"

He shook his head. "If I tell you, I'd have to erase your memory afterwards."

This was said with the usual accompanying humor but there was an undercurrent beneath the words that caught my attention. "You are a man of mystery, Wren."

Shrugging, he said, "I'm just a librarian."

"With friends in the FBI and insane hacking skills," I added, poking him in the shoulder. Seeing that some of his earlier discomfort was returning, I changed the subject. "So, do you want my chili recipe?"

Wren contacted his people in the FBI that night and two days later, we drove to Golden Gate Avenue to meet them. I ached to find out more about Wren's background, how he had the pull with the FBI to commandeer two agents—because that's what he did, friends or not—and arrange a private meeting with them over something as circumstantial as our case. But I knew that Wren would tell me if he was able to and if he decided not to, it was for a good reason, so, even though it went against my every instinct, I parked my questions for later.

We entered the building and waited at the reception desk for a few minutes before we were approached by a man and a woman wearing typical FBI garb: black suits atop white collared shirts, black ties, and equally dark polished shoes.

"Wren, it's nice to see you," said the woman. She shook Wren's hand but I saw warm familiarity in her blue eyes and tried not to feel tiny pin pricks of jealousy. This tall, slim woman knew aspects of Wren that I was in the dark about, and the knowledge irked me.

"Hello, Rebecca. Thanks for meeting with us." Wren turned to me. "Maya, this is Rebecca Smith. Rebecca, this is Maya Hartwell, the woman I told you about."

This addition smothered my jealous uprisings and when I reached out to shake her hand, it was with genuine friendliness.

"And this is Jack Miller."

Smith and Miller? Were those their real last names? They were generic in the extreme and I wondered whether FBI agents were assigned new, bland surnames upon their acceptance into the agency as I shook Jack's hand. He was tall and built like a swimmer, with broad shoulders and a thin waist atop long, lean legs.

"Nice to meet you, Maya," Jack said, holding onto my hand with both of his. His brown eyes were locked onto mine and I felt myself wanting to reach up and pat my hair, checking to make sure still in its chignon.

"Nice to meet you," I replied, feeling a bit breathless from his scrutiny. He was extremely handsome, wearing his all-American good guy charm with an ease that made it feel natural rather than contrived.

"Can we go somewhere and talk?" Wren asked.

The tone of his voice caused me to glance over at him. He was looking from me to Jack, a scowl on his face, and I smothered the pleased grin threatening to emerge on my lips. It seemed I wasn't the only one feeling jealous.

"Yes, this way," Rebecca said, motioning for us to follow her. We walked through a door and down a long hallway dotted with closed doors on either side. I imagined that criminals were being interrogated in some, international espionage being uncovered in others. Being an FBI agent seemed like such a glamorous and exciting profession; it was something I'd thought about during my time in the Marines, but my father's influence had eventually pushed me into law school and it was a decision I didn't regret. These people may find the bad guys, but I was the one who put them in jail and ultimately dealt out justice.

We entered one of the unmarked rooms and sat at a long metal desk with chairs around it. Jack offered me water or coffee, including Wren in the offer with an offhand glance that made Wren's cheeks go red, and nodded when we both declined. I wondered about their relationship; when Wren had told me he knew people in the FBI, I'd assumed they were friends, but that didn't seem to be the case with Jack.

"Let's get to it," Rebecca said with an efficient nod. "What have you got?"

Wren told her everything, from the Concerned Citizen to what we'd learned from Little John, and I felt marginally confident that we'd gathered enough evidence to catch their attention. When it was all laid out, the proof we'd garnered so far certainly seemed to substantiate our claims.

"A U.S. senator?" Jack repeated, his thick eyebrows raised. "And this guy has already been paid the initial fee to do the job?"

Wren nodded. "The funds were deposited into a Bitcoin account two days ago. And some time within the next two to three months the senator will die in what will look like an accident."

Jack and Rebecca exchanged glances.

"We can put the senator under surveillance for the next six weeks, under the claim that we've received information that puts him in danger," Rebecca said, tapping the desktop with her fingernails, "but the manpower we can commit to this is limited. Obviously, we aren't the CIA and can't go out-side international borders to put surveillance on the suspect in Mexico, and political figures don't like their movements monitored too closely for too long, no matter the threat, so our hands are tied." I felt my shoulders drop in disappointment, but Rebecca continued before I could voice my chagrin. "At least, officially. Unofficially, we can watch incoming flights, tap his phone lines and cell phone, and keep an eye on his schedule and monitor it for opportunities for accidents," this last word was accompanied with finger quotes.

I nodded. It was more than I'd hoped for, though it still put the senator in a certain amount of danger. Even under surveillance, a hitman as skilled as I knew ours to be could fly in under the radar and cut break lines or create the opportunity for other "freak" accidents. I felt compelled to add some of my own thoughts, to contribute something to the conversation.

"The most important thing is that we gather enough ev-idence to land this guy in jail for the rest of his life. The primary objective is to ensure the individual is incarcerated. Our optimal outcome would be to secure a conviction for attempted murder; however, while the perpetrator is serving their sentence, we can dedicate our efforts to gathering ad-ditional evidence that could potentially lead to convictions for his previous criminal activities. That would ensure that he remains imprisoned indefinitely, leaving no possibility of an early release." I didn't say that we were after the man who'd killed my father as I didn't want to seem too emotional, like I was making this a personal vendetta, but the thought was never far from my mind. "We need to have enough conclusive and incontrovertible proof that it will hold up in court."

Jack nodded as though completely agreeing with me while Rebecca looked at me askance, as though I was saying something so obvious it didn't need to be said at all.

Staring right at the other woman, I continued, "All this means nothing if we don't have enough to convict this guy. He could disappear without a trace and we'd never see him again. He's that good."

Rebecca still looked as though she thought I belonged at the kiddie table, but Wren and Jack were both in agreement.

"Absolutely, Maya. We'll be walking a fine line, what with making sure we gather evidence of the hit while ensuring that it doesn't happen, but I think we'll get there."

I smiled at Jack. "Right. All it takes is a little teamwork." I couldn't resist looking from Jack to Rebecca and adding, "Isn't that right?"

She smiled noncommittally at me before turning her attention to Wren. "Is the number you called us on the best way to reach you?"

He nodded. "Yes, I'll keep my phone nearby, day and night. Call me if anything comes up."

Practically purring, Rebecca replied, "Oh, you can be sure of that."

Wanting to roll my eyes at her obvious attempts at flirting, I stood and waited for the others to join me. We shook hands all around and Wren and I followed the two agents back out into the hall and through to the reception area.

Jack extended his hand again, grabbing mine with a gently yet firm grip. "I'll personally call you and let you know if anything of interest occurs."

"Thank you, Jack. I appreciate it." I held his gaze for several heartbeats before turning and exiting the building, Wren at my side. When we stepped onto the sidewalk and breathed in the warm, exhaust-filled air, I motioned Wren toward where I parked the car. "Let's go home. We have a lot to talk about."

"You're damn right about that."

I looked at him with a frown. His tone had been dangerously close to sulky, but I couldn't think of anything I'd done to warrant it. He, on the other hand, had been outright flirtatious with that floozy Rebecca while we were in the middle of an investigation. Very unprofessional.

We got into the car and I headed home. The traffic was awful, typical of San Francisco, no matter the hour, so I got right down to business. "Okay, so I think we should help Jack and Rebecca out by doing our own surveillance on the side. What do you think about—"

"You were sure being friendly with Jack."

I blinked at this non sequitur. "What?"

"It's nothing," he said, attempting to be breezy and light but coming across as petulant. "If you'd rather continue this investigation with him, that's perfectly fine. I'll just go home and—"

"Whoa, there. Wren, what is the matter with you?"

He shook his head. "Nothing. It's nothing."

I jerked the car into the parking lot of a fast-food restaurant and put it in park. "We are not going anywhere until you tell me what the hell is the matter. You've been acting weird ever since we got the FBI involved in this. I thought they were your friends."

Wren leaned his head back against the head rest and closed his eyes. "It's a long story."

Crossing my arms over my chest, I said, "I've got time."

Sighing, he opened his eyes and stared out the windshield. "Rebecca and Jack used to be an item. They'd been dating for a long time before I met either of them, but Jack never wanted to take the next step so she got angry with him and broke off the relationship. Then she dated me, just to make him jealous. They still have this off-and-on thing going that makes it very hard to deal with them, which is why I waited so long to ask for their help. We probably could've known a lot more a lot sooner if I'd contacted them at the very beginning of all this, but you see what they're like. She flirts with me to make him mad and he flirts with every woman in sight to make her jealous. It's ridiculous and straight out of high school, but there it is."

"You think he only flirted with me to make Rebecca mad?" I asked the question in a nonchalant tone, and Wren answered it the same way.

"Of course. That's the game they play with each other."

"It's just a game, huh? Then why did you get so mad that Jack was paying me so much attention?"

"I-I didn't get mad," he sputtered, shaking his head in denial.

"Couldn't Jack have flirted with me because he was genuinely interested in me?" I asked the question in the spirit of fun, of prolonging Wren's obvious discomfort, but found myself eager to hear his answer.

"No—I mean, yes. But probably not."

"I see." I knew I should drop the topic and move on to the more serious aspects of the legalities of capturing the hitman, but I couldn't help myself. "Do you think I'm ugly, Wren?"

He turned to look at me, his eyes open wide. "What? Of course not!"

"Do I have the personality of cardboard?"

"No!"

"Then why couldn't a man be interested in me because there's a lot to be interested in, rather than with the intention of making someone else jealous?"

"That's not what—you're twisting my words around!"

I was enjoying seeing him flustered; I knew my satisfaction stemmed from the way I felt watching him and Rebecca together, seeing another woman making eyes at Wren and being unable to do anything about it. It was outside my jurisdiction as partner in crime. My reaction was vindictive and beneath me—but real. I put my hand on the gear shifter and got ready to back out of the lot. "Okay, I'm sorry. Let's talk about something else."

"Wait." Wren put his hand on mine, stilling it. "You don't have to be sorry. I'm sorry. It's just that..." he trailed off, his lips pressing together in a grim line. "It's just that those two are from a past that I don't like to think about anymore. I put that stuff behind me a long time ago and seeing them again brought it all back." He let out a long exhale. "I apologize for acting weird."

"It's okay, I understand." I didn't, not really, but that was okay. "Let's go home. We've got work to do."

He nodded. "Yes, we do."

I pulled out of the parking lot and back into traffic, and smiled when I heard Wren mutter under his breath, "Jack Miller. What an asshole."

Chapter 13

Christopher McLaughlin scrolled through the document his contact had sent him, making notes when he saw an event in the senator's calendar that looked promising or a function with lackluster security that might provide him with an opportunity to slip something in the senator's drink, though this was harder to do than in the past. Tapping his pen against his teeth, Christopher mused over his options. There weren't many pharmaceuticals that could slip through the attention of today's medical examiners, but he knew of a few common herbs that, in the right doses, could cause heart failure. It had been a few years since he'd gone that route with an assignment, but he still remembered the exact dosage that would have the desired effect without being detectable.

Seeing a notification of a new email from his latest client pop up on his computer screen, Christopher set his phone down and clicked on the message. He frowned when he saw that the communication was filled with questions, how he was going to get the job done, when to expect completion, whether or not he'd received the initial payment.

Placing his fingers on the keyboard, he replied,

The assignment has been accepted. Questions are neither tolerated nor answered. You will know when job has been completed.

With a perfunctory tap of his finger, he sent his reply. People were so much more impatient nowadays; in the days he'd first branched out into the business of killing people, those who sought out his services were understanding and accommodating. They'd answer his ad, wire the initial payment, and he wouldn't hear from them again until the job was done and the final payment was sent. Now, his clients were controlling and obsessive, wanting constant updates and daily communications—not that he ever complied to these demands. He had enough saved to retire on his own island and not have to do another job for the rest of his life; he had no qualms about dropping clients and returning their deposit. It was the chase, the hunt, that kept him in the business of killing people. Because these weren't kindergarten teachers or priests he'd been hired to kill, these were men of dubious morals, men who'd make the pursuit the most satisfying; he made sure of that before agreeing to take on the assignments offered to him. The initial research he conducted before asking for the deposit payment served to uncover any skeletons lurking behind closed doors, and it was the presence of those secrets that helped Christopher decide whether or not he wanted to pursue the job. He wasn't out to kill the innocent—but neither did he consider himself a vigilante.

He sent a message to his contact in the senator's inner circle, asking for more in-depth reports as to the senator's personal schedule, before gathering up the sheafs of papers he'd printed detailing the private life of Senator Tim Collins. A spokesperson for gun control and women's rights, the good-looking politician seemed to be the perfect all-American family man he'd spent a lot of money and invested a lot of time to portray. What the average American didn't know was that Mr. Collins favored child pornography and had invested money embezzled from his family's construction business to support and create the dirty movies he preferred.

It had only taken Christopher three hours to find out everything there was to know about Collins—the dark web was a marvelous place to dig up dirt on even the most pristine of people—and even less time to decide that Tim Collins was a man worth killing. Now, it was all about manufacturing the perfect time and place to make it happen.

While he waited for his contact's reply, Christopher decided to make take a dip in the ocean and make a smoothie for lunch. He donned his swimming shorts and walked out of his cabana, which was so palatial it almost didn't deserve the humble name, and strode down the hill his house sat upon to the beach, swinging his arms and rotating his shoulders to warm them up for swimming. He waded into the surf, reveling in the warm water against his skin and the soft sand beneath his feet. Swimming was a part of his daily exercise regime, a routine which he only swerved from when assignments pulled him from home.

A healthy mind requires a healthy body, he reminded himself before raising his arms and diving beneath the next cresting wave.It was an oft-thought mantra that had guided him through life and even made an impression on his professional career. Some of the people he'd agreed to kill, he'd done so because they lived such slovenly lives that he couldn't help but think the world would be better off without them. Celebrities that did nothing but devour precious resources, drug-abusing billionaires with wives and multiple mistresses, the CEOs of companies that deforested virgin rain forests...the list of those he'd killed because they personally offended him was almost as long as those he'd assassinated for money. And neither caused him to lose sleep at night.

Refreshed and feeling energized after his mile-long swim, Christopher toweled off and entered his kitchen, which was a room where, outside of his office and bedroom, he spent the most time.

Slicing up a pineapple, some mangoes, celery, and a head of dark green kale, Christopher placed them into his blender with some fresh spring water and turned it on. He only ate organic produce and focused on live, raw foods when it came to his overall diet. His personal approach to nutrition was that the closer it was to its natural state, the better it was for you, and nothing was closer than raw fruit, nuts, and vegetables. He didn't drink coffee, only rarely imbibed in alcohol, and never put anything in his body that might make it less than the perfect machine he needed it to be. His penchant for fine scotch was the only time he lowered this high standard of living; perfection was for martyrs and saints—and he was neither.

He sipped his smoothie as he walked back to his office. When he heard his cell phone vibrate with an incoming call, he picked it up. Mikhail. He had few associates, and those he did have knew nothing about what he did for a living, though he thought that Mikhail might actually appreciate it.

"Γειά σου," he said, greeting the other man in his native Greek.

Mikhail returned the greeting before switching to English. "I've been trying to get a hold of you for weeks. Where have you been?"

An avid practitioner of yoga and leader of an underground environmental group that specialized in the demolition of whaling ships and deforestation equipment, Mikhail was

Christopher's closest acquaintance, one of the few he actually thought of as being a friend. "I've been busy with work."

"Ah, yes, the international man of mystery. Don't worry, I won't waste our time by asking what it is you do, because I know you won't answer." Mikhail laughed heartily and Christopher could imagine his big white teeth flashing behind his thick beard. "I had a question and you're the only man I know who might have the answer," Mikhail continued.

"Ask away," Christopher said, sitting behind his desk and leaning back in his chair.

"Where might one procure CL-20?"

Christopher's eyebrows lifted in surprise. "CL-20? What in the world do you want that for? That's the most powerful, non-nuclear explosive on the market."

"Ah ah ah," Mikhail admonished. "I cannot say what exactly I plan on using it for," he paused, "but there is a certain Brazilian president who needs to be reminded that the aboriginal forests he governs belong to the aboriginals, and not the private corporations who fund his lavish lifestyle."

Pursing his lips, Christopher ran through perspective sources in his head before naming some of them, checking his encrypted contact files for their info and rattling it off to Mikhail. "Let me know if you need any assistance. I've never used CL-20 before but I have a vacation home in Brazil that might work as a safehouse, should you be in need of one."

"Many thanks, many thanks. There is a woman with a beach house who has been missing me since I last visited her beautiful country, so I plan on staying with her."

Grinning, Christopher nodded. "I understand completely. Stay safe and let me know if you need anything." From past experience throughout their long friendship, "anything" could be money, a clean passport, or a quick exit strategy; he and

Mikhail had been through a lot since meeting on a tour of Turkey's untouched ecological biospheres.

"You got it. Adios, amigo."

"Adios, Mikhail." Christopher ended the call and finished his smoothie, thinking about his past exploits with the enigmatic Greek eco-warrior.

His reverie was interrupted when he got an email from his contact, who'd attached a document of Tim Collin's personal schedule, from his daughter's piano lessons to his dog's grooming calendar.

Every other Tuesday at Happy Tails, Christopher thought, stroking his chin. *Interesting.*

***

Two months later, Christopher had just finished with a six-mile jog up and down the beach when he heard his private email account, the one he used for his *Washington Post* ads, ping. He'd been on his way to the shower, walking past his office when he'd heard the tell-tale noise. Mopping sweat from his forehead, Christopher stripped off his shirt and laid it on the back of a chair as he sat behind his desk and opened the email.

I'd like to inquire about the lawnmower you have for sale. I have a neighbor, Jake Rawlson, who needs his lawn mown.

Personal information about Rawlson followed, making it easier for Christopher to Google the man's name and narrow down the search results. What he saw made his eyes narrow. Jake Rawlson was a farmer in Illinois who had been featured in his small town's newspaper for standing up to the corporation who'd been gobbling up neighboring properties and growing genetically modified crops. He said the constant crop spraying and wind-blown chemical fertilizers being used on the surrounding farms were polluting his land and making it harder and harder for him to meet organic standards. He'd been gaining a following of environmentalist lobbyists who were championing his cause in Washington, DC, which was making the corporation who'd invested money in its farming operations nervous. Christopher would bet money that the person who'd emailed him about taking care of Rawlson was an employee of the company, one who'd been given free rein to take care of the "problem."

He dragged the email to the folder he used to block further correspondence, cursing under his breath as he dropped the offending message into the deflection file folder. He hadn't killed a person he thought undeserving of it in years...six years, in fact.

It had been a rough time for him personally and professionally; his mother, who he hadn't spoken to in years but still kept tabs on, had died in a mugging gone wrong, and her lawyer had been ineffectual in the extreme, with the man who'd shot and killed her getting off with a slap on the wrist. Christopher had done more than slap the man on the wrist when he'd gotten released from his pitifully short prison sentence.

The experience had left a sour taste in his mouth when it came to lawyers, and when he'd been propositioned by gentlemen with mob connections concerning making a lawyer die in a "car accident", he hadn't hesitated. It had seemed like divine intervention, the universe letting him settle the score for the injustice done to his mother, so he'd taken the job even though he tried to avoid working for organized-crime clientele; they were messy and emotion-driven, but he'd needed the money after having to suddenly ditch an identity and the bank accounts tied to it.

He'd forgotten the man's name, the lawyer he'd killed, but he remembered chastising himself afterward for wearing his favorite watch. It was as good as a billboard to the right people, but luckily he'd never experienced any backlash from the oversight.

Pushing away from his desk, he was about to take that shower he'd come inside for, pausing when his cell phone flashed with a new text message.

Next week. An art gala. Minimal security. Surprise for his wife's birthday. Opportunity?

Christopher put his hands on his hips and sent his gaze to the ceiling as he imagined the scene.

I'm a waiter, carrying a tray of hors d'oeuvres. In my pocket is a capsule of snakeroot or oleander, concentrated. I circulate throughout the room, finding security and exits, deciding on my escape route before I even begin to focus on the senator. The time will come for a toast, to celebrate the pornographer's wife. Timing will be key. I'll only have moments to empty the capsule into his champagne glass, be at his side to offer it to him, and ensure he drinks it all. The poison will take effect immediately and I'll only have seconds to exit the room, using the chaos of the senator's collapse as cover. Then it'll be ditching the waiter uniform and donning my second disguise. Maybe I'll have a dog secreted near the entrance of the gala location. Just a man out walking his dog. Leave the dog where it will be found, get to airport, fly commercial to nearest international hub where my pilot will be waiting. Back in Mexico within hours of the senator's death by heart failure, with final payment to follow.

It was good but flawed. There were too many variables, too many things that could go wrong. He never set on a plan until the chance of success hovered around the ninety-five percent marker; knowing that strategies are only good until the first shot is fired, Christopher threw as many different scenarios and irregularities at each plan of action until he was satisfied that the possibility of success outweighed that of failure. Back to the drawing board. He liked the idea of the art gala, though.

Christopher bent over his desk and typed a message to his contact.

Art gala. No further communication until job is complete.

He hit the send key and walked out of his office, his head awhirl with potentialities and appropriate recourses. It was an exhilarating time for him, one of his favorite moments in the process of ending lives; the final countdown had commenced.

Chapter 14

The past few months seemed to happen within a continuum that both slowed and sped up time. I was left feeling alternatively impatient and indifferent, my work on the AME case occupying my time and keeping me busy while at the same time feeling like an inconvenience that I just wanted to be done with.

Wren left the first month after our vigil started. He'd been needed back at work and hadn't been able to stay away indefinitely. It was strange, how empty my apartment felt without him. I'd gotten used to him being there when I got home and saying goodbye to him when I left. Now, I had no one again and the knowledge poked and prodded at me like it never had before.

The final negotiations had just been completed, contracts signed and notarized, my clients starting to feel like they could celebrate their success, and I'd gone home from work feeling bursts of self-satisfaction when Wren texted me.

They got him.

I'd been pouring myself a celebratory glass of wine and almost overflowed the glass when I saw his message pop up on the screen of my cell phone. That could only mean one thing. Several weeks before, TJ had intercepted a conversation between the assassin and a mole in the senator's inner circle that had alerted us and the agents monitoring Collins's surveillance to the possibility of an upcoming gala in Dallas, Texas, being the setting for the hit. We'd been on tenterhooks ever since; the only way the assassin could be caught was by letting the scene play out just shy of the ultimate culmination—the senator's death.

I'd begged to be present at the gala, but had been told that my presence was a liability and that if I showed my face there I would be charged with obstructing justice and shipped to Guantanamo Bay. I'm pretty sure they'd been joking...I think. I'd managed to bury myself so deep in work that I'd forgotten that tonight was the night of the gala.

I just had time to set the bottle and glass down on the counter before my phone buzzed again, this time with a message from Jack. The agent had been good to his word, sending me updates that offered very little in the way of progress but were always full of up-beat remarks that conveyed positive developments. They were a little patronizing, but I appreciated the spirit in which they'd been sent.

I read Jack's text.

Suspect is in custody. More to follow.

My heart racing, I first texted Wren.

Get down here. Now.

Then Jack.

When can I speak to him?

My fingernails pattered on the counter as I waited for replies. The release of the anxiety I'd been living with for the past two and a half months made me jittery. I paced the floor of the kitchen, circling around the island as I obsessively checked my phone's screen for new messages.

"What are they doing?" I growled after checking for the twentieth time since I'd sent my replies. "I'm dying here."

I paused in my pacing, planting my palms on the wooden surface of the island and taking deep breaths. Working myself into a frenzy wasn't going to do me any good and it certainly wasn't going to make them text me back any faster.

When my phone did vibrate again, only seconds after I'd forced myself to calm down, I snatched it from the counter, my heart rate resuming its rapid rhythm.

On my way. Be there in four hours.

I grinned. The drive between San Francisco and Landsfield Ridge took five hours, and I knew Wren was letting me know he wasn't going to waste any time in getting here. We'd talked about him coming down here preemptively, in case the assassin did decide to use the gala as the location of his hit, but we hadn't been sure enough for him to ask for more time off of work, figuring that being five hours away wouldn't make a difference one way or the other. Now that it was happening, five hours seemed interminable.

I had to wait longer for Jack's reply. I'd resigned myself to the wait and was sipping on my almost forgotten glass of wine when my phone juddered across the counter. I grabbed my phone and felt my stomach drop as I read Jack's message.

Situation delicate. Protocol to follow. I'll let you know when circumstances allow for a face-to-face.

I gritted my teeth together. I couldn't believe the FBI was trying to backpedal after Wren and I had practically dropped a gift-wrapped assassin in their lap. How could they deny me access to him after all we'd done to make the capture as seamless as possible? Since Wren had the most pull, I decided to wait for him to get here before doing anything that would jeopardize my ability to be involved—like call Jack right now and scream invectives at him. I looked at the time and heaved a sigh. It was eight o'clock. Wren wouldn't be here until the middle of the night and I would have to wait until then before making another move. *I hate waiting.*

The next morning dawned clear and bright, no oceanic fog obscuring the ground and making the drive to the airport any more treacherous than my shaking hands and trembling legs already were. Wren had arrived four and a half hours after his last text, smashing the land speed record and causing my admiration for him grow even more. A man who would drop everything and break several traffic laws in order to come to your side was an invaluable asset—one I'd never had before and one I was growing increasingly reluctant to let go of.

Before we'd both fallen into our respective beds last night, Wren and I had talked about our strategy, how we were going to fly to Dallas, where the suspect was in custody, reinsert ourselves into the inner circle and be involved in ensuring that the assassin was brought to justice. Our talk had made me feel better, enough to sleep, at least, and we both pulled ourselves out of bed at five in the morning, wanting to clean up and get to the airport as early as we could. While he'd been on the road, driving to San Francisco, Wren had contacted Rebecca, using their past relationship as leverage to find out details: where the assassin was being held, the details of his capture, and what the next steps were.

Seeing as the capture and arrest happened in Dallas, it made sense that the assassin was being held in the local FBI head-quarters, and while she couldn't share much of the details as she claimed not to have them, Rebecca had told Wren that if he hadn't tipped them off to the last communique between the assassin and the mole in the senator's cabinet of advisors, Tim

Collins would probably be dead right now and the assassin in the wind.

"She congratulated me on TJ and told me again and again how smart I am," Wren said smugly as we turned into the airport. I'd gotten us tickets on the first flight leaving for Dallas/Fort Worth International Airport last night.

"I bet she did," I muttered under my breath, pulling into long-term parking.

"What was that?"

"Nothing," I said, at a normal volume. "You are the one who made this whole thing happen and I hope they acknowledge that publicly."

Wren turned to me with a frown. "What do you mean?"

"The assassin would still be free, killing people on a whim if not for you. You should be given a medal, be featured on morning talk shows, the works."

He shrank back into his seat. "No. I don't want any of that stuff. I don't want any of the credit. You can have it all."

Scowling at him, I put the car in park. "Okay, okay. We'll figure that out later." We got out and walked to the departure gate of our airline, my first-class status whisking us through check-in and into the lounge, where we downed cups of coffee and Wren ate a muffin. My stomach was too upset for food, though the two cups of caffeine I had didn't really help either.

We boarded our flight and settled into first class for the three-and-a-half-hour flight. Once we were in the air, I opened a book I'd brought, intent on keeping my mind busy, and Wren opened up his laptop and set it on the tray in front of him.

"Would you like anything to drink?" a flight attendant asked, offering coffee, sparkling water, mimosas.

"A mimosa? Is it free?" Wren asked, his expression suspicious, as though he thought the helpful man was trying to fleece him.

"Of course, sir. It is complimentary."

"Then, yes. I would like one."

Once the attendant had poured Wren a glass, I accepted a water, and waited for him to continue offering drinks down the aisle before turning to Wren.

"A mimosa? I didn't think you were the type."

"What, the type to drink in the morning?" He shrugged. "This is only the second time I've flown first class and I'm still trying to fit in. In all the movies I've seen, the actors who fly first class always get a glass of champagne or a couple of fingers of whiskey. Besides," he took a sip and closed his eyes appreciatively, "it's been a long couple of days, and I've earned it."

"You certainly have," I agreed, settling into my seat to watch him enjoy his drink.

The flight was uneventful, and when we arrived in Dallas, we stepped from the plane and were instantly pummeled by oppressive heat.

"Oh my goodness," I said, swiping a hand across my brow. "And I thought living by the ocean was humid." I could practically hear my hair *boing* as it drank in the moisture-laden air and lifted from my scalp.

"Yeah, I've only ever felt heat like this before in Florida," Wren noted, pulling the front of his shirt away from his body.

"When did you go to Florida?" I asked.

"Annual trips to Disney World," he said, passing me and leading the way toward the rental car stalls lining the arrivals terminal.

I shook my head. He was a man of many surprises, that was for sure.

We secured our rental car and drove to the FBI building, which, according to the directions, was on One Justice Way. *Fitting*, I thought to myself as Wren pulled into the parking lot.

After going through security and giving the names of the people we were here to see, Ms. Smith and Mr. Miller, we were ushered down yet another hallway dotted with closed doors—the FBI must use the same architectural plans for all their buildings—and directed into a room with one wall made of one-way glass. Rebecca and Jack were there waiting for us, and Jack pulled my seat out for me as we got settled.

"Congratulations are in order," Jack said, grinning at me. "We got your man."

With our help, I thought resentfully, but said, "Yes, congrats all around. Where is he? When can I speak to him?"

Rebecca shook her head. "We can't allow that, but I pulled some strings for you," she directed this at Wren, "and ensured that Ms. Hartwell would be involved with the legal side of the proceedings. As an aid to the lead prosecutor."

I shook my head. "No, not good enough. I'm the top attorney at my firm, not some legal temp fresh out of law school. I want second chair."

Shaking her head, Rebecca adopted a regretful moue. "That's not possible. We have our best legal team on the case and—"

Wren reached out and placed his hand on hers. "Rebecca, this was Maya's case from the very beginning. Putting her on the bench now would be unethical. She deserves the chance to take a swing at this guy. He killed her father."

"I'm aware of how much she helped with the discovery of evidence...not that we can use any of it in court," she shot a look at me that was full of contempt, "as it was obtained illegally."

"Rebecca, I think we can do something to ensure that Maya gets second chair," Jack said reproachfully. "She's earned the right. We never would have caught Christopher McLaughlin without her. That's the name he goes by, at the moment, but we're sure that he has other identities. We're looking into it."

I sat upright. "You're damn right you wouldn't've caught him without us."

Sitting back with a sigh, Rebecca waved a dismissive hand. "Fine. Jack, you know the prosecutor best so you can tell him he's got to deal with a second who has a personal vendetta against the defendant. Good luck with that."

Jack offered me a supportive smile. "Don't worry. I'll explain everything. There shouldn't be a problem getting you on the team."

I flashed him my biggest grin. "Thanks, Jack. You don't know how much this means to me."

He winked in return and I could see Wren fidget in his chair out of the corner of my eye.

"Is he going to be questioned? Is that why we're in this room?" he asked, gesturing at the large glass plate.

"Yes," Rebecca glanced at her watch. "They should be bringing him in shortly."

We made small talk, with most of the dialogue separated into two distinct conversations, with me and Jack talking to each other while Rebecca and Wren chatted. I tried to listen in on their conversation in moments of silence between me and Jack, but they spoke barely above a whisper, as though sharing secrets. It irked me, but I tried not to let it show.

Finally, the door in the room next to our opened and the man I'd seen disembark from the helicopter stepped inside, his hands cuffed behind him, followed by two agents.

After everyone was seated, and the assassin's handcuffs were secured to the tabletop, the questions commenced.

"So, Christopher...tell me, what's your real name?" asked one of the male agents. His black suit coat was stretched over muscled shoulders and his hair cut close, military style.

"The one I was born with?" Christopher replied, one eyebrow raised.

"Yes," the agent answered.

"I don't remember."

"You're going to have to do better than that," snarled the other agent. He was the exact opposite of his partner; his paunch burgeoned over his belt and his tie seemed to be trying to cut circulation from the roll of fat around his neck. "What's you real name?"

"Dear me, it was so long ago. I'm quite sure I just can't recall." Even with his hands cuffed, the assassin exuded confidence. He's assumed a casual position, one leg cocked and the other stretched out. He could've been sitting in a barber shop for all the concern he showed.

"I see," said the first agent. "I'm Special Agent Kent and this is Special Agent Abernathy. Now that we've introduced ourselves, let's get down to business. You're going to be charged with attempted murder, Mr. McLaughlin, and probably several counts of first-degree manslaughter, once we go through your home in Mexico and get into your computers. How does that make you feel?"

Christopher shrugged. "I feel like most who've been unjustly accused." He bared his teeth. "Angry."

"Unjustly accused?" I said incredulously. "I can't believe this guy! Why does he think he's here? He has to know we have piles of evidence that proves what he's done."

"That's the thing," Jack said softly. "We don't."

"What?! Didn't you catch him trying to kill Senator Collins?"

Rebecca shook her head. "We caught him holding capsules filled with enough oleander to kill an elephant. That's pretty much all we've got."

"But the information from his computer, everything that TJ has access to, that has to be enough to put him away for four lifetimes!" I was on the edge of my seat, ready to jump to my feet and...I didn't know what I was ready to do but I wanted—needed—to do something.

Seeing my frustration, Wren laid a hand on my shoulder. "It's okay, Maya. Even if he doesn't confess, you'll be questioning him in the courtroom. He won't stand a chance."

I nodded reluctantly, relaxing back into my chair. I'd get my chance, and I wouldn't waste it.

***

In a dark backroom that smelled of sour wine and spilled beer, Luca Rossi sat on a plush chair, his fingers steepled in front of his face. Before him were three men, each as different as the seasons, though they were brothers. The siblings were staring at Rossi with intent expressions that manifested inconsistently throughout their disparate facial features—the one with a heavy, Cro-Magnum brow had it lowered so far that his eyes were barely visible, the one sporting a long, thin mustache had run his fingers along it so much that the ends were frayed, and the one with a glass eye had closed it, to see his boss better.

"Let me get this straight. They caught our gardener?"

The three brothers nodded.

"That is going to put a serious damper on our future business endeavors. We use that gardener as leverage to make sure that everyone does what they say they're going to do, and without him, I'm worried about certain people getting ideas about certain things." Rossi looked at each of his men, searching for signs that they understood what he was trying to say. When he didn't find any, he sighed. "What I mean is that people are going to start wondering if I have the pull that I've always had, without having the gardener in my back pocket." He paused. "That's bad."

The three brothers nodded, seemingly the only response they were capable of.

"So, what I want you to do is fix it. Get in a plane to Dallas and put some pressure on the lawyers. I want them to realize that they'd be better off, health-wise, you see, if they backed as far away from this case as they can."

Before spinning on their heels and exiting the dank backroom, the three brothers looked at each other, communicating without words, bobbing their heads in unison.

"Now to take care of that rat Little John," Rossi growled into the darkness.

Chapter 15

Three weeks earlier
Chetumal, Mexico

Christopher couldn't shake the lingering sense of trepidation that weighed his thoughts down as though they'd been covered with a thick wet blanket. Figuring the source of his apprehension lay in the method he'd chosen, as current biotechnology might be able to detect the poison during the senator's autopsy and therefore ensure that murder, rather than a weak heart, was the cause of death, he dug a little deeper, spent more time researching Tim Collins for possible avenues of "accidental" death.

When he stumbled upon notes from the senator's recent doctor's visit provided by his contact, Christopher almost leapt out of his chair. There it was. The path forward was as clear as the cut-crystal glass sitting next to his computer: the senator had a pacemaker.

His thoughts afire with potentiality, Christopher leaned back in his desk chair, cupping the glass in his hand as he let the possibilities unfurl. Pacemakers were implanted into patients' chests with the intention of aiding the heart in controlling the heartbeat; the technology had been perfected, what with recent medical advancements, but the ways in which a device planted in someone's chest could be used to kill them were numerous—and not a few of those ways would be indetectable as being the result of foul play.

He mentally discarded the idea of using poison. The outdatedness of it had both its advantages and disadvantages, but he felt suddenly inspired by Mikhail's recent call. Explosions could be big...and they could also be barely detectable but still powerful enough to cause a pacemaker to malfunction, mini EMPs, also known as electromagnetic pulses.

I'm a waiter still, but this time I don't have poison capsules secreted on my person. No, I have something much more difficult to detect. A device that can emit a controlled electromagnetic pulse, one strong enough to affect surrounding electrical devices. I'm sure Mikhail has contacts able to craft something that would fit the bill. The gala is still the best setting for the hit, and it's a week off yet. Plenty of time for that Greek to pull a rabbit from under his hat—especially after I helped him with his CL-20...so, as I near the senator, I activate the device, dropping the tray full of champagne flutes I'm carrying at the same time, as though Collins flails wildly as his heart gives out. The resultant noise and confusion are exactly what I need to cover my escape. Cue the change of appearance and awaiting dog, and I'm free. In the clear, millions of dollars richer.

As his mind picked through the plan, looking for deficiencies, one became immediately apparent. How was he supposed to get the device past security? There would be metal detectors on sight, and no one would get close to the gala's interior without having gone through several.

Christopher frowned. Could the device be made out of some polycarbonate? This brought about another line of questioning. Was he too focused on the gala, too intent on making it work that he was jeopardizing his chances of success? He took a sip of scotch, letting the liquid play over his tongue before swallowing it.

A seasoned professional, Christopher knew that the first—or second—plan wasn't always the best. Sometimes it took countless days of planning and problem solving to make a hit work. But they always did, in the end. They *always* did.

***

"Wow, would you look at that," Wren said, scrolling through the news feed on his phone.

"What?" I asked distractedly. I was pulling my hair back into a tight bun and stray strands kept escaping, causing me to have to start over. My hair wasn't usually so unruly—it was my shaking hands that were the problem.

Wren's hotel room was adjacent to mine, but we'd taken to meeting in the morning to go over the aspects of the case over cups of coffee.

"The president of Brazil's house went up in a huge explosion this weekend," Wren said. "They're saying the bomb was planted by the opposing political party and are investigating the nature of the explosive device that was used. Apparently, it's pretty rare."

"Huh, interesting," I said, barely following what he was saying. Today was the first day of Christopher McLaughlin's—whatever his real name was, I only thought of him as Christopher—trial, and my nerves were making even the most simplest tasks difficult. Pulling up my pantyhose without ripping runs into them had taken me nearly ten minutes. "Are you ready to go?"

Wren squinted at his phone. "Maya, it's six o'clock in the morning. The trial doesn't start until eight."

"I know, but I want to be there early so I have a chance to prepare. Get your shoes on while I go and get the car warmed up." Fall had brought cooler weather, for Dallas, and I'd woken up to a light frost fringing the window of the hotel room. I wanted to get the defrost going in the rental car so the moment Wren was ready, we could leave.

He grunted, his eyes still fixed on his phone, as he stood up from the table and walked out of the door to go to his room.

Rolling my eyes, I grabbed my travel mug of coffee and left the room, taking the elevator down to the hotel lobby and nodding at the security officer manning the reception area before exiting the building. I trotted toward the blue rental car I'd picked up at the airport, but pulled up short when I saw three men loitering near the front of it. One of them was bent over, almost fully hidden by the hood; I'd only managed to catch sight of him when he'd lifted something metallic in his hand and it had caught the beam of the streetlamp above them.

"Hey!" I shouted, marching toward them. "Get away from there!"

The man crouching down stood and three heads swiveled to look at me before turning to regard each other. They neither spoke nor moved away from the car, and I felt something feral start to stir in the pit of my stomach. Who were these men and what were they doing? Mentally shrugging my shoulders, eager for a fight, the civilized side of me knew that if I were to get hit in the face, it would distract the jury and possibly lose us the case, so I dipped a hand into my briefcase instead, intent on grabbing the pepper spray canister I kept clipped to an inside pocket, when I heard footsteps behind me. *Another one!*

I turned, pepper spray in hand and ready to shoot a stream of the burning liquid, and barely escaped hitting Wren in the face. I jerked my finger off the trigger just in time.

He looked from me to the men, a scowl furrowing his forehead. In the illumination of the streetlamps, the shadow of his brow made his face menacing and fierce. "What's going on here?" he demanded, directing his question toward the silent men standing by the rental.

With another glance at one another, the men turned on their heels and hustled away, disappearing into the darkness of the early morning.

I was breathing hard, adrenaline coursing through me. I'd thought for sure there was going to be a confrontation between us and the men—and they'd looked dangerous. Even though I knew the brand of pepper spray I'd chosen claimed to be able to stop a bear in its tracks, I hadn't been sure I'd be able to get all three of them at the same time.

"What do you think they were doing?" Wren asked, slowly walking toward the car, his head swiveling.

"I don't know. One of them was crouched down and had something metal in his hand, but I couldn't see what he was doing."

"Hmm," Wren said. "Let's go take a look."

We walked over, Wren approaching slowly, on the tips of his toes as though worried about spooking a wild animal crouched beneath the car.

"Why are you walking like that?" I asked. My voice was barely above a whisper; his caution affecting me more than I thought.

"Because I don't want to cause any vibrations that might make a bomb go off."

"What?" I shouted, all thoughts of care disappearing. "Why do you think there's a bomb?"

Wren looked at me. "Think about it, Maya. Those were unsavory characters acting suspicious near the car of one of the lawyers of a high-profile case. They could've been planting a bomb, with the intent of intimidating the prosecution or stalling the process indefinitely."

"You only think that because of what you read on the news this morning," I retorted. "You've got bombs on the brain. Besides, it's a rental. How could they've even known it was mine?"

Wren shrugged. "Better safe than sorry." Placing a hand gently on the car's hood, he peered around it to the side where the men had been standing. He frowned, sniffing the air. "You smell that?"

I came to stand beside him, wrinkling my nose. "It smells like fish."

"That's brake fluid," he said, crouching down to touch his hand to a dark splotch on the asphalt. Rubbing his thumb and forefinger together, he shook his head. "Yep, just as I thought. They cut your brake lines."

I blinked. Why would anyone want to...I turned to look down the street. The surroundings were flat, as Dallas was devoid of the hills that made up my adopted hometown of San Francisco, but I still couldn't see anyone suspicious. "There were trying to kill me," I said on an exhale, feeling stupefied.

Wren straightened, nodding. "Or at the very least hurt you so badly that you couldn't continue trying the case."

"But why me?" I said, my mind reeling. "I'm just the second chair—"

Before I could finish the sentence, Wren had stuck his hand out. "Your phone. Give me your phone."

Numbly, I dug into the front pocket of my briefcase and handed him my phone. "Who are you going to call? The police?"

"I'm calling the lead prosecutor. He's in your contact list, right?"

I nodded, picking up on Wren's line of thought. "Yes, Paul Henderson."

He tapped the screen before handing me the phone. "Tell him to call a cab, ride the bus, walk, to do anything but drive his own vehicle, rental or not, to work today. They aren't targeting you specifically, they are going after everyone involved."

When a sleepy voice answered my call, I opened with an apology before explaining why I had woken him up. "Paul, my car's brake lines were cut this morning. I think the trial has caught the attention of the mob."

A true professional, Paul instantly roused. "Call the police. They may have done more than just cut the lines. Make sure before you go anywhere near the car." He took a deep breath. "Why do you think it's the mob?"

I told him about Little John and Luca Rossi, how they had connections to Christopher. "It makes sense that they wouldn't want to lose his services as before he'd been captured he had a one-hundred-percent success rate."

"Hmm. That would have been nice to know that ahead of time, Maya."

Shame and pride warred for the right to offer a rebuttal against Paul's comment, and it was with some effort on my part that I swallowed down pride and said, "You're right. I honestly didn't think it was relevant to the case or else I would've mentioned it."

"We'll talk about it more later. Since you caught those men by your car, I gather you were on your way to the courthouse?"

"Yes, I wanted to get there with plenty of time to prepare."

"Okay, call me after you're done with the police. I'll meet you there." He sighed. "I guess I'd better call a car to take me to the courthouse, if we're dealing with the mob tampering with vehicles. Since today is the first day of our arraignment and Judge Mailor is residing, I shouldn't need you so don't worry if you're late."

His insistence that he wouldn't need me made my jaws clench. Whether or not we were dealing with a lenient judge, it shouldn't matter; a second chair wasn't an unimportant member of the proceedings. I was about to begrudgingly say my goodbyes when he continued.

"And, Maya?"

"Yeah?"

"Is there anything else you want to tell me about this case that I might not already know?"

I swallowed, my mind whirring to our trip to Mexico, the Concerned Citizen's video, and the incriminating watch. "Let's talk at the courthouse," I said, dodging the question. "I'll get there as soon as I can." There was too much to get into over the phone, though I figured it was time to lay it all out for Paul.

We said our goodbyes and I called the police, who said not to call a tow truck as they would collect the car after they'd had a chance to look it over for any surprises.

Exhaling noisily through my lips, I looked over at Wren, who was tapping away at his phone's screen.

"The police are on their way. I guess there's nothing we can do but wait until they get here."

He nodded, glancing up at me. "Okay."

"What are you working on?" I asked, bored and resigned to wait.

"I'm checking to see if TJ has found any connection to the mob on Christopher's computer."

"Any luck?"

"Nothing so far, but I'll keep looking. I figured it would help us out if I could find something, as maybe occupying the mob's time with their own legal troubles would make them leave you alone." He looked at me from beneath his eyelashes. "I can't have anything happen to you, Maya."

The intensity in his gaze made my heart beat faster and I tried to look away from it, but found that I couldn't. I raised the corners of my lips in a tremulous smile. "I'll be fine, Wren. It'll take more than three goons to hurt me."

He stared at me for several seconds that stretched into small, disparate eternities of time before turning his attention back to his phone. In that immutable moment, I'd been sure he was going to kiss me and felt mildly disappointed when he didn't—then felt extremely disconcerted at my disappointment.

I cleared my throat. "I think I see flashing lights. Good. I can't wait to get this over with so we can turn our focus back on the case."

"Yeah," he agreed noncommittally. "The case is most important."

Even though I was facing away from him, looking down the street and watching as the flashing lights in the distance grew brighter, I could tell he was staring at me again. The knowledge made my skin prickle in a way that wasn't totally unpleasant.

Chapter 16

When we eventually got to the courthouse, half the morning had gone, used up in answering questions and offering explanations as to why anyone would be so invested in impairing my health that they'd cut my brake lines. Because that's all the police discovered, much to Wren's chagrin. There were no bombs secreted amongst the metal workings of the engine, no TNT strapped to the muffler.

I gave the police as little as possible, hesitant to make connections between my work and the sabotage; creating new chains of evidence that touched the inquiry against Christopher, even peripherally, could cause delays. Even knowing that the police were just doing their job and that I had been the one to call them, I still parsed out information as sparingly as I could. To check my car out more thoroughly, they called in a tow truck and had it pulled to the nearest evidentiary car lot after taking my statement.

As we entered the lofty entrance of the Superior Courthouse, offering the security guards our briefcases and the contents of our pockets, I was trying my best not to hustle the guards into moving faster. My plans for arriving early had been completely dashed and frustration mixed with impatience made my attitude more curt than it usually was.

"Yes, yes, I'm sorry. I forgot I had change in my pocket," I said, exasperated. I held it up in my palm, showing the blank-faced guard who'd pulled me to the side after I'd set off the metal detector. "Can I go now?"

"Easy there, stormtrooper," Wren said, grinning at me. "The poor guy's just doing his job."

"I know, I know," I said with a sigh. "It's just that—"

"I know, I know," he said, mimicking me. "Come on, be nice to the security guard so he doesn't hold you in contempt or something."

I rolled my eyes at him before pasting a smile on my face and addressing the frowning guard. "I'm sorry, it's just that I'm late. I know you hear that a lot..."

"I do," he answered, his voice even.

"Can I go through now?" I beamed at him, really putting effort into it.

"Yeah, yeah. Go through."

I snatched up my briefcase and hurried through the cavernous main foyer of the courthouse. From the main entrance hall, branches of the building spread out in different directions, like the arms of an octopus, and I marched down the one pointing west. I'd studied the layout of the Dallas courthouse last night, so I'd know exactly where to go. I saw Paul sitting on a bench along the wall, a laptop open in his lap and a pen hanging from his mouth.

Halfway down the hall, I turned to Wren. "We're going to go over some preliminaries. Why don't you go and get some breakfast? I'm sure you're starved."

Wren nodded. "Do you want me to bring you back anything?"

I shook my head. "No thanks. I'm too amped up to eat. But you enjoy yourself."

As I watched him walk away, I marveled at the empty feeling his absence instantly left me with. What were we going to do after this was all over? He would just go on living in Landsfield Ridge and I would continue on with my life in San Francisco? I pushed the thought aside. There was too much to worry about now without my adding to it.

I came to stand next to Paul and, noticing my presence, he looked up at me.

"Maya, I'm glad you made it. Did the police have anything they could tell you about your car?" His ruddy face—I envisioned him being a sailor in his free time, his thick hair pushed this way and that by the wind, the sun bright on his lined face—was somber, far more than my own predicament accounted for, I thought.

"Not really," I said with a shrug. "Is everything okay? You look..."

"Well, Maya, I've got good news and I've got bad news. Which do you want first?"

My heart sinking deep into my rib cage, I exhaled. "The bad news. It's always best to hear that kind first."

"Judge Mailor was in a motorcycle accident during the weekend. Apparently, he's a member of an overweight, mid-life crisis biker club and they had a ride through the hills this weekend. I don't know the details," Paul shook his head, "but his bike went down and Mailor tumbled down a hill, hitting most of the trees on it on his way down. He's in traction and we've been assigned a new judge." Paul paused and I felt my breath hitch in my chest. It felt like although the accident may have been bad news for Judge Mailor, mine was yet to come.

"We've been assigned the Honorable Judge Gilbert Houston." Paul, who was a local attorney and knew all of the judges, quickly filled me in.

I felt my spirits sink. Most of the judges attorneys come across are as neutral and impartial as they're supposed to be; they try cases with clear heads and offer fair hearings without too much input. Some judges take a more active approach; if they have questions, they ask them, making sure that the jury has all of the information available to them so as to ensure a fair trial. And then there are the judges that are notorious for their apparent hatred of their chosen occupation. They are the judges of lore, the ones who lawyers speak about behind raised hands, the ones who have never stopped being lawyers even though they now wear the robes of judgement. And it isn't just that they wished they were still active participants, these judges think they could do the attorney's job better—and often point that out during the trial, undercutting the prosecuting lawyer's standing with the jury and making the defending lawyer feel as though their client were destined for the electric chair, guilty or not. One guess as to which group Gilbert Houston belonged to, according to Paul.

"Wasn't pleased?" I repeated incredulously. "This is devastating to our case! From what you told me, Houston is notorious for mistrials and hung juries."

Paul moved his wide shoulders uncomfortably, as though his suit jacket were too tight, before tucking his laptop back into his leather briefcase and coming to his feet. "I just got the news this morning. Houston is just finishing up a trial, so our first court day has been moved to Wednesday. I waited here for you because I wasn't sure if you'd answer my phone call, what with you being occupied with the police and I wanted to give you the news in person, anyway." He assumed a tight-lipped smile. "At least we have another two days to prepare before we have to deal with Houston. That was the good news, by the way."

I rubbed my temple with the tips of my fingers. "I'm sorry. This is a lot to process. I just can't believe we have to deal with that..." a thought occurred to me, produced by Paul's mention on my dealings with the police. "Do you think that Mailor's accident could've been caused by foul play? By the same people who cut my brake lines this morning?"

"I don't know," Paul said, hoisting the strap of his briefcase onto his shoulder in preparation of leaving. "It's going to be hard to prove, either way, especially if Mailor never regains consciousness. Even if it was, the outcome wouldn't be any different, so we have to work with the cards we've been dealt. I'm going back to my office, to work on my opening statement. Would you like to join me or do you have things to do?"

I blew a gust of air through my lips. "Knowing that we're going to be dealing with Houston, I think I better go back to my hotel and do some thinking about what's the best way to move forward."

Paul patted me on the shoulder, his gaze moving beyond me as his attention wandered, his thoughts no doubt taken up with the new challenge that Houston presented. "Don't worry about that. Leave the thinking to me. If you want to type up some notes about our evidentiary exhibits, that'd be very helpful." With one last pat, he moved past me—which was lucky for him because if he hadn't, I would've been very tempted to jam my knee into a very sensitive part of his anatomy. *Leave the thinking to him?* I thought incredulously, my eyes boring into his retreating back. *I'm the second chair on this case, not his legal secretary.*

Stewing in a soup of animosity and wounded pride, I barely registered the fact that I'd exited the courthouse until a cold gust of air blew a stray sheaf of hair across my face. I looked up and down the street, wondering where Wren had gone. I needed him now more than ever; if I was to hold up against everything Paul had told me about what Houston would throw at us, I'd need to make sure every i was dotted and every t crossed—and no one was better at details than Wren.

Seeing him walking down the sidewalk toward me, I raised my arm in greeting and hurried to meet him. After telling him of the newest development, excluding the way Paul had dismissed my help, Wren adopted a concentrated frown.

"The judge sounds like a real pain in the ass." He raised a paper bag that was streaked with dark splotches of grease. "I got breakfast for us right here. You want to head back to your hotel room and put our heads together on how to deal with him?"

I nodded gratefully. "Yes, please."

As we walked slowly, waiting to catch the attention of a passing taxi, I wondered aloud if Judge Mailor's motorcycle accident had been anything but.

Wren shook his head. "It's going to be hard to prove, if it was."

"That's what Paul said. But, if it was foul play, how would they know that the case would be reassigned to Houston?"

"They probably didn't. If someone forced Mailor off the road, I'm sure all they were concerned with was causing hardships for the continuation of the trial. If accidents don't work, I'm sure they'll start using less...indefinite methods to get their point across."

"Like cutting my brake lines?" I offered.

"Like cutting your brake lines," Wren agreed with a nod. He turned and lifted a hand to call an approaching taxi. After we climbed inside and gave the driver my address, Wren shifted in his seat to face me. "So tell me more about this Judge Houston."

I rubbed a hand over my eyes. "Well, Paul said that the last time he presided over a trial, he made the lead prosecutor cry."

"Oh, that poor woman."

I lifted my eyebrow. "It was a man. He quit being a lawyer shortly after the trial—which he lost."

"Oh," Wren said quietly, his eyes wide.

"Yeah, oh."

The hardest case of my life had just gotten a lot harder.

***

Two weeks earlier

When Christopher saw a strange number pop up on his screen, he felt the tell-tale tingle between his shoulder blades that alerted him to something on the wind, that some new development was forthcoming—and as he never knew whether the intuitive prickle heralded good or bad news, his tone upon answering the call was cautious. Very few people had this number and those who did never called unannounced.

"Hello?" He injected a healthy amount of Scottish brogue into the greeting; he was supposed to be from Scotland, after all.

"Hello. Am I speaking to..." a short silence, "...Christopher McLaughlin?"

Christopher swallowed. So, it seemed the news was bad.

"That depends on whom I'm speaking to," Christopher replied, running his fingers along the hem of his swim shorts. His tropical surroundings, the raucous macaws and the susurrus of water brushing against sand did little to ease his newfound anxiety. He'd just recently finished forming his plans concerning the senator job and hoped that whatever this call was about didn't affect them. Reconfiguring his plans once he'd mentally undertaken them was such a bother.

"I'm a friend, I can assure you of that." The voice was a man's, confident and self-assured, but Christopher couldn't match a face to it.

"I have very few of those, even fewer who have access to this phone number."

"Then let's say I'm your newest friend. One you didn't even know you had." The man cleared his throat. "I'm calling to let you know that you've become a suspect of interest to the FBI."

Christopher's eyes opened wide and even though it was futile, he glanced at his surroundings, searching for someone or something that didn't belong. All he saw was his cabana, dock, and the sunlit beach stretched out before him. "Why would I be of interest to the Federal Bureau of Investigation? I'm not even a citizen of the United States. As a boring, middle-aged Scottish businessman, maybe I should feel flattered." He paused. "But I don't. In fact, I feel as though I should report this call to Interpol."

The man laughed. "Oh, that's good. You're good, Mr. McLaughlin. Very convincing. The thing is...it's too late for lies. You've been found out. Your home in Mexico has been discovered and your contact in Tim Collins's inner circle has been arrested for conspiracy and fraud."

Christopher felt his throat constrict and took a drink of water from the table next to him. Only minutes before, he'd been relaxing under an umbrella, drying off after his swim, and now...now he was being told that his very existence was endangered.

"Why are you telling me this?" he asked. "And who is, what was that name? Jim Collins?"

"You keep playing your little games, Christopher, and see where they get you. I'm the only one willing to go out on a limb and help you out."

"Yes, and that begs the question why. Who are you and why are you telling me this?"

"Let's just say that you and I have some of the same friends. People who are invested in you staying out of prison. I always keep our friends informed when new and interesting suspects are brought to my attention and when I saw in your casefile that you had possible connections with said friends, I brought your name and the suspicions against you to their attention. They were not pleased. They ordered me to help you out of your predicament. Hence, this courtesy call. Watch your back, moving forward, Christopher."

Pursing his lips, Christopher thought about how to respond to this warning, but he was saved the trouble when the other line disconnected.

Hmm. Interesting. He mused over this recent development. *How to proceed...* He listened to the surge of the incoming tide, the soft splash of waves hitting the sides of his docked boats, and after a few minutes of contemplation, the corners of his mouth lifted as he slapped his thigh. The fact that he was under suspicion raised the stakes, added the flair of danger to an already precarious situation. He was into it. He even thought he saw a way to make it work in his favor.

"Catch me," he whispered as he stood, "if you can."

Chapter 17

Wednesday dawned clear and cold, and I wished that my mind was as crystalline as the sky above as Wren and I waited to catch a cab downtown. The past two days had been full of stress and frayed tempers—on my part; Wren, on the other hand, had been nothing but supportive. The flairs of temper had occurred when he'd gotten the bright idea of role playing the courtroom experience, with him playing the part of Judge Houston, of course.

The second time he'd called me a pejorative word that put the morals of my mother and father in question, I'd slashed my hands through the air. "Enough, Wren. Judge Houston might be bad but he'd never use a word like that in a court of law. You're overacting."

Wren had merely shrugged. "If we prepare for the worst, we'll be pleasantly surprised when it's not as bad as we thought."

"Yeah, but this isn't helpful. It has to at least be realistic in order for it to be effective."

"So I have to make you cry, is that what you're saying?"

I'd shaken my head and called for a break. Needless to say, we hadn't tried the role-playing tactic again. I'd focused on the trial, how to break down the defense's case and leave no doubt in the jury's mind as to Christopher's guilt. It was proving to be more difficult than I'd anticipated; I didn't fully understand what had happened the night he'd been arrested. I couldn't understand his motives or the outcome he'd expected. I'd ended up going around in mental circles, chasing my tail and the vague outline of thoughts that didn't make sense, no matter how much I tried to force them to. Now that the day we'd tried to prepare for was here, I felt a mixture of excitement, despair, and regret. Maybe I should've let Wren play the part of Houston once or twice more...no, I was ready for this. I wasn't going to let one crotchety old man get in the way of seeking justice for my father's death.

It wasn't until Wren said, "Technically, Christopher isn't being charged with your father's death," that I realized I'd spoken this last aloud.

I barely managed to restrain myself from rolling my eyes. "Yes, I'm quite aware of that." I held up a hand and listed off the things Christopher had been charged with. "Attempted manslaughter, assault, reckless endangerment, and conspiracy."

"Yeah, but how many of those do you think will actually stick?"

I scowled at him. "Are you questioning my capability as a lawyer?" I felt more shaken than I let show. It was as though he'd been reading my thoughts, seeing the misgivings that I hadn't voiced aloud. When he shook his head, his eyebrows lifted in alarm at my tone, I continued, "They'll all stick." Giving into the misgivings I'd been trying to smother, I added, "I think."

"Remind me what you have in terms of actual evidence?"

We got into a waiting taxi and I answered Wren's question with one of my own.

"How much will Judge Houston allow, you mean?" I shrugged. "That's up to Paul, I guess." This was said with more than a little resentment. The lead prosecutor had continued to treat me like his secretary, sending me on errands and having me take notes during his meetings with our expert witnesses. I'd given him the video featuring Christopher wearing the watch, the list of people who owned one of the expensive time pieces, and all of the other pieces of evidence Wren and I had gathered during our investigation. Watching the video of my father's death again had been hard, but knowing that Christopher was in custody made it a lot easier than it had been.

"You being on the witness stand will be a big help," I said, tucking my chin into the collar of my jacket. "You're our main expert witness—"

"Wait, what?" Wren interjected. His face had gone deathly pale, the blood draining from it with a suddenness that made me thrust my hand out, ready to catch him if he fainted. "I thought I told you I didn't want to be involved."

I scowled at him. "You said you didn't want any of the media attention, you didn't say anything about being involved in the case itself." I softened my expression. "Wren, I need you to testify."

He shook his head violently. "No, I can't."

"Why not?" I tried to ask this gently, in a concerned tone—which was hard because I wanted to scream it at the top of my lungs. "Why have you even been coming to the courthouse with me if you weren't going to testify?"

"I was going to tell you Monday morning. I had planned on flying back to Landsfield but when I found out that you were being targeted by the mob," he shrugged, "I changed my mind."

"So you'll stay here to protect me but you won't help me win this case? I don't understand."

You're going to have to trust me," he mumbled, red staining his pale cheeks. He avoided meeting my questioning gaze, and I knew the growing crimson blotches on his face stemmed from embarrassment and regret. Unfortunately for him, the knowledge didn't soften my attitude towards him.

"Trust you?" I said, almost shouting. "Trust you? Wren, this is the most important case of my career—no, make that my life—and all you can say is that you want me to *trust you*? I barely even have a case without you!"

He finally met my glare. "I have my reasons, Maya."

I threw my hands up into the air. "How great for you. I'm so glad you have your *reasons.* Are you able to share them or are they secret reasons that you can't tell anyone about? Because you know what? You seem to have a lot of secrets, like your past and your relationship with Rebecca and your—"

"Maya, do you have any idea how much time I've had to take off work to help you with this case? I don't know about in San Francisco or Dallas, but in Landsfield Ridge we don't have the climate for money trees. I have bills to pay and a mortgage and obligations to the library. My life doesn't revolve around you!" His voice had been growing in heat and volume throughout this tirade and by the time he was finished, everyone in earshot on the trolley was staring at us, enjoying this early morning spectacle.

His words hit me with an almost palpable force. I *had* been acting as though he had nothing better to do but help me out. He had a life outside of the drama I'd involved him in and I'd forced him to drop everything for the past couple of months, expecting him to be embroiled in a trial that might go on for even longer.

"I'm sorry, Wren," I said, biting at my lower lip. "You're right. I've been so selfish." The last thing I wanted was for him to feel taken advantage of; he meant so much more to me than that.

"I'll go with you to the courthouse, Maya, because I want to make sure you're safe, but I can't testify. I can't be involved." His expression was solemn, and I nodded, feeling chastised and embarrassed at my selfishness.

"If you have to go back home, Wren, you can. You don't have to stay here. I'll be fine."

He sighed. "I do have to go back home, Maya. I'm so sorry. I'll ride with you to the courthouse, to make sure you're okay, but then I'm taking the cab back to the hotel to get my things and going to the airport."

When we got out of the cab, the courthouse a block away, it was with the friendly companionship we'd always enjoyed, but I couldn't help but wonder at his insistence on returning home. What was Wren hiding?

***

One week earlier
Dallas, Texas

Christopher adjusted his tie, looking around the room of well-dressed, neatly coiffed people, and idly wondered which ones were actual art enthusiasts and which were FBI agents. Carrying his tray of canapes, it gave him the perfect excuse to circulate throughout the room at a leisurely pace, watching the interactions between gala guests. He'd gone to the kitchen and had his tray refilled twice before he'd picked out the agents; it wasn't hard, they stuck out like ungainly giraffes amidst sleek gazelles.

Even though it was an art gala and everyone was wearing black, from the women in their slinky black dresses and the men in their black suits, the agents wore black without the benefit of grace and style. They tugged at the cuffs with impatience, stuck fingers between their ties and their thick necks, their heads, topped with cheap haircuts, swiveled as though on sticks. Christopher, enjoying the spectacle, made sure to keep plying them with champagne flutes and salmon sandwiches. He felt safe behind his thick glasses and unfortunate dental work, his hunched, awkward shoulders and his shining bald head. The informant who'd called him hadn't said they knew what he looked like, only knew that he was going to target the senator; he'd never shown his face to the inner-circle snitch and the face that went with his Christopher McLaughlin identity wasn't his, so he felt close to invisible as he wafted through the gala, just another current of air drifting through the overly perfumed room.

He stayed away from the senator for the first two hours of the gala, content with watching the FBI agents watch Tim Collins as he went over the plan in his mind. It was far from the original but he was still pleased with it. Pills rattled in the prescription bottle he carried in his pocket, supposedly treating a rather embarrassing medical condition that he'd explained to the security guard in excruciating detail. He figured as the night drew to a close, after numerous glasses of champagne and the few glasses of whiskey he'd seen the senator imbibe, Collins would be in such a jolly mood that the final toast celebrating his wife would be downed with gusto—without worry or care if the coloring or the bubble content was different than in previous glasses.

Stifling a bored yawn, Christopher held his tray out to one of the three agents canvassing the room. They were just as fatigued as he was pretending to be, being on their feet for hours past their usual clock-out time, and he was counting on their tiredness and boredom.

Finally, it was time for the final toast. Christopher meandered over to the senator, a single flute of champagne left on his tray. Nearing the shorter man—politicians were always smaller than they appeared to be in pictures or on tv—Christopher looked left and right, his nervous expression causing the lines in his forehead and around his eyes to deepen. Dipping a hand into his pocket, his pinky finger caught on the exterior lining, and he fumbled around before finally extracting the bottle of pills. Biting his lower lip with his fake teeth, feeling the crooked ends dig into his soft skin, Christopher opened the bottle and dumped out two pills into his palm, dropping the bottle in his haste. The sound of the plastic bottle hitting the ground was drowned out by the sounds of celebration around him, and as he ducked down to pick it up, out of the corner of his eye, he saw all three agents making a beeline toward him.

Consciously loosening the muscles in his back, Christopher gave way when the first agent jumped on him, falling to his hands and knees with an audible grunt. Screams and shouts of surprise echoed through the tall-ceilinged room, mingled with the muffled curse words the first agent uttered when the second and third agents jumped on top of the huddle.

At the bottom of the pile of flailing arms and legs, Christopher let his mind go blank. Those gathered around the impromptu scrum were forced back as the agents got to their feet, yanking him to his feet and securing his arms behind his back.

As federal agents, they didn't feel the need to read him his Miranda rights, merely marched him from the room with alacrity. Christopher couldn't help the smile that tugged at the corners of his lips. Yes, everything was going just as he'd planned.

Chapter 18

There was so much I didn't understand about the case, so much that didn't add up, that my notebooks were full of questions, rather than pertinent lines of inquiry. It was these notebooks that I pulled from my briefcase and set on the long wooden prosecutor's desk, glancing over at Paul and wondering whether he felt the same trepidation I was mentally struggling with. Our preparatory meetings hadn't given me an inkling as to any concerns he might have; he was confidence itself, barking out commands and statements he expected me to write down—and for my part, I *did* write them down, but with question marks rather than the exclamation points he used when speaking his thoughts aloud.

I pressed my palm against my stomach, trying to quell the first-day nerves that were battering my insides. *What was going on with Wren?* I thought, trying to keep my mind busy as I arranged my pencil next to my tattered notebooks and opened my laptop, touching the power key until the screen lit up. *He's acting like he's on the lam or something. But that couldn't be...could it?* Mentally ridding myself of these unhelpful and confusing thoughts, I focused on the task at hand: today's opening statement.

Paul was slated to deliver ours, though I'd had a big hand in preparing it. He was one of those people who listen intently to the ideas of others, think for a moment, then make grand pronouncements of the same idea they'd just been given, passing it off as their own. It was infuriating and demeaning and totally annoying—but there was nothing I could do about it. If I wanted to be involved in the trial, this was the only way. I'd choked down my pride and pasted on an empty-headed smile throughout most of our prep meetings. Today, sitting in the courtroom, awaiting the arrival of Judge Houston, I regretted my hesitancy, my reticence. It wasn't representative of who I was as a person or as a lawyer. I had a voice, an intelligent, informed one with years of experience to back it up—so why was I letting Paul steamroll me?

As the bailiff called for everyone to rise, I gained my feet, watched Judge Houston march into the courtroom as though he were storming a castle, and felt my stomach drop into my sensible patent-leather shoes. As the reality of my situation set in, carried forth by the admittance of Houston into the expansive room, a flash of inspiration allowed me to understand why I'd taken the passenger seat in this trial: I had too much to lose. From the very start of all this, those emails from the Concerned Citizen, to the discovery of the watch and narrowing down of the list of suspects, to our reconnaissance of Christopher's Mexican hideout, it all reduced down to one thing. Finding my father's killer and bringing him to justice. Closure after the past six years of mourning his loss. I was lucky to even be a part of this trial. I knew that and Paul knew that and I think he used it to his advantage, treating me as less because he knew he could. Very few people can resist taking advantage of those holding a lesser position than they and Paul wasn't one of them. I didn't blame him. All I could do was take what I had and run with it. And that's exactly what I intended to do.

"Okay, here we go," Paul muttered to me under his breath as the proceedings got under way. The defendant was brought in, his hands fettered behind his back and unshaven stubble growing on top of his head. I hadn't seen him since that day in the FBI field office and was surprised to see that he looked no worse for wear after the time he'd spent in custody. He looked well-fed, fit, and disconcertedly content. Nothing like a man facing an attempted murder trial. Again, I couldn't help but wonder why.

After Christopher sat, the charges against him were read and I silently followed along in my head. *Attempted manslaughter, assault, reckless endangerment, and conspiracy to commit murder.* Then, the defending attorney was asked for his opening statement.

"And, counselor, make it short and succinct," Houston said, eyeing the tall, thin lawyer with a malicious gleam in his eye. "I don't want to know about every good deed the defendant has ever done, about the charities he gives money to or the stray animals he nurses back to health. Keep to the point, if you please."

The gangly attorney nodded, seemingly unphased by the warning, but I saw his Adam's apple bob up and down in his throat as he swallowed.

"Ladies and gentlemen of the jury, we're here today to decide the innocence or guilt of this man," he indicated to Christopher with a practiced gesture. "This is not something that should be taken lightly. The charges being brought against him are serious offenses, some carrying substantial prison sentences that would change his life forever, long after he was released." He strode across the room, his hands clasped together behind his back. "The prosecuting attorney will try to convince you of his guilt, that Christopher McLaughlin attempted to murder a well-known politician, that he came to that gala in Dallas, Texas, with malicious intent. But, ladies and gentlemen, that is far from the truth."

Even though both parties knew that Christopher wasn't his given name, there wasn't enough evidence to name him anything else, so it seemed as though his latest identity had stuck.

"The truth is that my client was tasked with the performance of a harmless prank. He was paid to put a drug in the senator's drink that would make him appear drunk and disorderly, make him act in a way that would be damaging to his campaign. Now," the lawyer adopted a chastising expression as he turned his attention to his client, "this isn't something that should be taken lightly. Drugging someone is a serious offense, one that, rightly so, is punishable by substantial fines and up to a year in prison. But I ask you," he turned back to the jury, "is slipping a mickey into a flute of champagne something that should forever damn my client as a felon? The senator's health was never in any danger, though his bottom line might have been, if his constituents had taken offense to his actions while under the influence of the drug. But this trial isn't about what might be, it's about what is.

"My client was attacked by the FBI agents at the gala, suffered extreme bodily injury at their hands, and is currently suffering the mental anguish at the prospect of a ruined life. All because of a prank. It's not right. It shouldn't be condoned. Not by you, the members of the jury, and not by the prosecuting attorneys, and not by the esteemed judge who has been given the authority to preside over this trial. I ask you to open your minds and your hearts as you listen to the evidence that will be presented to you. I ask you to question the validity of their claims," he pointed a long, narrow finger at Paul and myself, "and ensure that there is no doubt whatsoever in your mind as to Christopher McLaughlin's guilt before you make your decisions. Not even an inkling. Because a man's life and livelihood is at stake, his future and his present. Christopher McLaughlin *is* guilty...of a harmless prank. Nothing more and nothing less. Thank you."

As he stepped back behind his desk, he laid a hand on Christopher's shoulder, giving him a somber yet confident look as he sat. I wanted to applaud. It had been a great performance. Christopher had obviously done his homework when he'd hired his lawyer; he'd laid down framework that had the potential of discounting everything we as the prosecutors would offer in terms of evidence. Even the use of the word "mickey" had made what Christopher had done seem like a harmless prank rather than a serious crime.

Judge Houston, who'd been watching the defending attorney with a moue of distaste, turned his attention toward Paul.

"Counselor Henderson, the prosecution may give their opening statements. And consider the same warning that I gave Mr. Colby and apply it to yourself." His thick gray brows dropped low over narrowed eyes. "Not that it made a difference."

Paul gave the judge a disarming smile. "Absolutely, Your Honor." When the judge met his grin with a frown that threatened to grow into a snarl, Paul hastily stood and stepped around our desk, turning his gaze toward the jury. As he gathered himself, I scanned those seated in the jury seats. As usual, they offered a variety of humanity: from an aged woman with a scarf tied around her tightly permed hair to a young housewife wearing an anxious expression, as though she were cataloguing all of the chores that were not getting done in her absence, to a paunchy man who looked as though he belonged in the seat of some big piece of construction or demolition machinery. We'd gone through the jury selection together, with Paul insistent on trying to choose as many men, no matter their race or creed, as were available—even though I told him again and again that women were just as capable of finding the defendant guilty as a man was. Maybe even more so; women weren't as prone to playing pranks as men, due to the innate maturity childbearing and rearing forced upon us. But, as usual, he'd ignored me and picked who he wanted to pick, with the result being a two-to-one ratio of men to women sitting on the jury panel. I hoped that wouldn't come back to bite us in the ass.

"Ladies and gentlemen of the jury," he began, coming to stand in the middle of the open space between the lawyer benches and the judge's raised dais, "make no mistake about it. That man," he pointed at Christopher, "tried to kill a prominent US politician. We have expert testimony that proves that the substance found in the capsules Christopher McLaughlin had on his person would have stopped Senator Collins's heart. You will hear that testimony in the upcoming days and weeks of this trial, but I want to give you the opportunity to think about the premeditation that went into this 'prank' the defending attorney wants you to believe that the attack on Tim Collins was. Christopher assumed a costume, changed his appearance, and went to that art gala in Dallas with the intention of killing the senator because he was *paid* to do so. He was given money in exchange for ending a man's life, ladies and gentlemen. That's called assassination. That's called first-degree murder. That's an offense punishable by life in prison and that's exactly the crime that I'm going to ask you to convict Christopher of. This was no prank, no friendly joke between political rivals.

This was the premeditated execution of a plan to end a man's life.

"By calling this unlawful and deliberate act of violence a prank, the defending attorney would have you believe that Christopher was just a fun-loving guy who got caught before the joke could be completed, like a mischievous child trying to put a whoopie cushion on his grandpa's chair or a college boy who'd been charged with completing a prank before he could be admitted to the fraternity. But this isn't the case."

As Paul continued comparing what Christopher had done with different pranks and practical jokes, I silently urged him to shut up. The more he brought up the resemblance, the more Christopher's crimes were actually starting to look like pranks. I'd warned him against this, reminding him of the old adage that if you wanted someone to think of a pink elephant, all you had to do was tell them not to.

"Remember, as you listen to the testimonies of the expert witnesses and speak to the FBI agents who were present at the gala, the facts of the case: one, that Christopher was paid to do harm to another human being, it was no mere prank. Two, that he spent a lot of time planning, from his costume to his appearance. This was no spur-of-the-moment incident. And three, that if Tim Collins had ingested the contents of those pills, he would likely have died from heart failure—an outcome that would've suited Christopher just fine, as that is exactly what those who put him up to this prank wanted." Paul surveyed the jury, looking up and down the two rows of aisles and making sure to make eye contact with every member who was returning his gaze. "Pranks are harmless and amusing. This was not a prank. This was attempted murder.

"Thank you."

I didn't feel so much like clapping as Paul sat down beside me, unless it was clapping my palm against the side of his face. How many times had he used the word "prank" to describe what Christopher had done? Even as he was adamantly denying the fact that it was a joke, he kept using the phrase in reference to the events at the gala. What did he expect the jury to think? I would've taken a completely different tack, one that steered away from pranksters and practical jokes and focused on Tim Collins's family and his positive influence on the political climate, how devastated both would have been had he drank the substance within those pills and succumbed to the heart condition that I would have revealed to the jury. But had Paul listened when I told him that that was the way we should steer our opening statement? No. He had gone his own way and now that jury was going to liken Christopher to a mischievous man with nothing but lighthearted gaiety on his mind, rather than a ruthless killer.

"Now that *that* is done with," Judge Houston said, making it sound like he'd just undergone a visit to the dentist, "we can move on." He waved an imperious hand at our table. "You may call your first witness."

I cleared my throat, looking out of the corner of my eye at Paul. This was another point we'd argued back and forth on: who to call first. I'd wanted to focus on the medical expert, relying on her to back up our assertion that ingesting the pills would've killed the senator, while Paul had wanted to call the informant the FBI had arrested, the frustrated young man who hadn't risen as high as he'd wanted as fast as he'd wanted, and so had been feeding Christopher information about the senator's private life and schedule.

Paul took his time returning to a standing position, adjusting his tie and smoothing the crisp pleats on his pants before speaking. "The prosecution would like to call Ryan Gorst to the stand."

I bit my lower lip, almost drawing blood. It looked like the informant was going to be our first witness. *You're such an ass, Paul,* I thought, forcing myself to release my lip before my lipstick was tinged with the crimson of my blood.

Chapter 19

As Ryan Gorst shambled up to the witness stand, my hands clenched into fists on my lap. He was not the way I would have opened the presentation of our case; he was a snitch and a disreputable character but didn't look as sleezy as I knew him to be. His hair was slicked back and appeared to be covered in motor oil, but his cheeks were smooth and hairless, making him look younger than he was. He had a way of posturing that always made me think of a featherless peacock; he still paraded around, waiting to be noticed, but had nothing to back his self-confidence up with.

I grabbed my pen and readied myself to take notes. If I thought that Gorst was on his way to ruining our case before we even had a chance to start, I was ready to scratch down a message to Paul. Our lead prosecutor was slowly making his way toward the witness stand, his hands clasped behind his back.

"Mr. Gorst...may I call you Ryan?" Paul asked.

"Sure," the witness said with a shrug.

"Thank you. Ryan, can you tell us about your involvement with Senator Collins?"

"Sure," Ryan repeated, shifting in his chair. "I was in charge of Tim's schedule. I made new appointments, made sure that he kept old ones, and generally kept track of where he was supposed to be and when he was supposed to be there."

"I see," Paul said, a thoughtful frown creasing his brow. "You said 'I was in charge,' does that mean that you are no longer in charge of Senator Collins's schedule?"

Ryan adopted a disgusted sneered. "Yes, I mean, no, I'm no longer in charge. I was fired."

"Why were you fired, Ryan?"

He shifted in his chair again. "Because of a misunderstanding."

Paul waited, his expression the epitome of patience. When Ryan didn't offer any further explanation, he said, "Do you think you could elaborate on that?"

Ryan sighed. "They said that I was feeding classified information to that guy," he pointed at Christopher, "but I wasn't doing anything like that at all." He slouched back in his chair, his arms crossed over his chest. "I don't even know that guy. Never seen him before in my life."

"Were you arrested, Ryan?" Paul asked, changing tack.

"Yeah."

"What were the charges?"

"Conspiracy and fraud and other stuff like that. It was all ridiculous, though. I didn't do anything wrong."

Paul walked back to our table and grabbed a sheet of paper from it. "It says here, on your arrest report, that you were arrested for conspiracy to commit a crime, allegations of fraudulent activity, and embezzlement." Looking as though he were confused, Paul idly tapped his thigh with the paper. "Those are pretty serious charges. Why would you get accused of those crimes if you didn't do anything wrong?"

Ryan sighed, his eyes rolling. "Because I *might* have been feeding the senator's schedule to a political reporter who paid me for the information. But, I mean, it's public knowledge, not classified or anything. And, for the record," he looked over at the jury, "I don't know how that money made its way to my account. I was framed."

Since no one was looking at me, I let my own eyes roll around in their sockets. The embezzlement charge was the one with the most evidence behind it; Ryan Gorst had been accepting contributions from Tim Collins's constituents without the senator's knowledge—and had been putting it his own bank account rather than that of the campaign. But that wasn't why he was up on the stand; what we wanted to prove was that he had been feeding information to Christopher, knowledge that the assassin used to plan his hit.

"This political reporter you mentioned," Paul said, tapping his chin and looking pensive, "how do you know it was a reporter? How did you two meet? Did they reach out to you or did you reach out to them?"

"He got a hold of me. By email."

Paul nodded. "And what did he write? How did he introduce himself?"

Ryan rolled his eyes again. "He said his name was Victor Francis and he introduced himself as a political reporter, which is why I assumed he was one."

"A reasonable assumption to make," Paul replied. "Did you ever meet in person?"

"No, just through email."

"What kind of things did you write about in your emails? What did this Victor want to know? About Senator Collins's political stance on important issues?"

Ryan shook his head. "No, he wanted to know about Tim's schedule, where he was going to be and when, stuff like that."

"Did it ever occur to you that a political reporter focusing on something other than Senator Collins's politics was strange?"

Shrugging, the witness said, "I didn't think too much about it."

"Why was that? Because he was sending you money for the information you were giving him?"

"Objection!" the opposing counsel said, rising to his feet. "Leading the witness."

Judge Houston, who looked like he was having a hard time staying awake, waved this away dismissively, but said, "Sustained. Rephrase the question, Counselor."

"Were you receiving money for the information you were sending to this political reporter?" Paul asked, after giving a gracious nod to the judge.

Ryan squirmed in his chair.

"Remember that you swore to tell the truth, Ryan," Paul reminded him gently.

"Yes, he sent me money every time I told him about Tim's schedule."

I nodded to myself. We'd obtained Ryan's bank account records and were able to prove that deposits into his account coincided with emails he'd sent to an encrypted email address. The address had been registered under the name Victor Francis, but, thanks to TJ, had been found on Christopher's personal computer. Whether or not we'd be able to use that information was going to be up to the judge; it was evidence that we were planning on using later on in the trial, the authentication of which would mean asking for a private meeting with the opposing counselor and Judge Houston. I had planned on presenting Wren as the expert testimony to back up TJs use but would have to come up with another way of supporting the computer spyware, now that he'd refused to participate.

"Did you tell Victor about the art gala in Dallas?" Paul asked.

"Yes."

"You told Victor that the senator was going to be present?"

"Yes."

"How soon after telling Victor about the gala were you arrested?"

"Objection! Relevance?"

"I'm trying to establish a timeline of events, Your Honor."

Judge Houston looked back and forth from Colby to Paul, his eyelids heavy. I frowned. He didn't have the usual bulldog expression that he usually wore while presiding; I wondered why. He'd stormed into the courtroom with all his usual vigor, but it was as though the longer the questioning went on, the more fatigued he became.

"Overruled."

Paul nodded his thanks and turned back to Ryan. "How soon after telling Victor about the gala were you arrested?"

"A couple of days," Ryan answered with a shrug. "The police came barging into my office at work, saying that I was under arrest. It was embarrassing."

"I'll bet it was," Paul said. "Not as embarrassing as having to give back all the money you'd embezzled, though, was it?"

"Objection!"

"Question rescinded," Paul said quickly, before Houston had a chance to chime in.

I had to admit, he'd done a great job with Ryan so far. Paul had established the fact that Ryan was an unsavory character who'd sold out the senator—and bamboozled quite a few wealthy political supporters—before his arrest for charges unrelated to the trial at hand. What he had yet to establish was the fact the Christopher McLaughlin was Victor Francis. I waited for him to start making the connections, laying out mental paths for the jury to start wandering down, with the destination being Christopher's masquerade...and waited. He couldn't say outright that we had evidence on Christopher's computer, that had to wait until we could find a private moment to speak with the judge, but he needed to start pointing the jury in that direction.

But instead, Paul focused on Ryan's association with Tim Collins, how long they'd worked together and their personal history. I mentally urged him to move on, that he was losing the jury's attention, but he doggedly kept the questions centered on Collins, rather than Christopher. Finally, I snatched my pad of paper closer and wrote, in capital letters, FOCUS ON THE DEFENDANT! The next time Paul ambled by, I subtly pointed at the note, but he merely glanced at it and continued on his way, not changing course physically or mentally.

By the time he said, "I have no further questions, Your Honor," I was practically shooting steam out of my ears I was so angry. He'd done nothing to introduce a connection between Victor and Christopher, which was the whole reason Ryan was one of our witnesses.

Colby stood up and walked around his table. Addressing Ryan, he said, "Mr. Gorst, did you ever meet Victor Francis face to face? Did he ever send you pictures of himself?"

"No."

"Does this man," he gestured to Christopher, "look like Victor Francis?"

Ryan shook his head. "I told you, I never met the guy. Victor could look like Santa Claus, for all I know."

"Did Victor ever describe himself to you, give you any indication of his background, interests, or hobbies?"

"How many times do I have to say it? We talked about Tim's schedule. That's all. I don't know anything about Victor Francis."

"No further questions, Your Honor." Colby shot an exultant look at us before resuming his seat next to Christopher.

Judge Houston yawned and called for a recess for lunch. He stood, those in the courtroom stood, and as he walked out of the room, I turned and glared at Paul.

"What are you doing? I thought we talked about establishing a relationship between Ryan and Christopher."

"It's a relationship we can't prove unless Houston permits us to use the files from Christopher's computer—which we don't even know whether or not he's going to do." Paul's back was almost painfully straight with affront, and his expression was an interesting mixture of surprise and outrage, as though he couldn't believe my audacity. *I* was questioning *him*? "If you don't mind, Maya, I'd like to conduct this trial in accordance with my twenty years of experience as a prosecutor."

I had to clench my jaws together in order to keep a very disrespectful remark concerning what I thought his twenty years had taught him about dealing with witnesses and juries—which was very little. I knew I was here only because Jack had pulled some strings and done me a favor; I had to rely on Paul's mercy to stay on the case and calling out his ineffectual questioning wasn't the best way to do it.

"Yes. Sure, Paul. Whatever you say," I replied, wanting to bite my tongue off rather than offer these placating phrases of surrender.

If Paul heard the anger in my voice, he didn't show it. He merely nodded and straightened the papers on the desk. "I'm going to grab some lunch. I'll meet you back here in an hour."

I watched him walk away, my mind wrapped up in how the hell I was going to survive this case without imploding, until my phone rang.

"Hello?" I snarled.

"Maya, you sound like you want to kill someone. Is everything going okay?"

I turned my attention from Paul to him. "I don't know." I gave him a quick rundown of the day and asked, "So, what do you think?"

Wren sounded uncomfortable when he answered. "Why don't you go somewhere and grab a bite to eat and we can chat there. I don't want you to miss lunch."

Nodding, I stood, leaving the courtroom and walking out of the courthouse. I took a deep breath of the cool fall air and instantly felt better. As I strolled toward Patty's Diner, which I took to be a favorite of lawyers escaping the pressures of the courtroom, as it was filled with suits, I started to think more positively about how the day had gone so far. We'd established that Ryan was an unsavory character who only cared for his bottom line, which would come in handy when we called him back to the stand and revealed evidence directly connecting him to Christopher. The distasteful impression Ryan had made would inevitably leach off onto the defendant, making him look even more guilty than he already did.

They found the pills in his pocket, I reminded myself. *It shouldn't be too hard to establish the fact that he's guilty of conspiracy to commit murder. You've practically got this in the bag already, Maya.*

I grabbed a corner booth, weaving through the crowded diner, and picked up the laminated menu off the table. I hadn't been eating much lately, what with the stress of worrying about the mob and the trial, so as I perused the sandwiches on offer, I felt my mouth start to water.

"Grilled cheese, tomato soup, and coffee," I ordered, handing my menu to the waitress.

"That sounds good. I wish I could have the same," Wren said. "Oh, and order an Oreo milkshake. You'll need something sweet afterwards."

I smiled at the phone, enjoying the lighthearted conversation. "Okay. That does sound pretty good."

I sat in companionable silence with my phone—and, by proxy, Wren—for a while, enjoying the murmurs of the various discussions going on around us. Most of it pertained to law, but here and there I heard snippets of personal exchanges.

"And I told her that I wasn't going to pay child support for her dog! Can you imagine? She tried to tell the judge that since that little weasel-faced chihuahua was her emotional support animal, I should be the one to pay for its vet bills. Can you believe that?"

Grateful that none of my romantic forays had ever gone as far as marriage, I turned my attention back to Wren and asked, "So, how do you think we did today? I know it's based off of my second-hand commentary but I hope I gave you an idea of how things went."

Wren said, "Well..."

I frowned. "Spill it."

My food arrived, but I didn't touch my meal as I waited for him to explain his comment.

He sighed and said, "I thought you guys were going to start pointing fingers at Christopher from the very beginning. From what you said, it sounded like Paul focused more on just establishing that Ryan guy's guilt. Which, by the way, you certainly did. It sounded like he came off as a creep."

Sighing, I tore off a bit of crust from my sandwich and nibbled at it, my appetite gone. "I know. That was the plan, but Paul decided to take it another way, to wait until the judge allowed for the inclusion of the evidence from Christopher's computer."

I know the tone of my voice implied what I thought of Paul's direction, so I didn't add anything more—especially since what I wanted to add was how much Wren's testimony would help with the support of that evidence.

"Does Paul know what he's doing?" Wren asked. "Do you feel good about working with him?"

I shrugged. "I would feel better if I were the lead on this case, rather than the second. He's a bit of a chauvinist, to be honest. I know he thinks I belong behind a secretary's desk, not sitting beside him at a trial."

Wren was silent for a moment. "Who is the next witness?" he said, when the silence had stretched out for too long.

"We are planning on calling one of the FBI agents who was at the gala to the stand next." I dropped the bit of crust into the red depths of my soup. "Hopefully, Paul sticks to the plan with *that* witness."

Chapter 20

"Your Honor, the prosecution would like to call Travis Lindley," Paul said.

The rest of the lunch break had been uneventful, with me and Wren batting ideas back and forth over the phone, and now that court had reconvened, I felt as though I'd benefitted from talking with him. It had served to fill my head with positive potentialities, rather than negative thoughts concerning the way Paul had been treating me so far. Glancing up at the lead, I noticed that he had a dab of something dark red on his tie, ketchup? Feeling quietly happy at this little detail, I refrained from mentioning it to him as he rounded our desk and walked toward the waiting witness.

"Travis, do you think you could tell the court a little bit about your professional background?"

The FBI agent nodded, his wide, clear-cut jawline casting his thick neck in shadow. "I've been an agent with the Federal Bureau of Investigation for twelve years. In that time, I've apprehended many who were suspected of plotting and carrying out assassination attempts." He shrugged. "This being the latest."

I liked the way he casually included Christopher into the assassination narrative. It would be easier for the jury to make mental connections between assassinations and the defendant. I settled back into my chair; this was starting off good.

"Can you tell me about that night in Dallas? At the gala? Walk us through the event and Christopher's apprehension."

Travis nodded before speaking. "Me and two other agents were told to watch out for a man with his physical description. We had a photograph but we were worried about the level of disguise he would use, luckily for us he didn't go too far with it and we recognized him quickly" he nodded toward Christopher, "because he was planning on going after the senator."

"Objection, Your Honor. I'd like to point out that Travis is merely an FBI agent and has received no training in facial reconstruction based on verbal descriptors."

I gave the defending counsel a wry look. The man was obviously reaching for reasons to discount Travis's testimony; if the jury members had a brain in their head they would see that, too.

Judge Houston, who looked as though he'd had lunch in a boxing ring, the half circles under his eyes were so dark, waved this past. "Sustained."

"Apologies, Your Honor. Travis, could you share with the jury the description you were given? Who were you supposed to be looking out for that night?"

Travis shifted his attention from Paul to the jury. "I was told to keep an eye out for a very fit guy in his early forties. We assumed he'd be in some kind of disguise, but we were told his hair and eyebrows were originally dark, his eyes blue. We spotted him right away, one of the waiters."

Paul lifted a hand to forestall the agent. "How did you know he was a waiter? How could you be sure?"

"Have you seen people lately?" Travis's voice was half apologetic and half shameless. "It's pretty hard to find ones that are very fit anymore. When I saw him," he gestured toward Christopher, "I knew right away that he was the guy we were looking for."

Out of the corner of my eye, I watched Colby, wanting to see if he was going to let that statement slide. He looked annoyed, but didn't stand to offer any objections. Maybe he'd learned that trying to make a clean-cut Federal agent out to be a bad guy wasn't such a good idea.

"Could you point out the person, if he is in fact in this courtroom, who fits the description you were given that night?"

Unerringly, Travis pointed at Christopher. "Him. He'd shaved his head but his eyebrows were still dark and you could tell beneath his costume that he was in very good shape. He was the only waiter circulating the room who wasn't sporting a belly."

"What did you do next, after you'd identified the person you'd been told to look for?" Paul asked.

"We'd been told to keep tabs on him but not approach unless it looked as though something was going down, unless the senator was directly threatened. When I saw him approach the senator and tuck a hand into his pocket, I made an informed decision and dissuaded him from coming any closer to Tim Collins."

Paul and I had talked about this moment, about how to approach the fact that Christopher had been forcefully taken down to the ground. We didn't want the jury to feel any sympathy for him or think that he'd been brutalized in any way. We'd coached Travis on his reply, to make sure that he didn't use any words or phrases that implied unnecessary force.

"I see," Paul said thoughtfully. "After the suspect was in custody, what did you find in his pockets?"

"We found a bottle of unmarked capsules filled with an unknown substance."

"Did the FBI run tests on the substance within the capsules?"

Colby jumped to his feet. "Objection. The witness isn't a forensic expert, nor is he qualified to offer his opinion on test results he didn't perform himself."

"Sustained," Houston said, the second half of the word almost drowned in a yawn.

"Once the suspect was in custody, did he say anything?" Paul asked, a slight frown on his face. He was looking back and forth from Travis to Houston, his attention on the FBI agent only long enough to ask his question before turning his attention back to the judge.

"He said that it was just a joke. That the pills were just supposed to make the senator look drunk. He said that the last thing he'd want to do was try and kill anybody."

Paul nodded. "We'll come back to the last part of that statement shortly but first, I'd like to ask you a question based upon your twelve years of experience. How many of the people you've apprehended actually confess to their crimes once they've been caught?"

Travis chuckled, displaying straight white teeth. "That'd be none. Not a single one."

"I suspected as much," Paul said, a small grin on his lips. "Now, back to what you said about the pills killing anyone. What did you mean by that?"

"The capsules were full of an herbal powder capable of disturbing or arresting the heartbeat of the person who ingested them. In a normal person, they would just cause an irregular heartbeat, but in Senator Collins, it could have been deadly."

Colby again jumped to his feet. "Objection. The witness is not a medical examiner or an expert in herbal pharmaceuticals."

Paul turned to address the judge. "The contents of the capsules aren't up for debate, so an expert isn't necessary to tell us what was in them. He was the agent assigned to the case, he has access to all of the facts, and he has twelve years of experience with the FBI. I think he's capable of remembering the contents of a report correctly."

"Sustained."

This time I could see the anger on Paul's face at the judge's ruling. He cleared his throat and tried again. "Travis, are you aware of the senator having any medical issues?"

"Yes."

"Could you tell the court, without inference or conjecture, what you believe the senator to be ailing from?"

"I was told that Senator Collins suffers from a heart condition and that he has a pacemaker."

"And it's your understanding that the contents of those capsules could be deadly to a person suffering from a heart condition like the senator's?"

"Yes."

Before Colby could leap to his feet again, Paul dismissed the witness. "Thank you, Travis. I have no further questions."

Colby was standing and moving around his desk before Paul even had a chance to sit at ours.

"Travis, let's go back to your earlier statement, the one about it being easy to spot an in-shape person versus one who isn't. What exactly were you implying?"

Travis shifted in his chair. "I wasn't implying anything. I was saying that in a room full of ten people, nine of those will be overweight and only one will be fit. We were told to be on the lookout for a suspect who took care of himself, and there was only one person at the gala who fit that bill."

"None of the gala attendees were in good shape? None looked like they took care of themselves?"

"Well, yes. Most of the people at the gala were in good shape. People with money generally can afford to be."

"I see. Why didn't you tackle any of them? You couldn't have known that Christopher would be a waiter versus an art aficionado. Are waiters the only type of people who you suspect of being guilty? Because of their tax bracket, you assume they need the money and are therefore willing to do anything to get it?"

"Objection!" Paul said, pushing himself to his feet. "He's both leading and badgering the witness."

"Overruled," Houston said, sitting back in his chair and steepling his fingers in front of his face.

"Jesus Christ, we're getting slaughtered," Paul muttered as he resumed his seat. "Houston hasn't ruled in our favor at all today."

"Go ahead and answer the question," Colby said, folding his arms across his chest and looking at Travis grimly.

Travis sighed, knowing he'd backed himself into a corner. This was turning into a discussion on class distinctions, which was definitely not good. You rarely find wealthy people on juries because they usually figure out a way to buy themselves out of jury duty.

"We figured he'd be dressed as a waiter because they usually go undetected in a crowd. No one looks at waiters, no one makes eye contact with waiters. It was the safest bet. One that turned out to be correct, by the way."

Stick it to him, Travis, I cheered silently.

"So if you're fit and wealthy, you're not a criminal, but if you're an in-shape guy who makes ends meet by serving at high-end events, you're automatically a suspect? Seems like your profilers need to enter the twenty-first century, Travis. Nowadays, rich people can be guilty of crimes, too." Colby uncrossed his hands and turned, as though he were finished with the witness. Before he could, he paused as though re-membering something and faced Travis once more. "I wonder, if one of the gala attendees had approached the senator with a pocketful of pills, would you have almost given them internal bleeding too? Or is that a tactic you save only for the blue-collar suspects?"

"Objection!" Paul shouted. "Your Honor, that line of ques-tioning is ridiculous. Travis was doing his job. Nothing more and nothing less."

"Sustained."

"Your Honor, I sincerely ask that you—"

Paul was cut short when Houston slashed an impatient hand through the air. "Sustained. If you continue to expostulate out of turn, counselor, I will hold you in contempt."

After a quick glance at us, Travis said, "My only objective was the senator's safety."

Colby stared at him for a long moment before nodding slow-ly. "I have no further questions."

As Travis was led from the witness stand, Paul and I huddled together.

"Travis is a cool operator," I said. "That's the only thing that saved us there."

Scrubbing a hand across his face, Paul nodded. "Houston is worse than I thought he'd be. He sustaining everything that prick Colby is saying. Maybe we should call for a recess and see if he's in a better mood tomorrow."

"No," I replied, shaking my head. "We can't end the day like that. Let's call the forensic expert to the stand. That way we can at least establish that the capsules contained deadly poison, rather than a harmless intoxicant."

"Good idea."

As Paul stood and called our next witness, I wondered at his sudden change of heart when it came to listening to me. I thought it must be Houston, and the way the judge was shaking his confidence. Whatever the reason, I was glad for it.

The forensic expert took the stand and Paul led her through her qualifications and experience before getting to the heart of the matter.

"Did you examine the capsules found in the defendant's pocket?"

"Yes, I did."

"Could you tell us what the capsules contained?"

The older woman nodded graciously. "They contained a potent mixture of bitter orange, St. John's wort, and oleander."

"And for those of us who don't know, what are the constituents of these particular substances?"

"They are all herbs and plants that have been proven to affect those with heart conditions. Bitter orange in high doses can cause irregular heart palpitations. St. John's wort is also considered dangerous to those with preexisting heart conditions. Oleander is a common shrub that is extremely toxic to humans. One leaf can kill a grown man." The forensic expert paused for effect, just as we'd told her to. "The capsules contained the powdered equivalent of three oleander leaves."

"I see," Paul said, his brow furrowing. "So, your assertion is that the pills could be considered deadly if they were to be consumed by someone with a heart condition?"

"Very," she said coolly.

"I have no further questions, Your Honor."

Paul walked back to our table and sat. We hadn't wanted to leave out the fact that Senator Collins had a heart condition, but we had to wait until his physician was available to supply testimony, and she hadn't had time in her schedule until Friday, two days from today. We figured at least establishing the deadliness of the pills would work to chip away at the idea that slipping them into Collins's drink was a mere prank.

"I have no questions for this witness," Colby said.

Paul and I looked at each other in confusion. How did he plan on refuting what our expert had just said without questioning her? The reasoning behind his actions immediately became clear when he continued to speak.

"The defense would like to call Dr. Timothy Piper to the stand."

Since he had declined questioning our witness, he had the right to call his own in order to refute our expert's testimony—unfortunately. "Oh, shit," I growled. He had his own forensic expert. This was not going to be good.

A portly man who carried his weight around his mid-section, his round stomach straining against his leather belt, waddled up to the stand. Once again, bona fides were established before the real reason behind his presence was revealed.

"Dr. Piper, have you had much experience in dealing with herbal constituents?"

"Oh, yes. I've performed numerous drug trials for pharmaceutical companies involving many different plants and herbs. I'm well acquainted with most of them."

"What can you tell us about bitter orange?"

Dr. Piper cleared his throat. "Well, it's been traditionally used as a blood purifier and recent studies have shown that it works well as a sedative for sleeping disorders."

"What would happen to someone who ingested bitter orange?"

"Well, they would sleep better."

Soft chuckles emanated from the jury stand as I ground my teeth in frustration. Colby had chosen his expert well; the guy practically oozed a jolly, good-humored aura.

"Would they become woozy, maybe even appear drunk?"

"Oh, quite possibly, yes. Especially when taken with alcohol."

"Have you ever been to an art gala before, Dr. Piper?"

His apple cheeks bunching in a smile, Piper nodded. "Oh, yes. My wife is a lover of the arts."

"And do they generally serve alcohol at gala events?"

"Objection," Paul crowed. "Relevancy?"

"Overruled," Houston said, his eyes lidded.

After being directed to answer the question, Piper grinned sheepishly and said, "I'm not a patron of the arts, so the alcohol served is usually the only reason I go to such gatherings."

"Thank you, Doctor. Moving on, what can you tell us about St. John's wort?"

"It's used as a mood elevator, often in treatment for those suffering from anxiety."

"Would it make you appear drunk?"

Piper smiled again. "It wouldn't make you look sober, especially when mixed with alcohol. People who've ingested St. John's wort often feel very content and happy. Mixed with alcohol, the feeling would be amplified."

"I see. And lastly, what can you tell us about oleander?"

"It's a shrub often used to foliate highway dividers, especially in California. It's been used in treatment of asthma and diabetes, with some success."

"Do state authorities often use deadly plants to decorate its thoroughfares?"

"I don't know. That falls outside of the purview of my training and education."

I rolled my eyes; even the man's ignorance was adorable.

"If oleander has been used to treat asthma and diabetes, I find it hard to believe that it's a deadly poison," Colby said, looking from Piper to the jury.

"It's not," Piper said distinctly. "It's actually quite an attractive plant."

"No further questions, Your Honor."

Paul leapt to his feet and questioned the doctor at length, but only managed to get the rotund man to admit that, in certain high dosages, most herbs could be considered poison. Knowing that it would be damaging to our case to make it look as though we were badgering the kind-looking older man, Paul announced he had no further questions and strode angrily back toward our desk.

"Well," I said, trying to appease him, "at worst, our expert testimonies were a draw. We scored a point and they scored a point. But when we have Collins's physician on the stand, our expert will be infinitely more relevant."

"If Houston doesn't sink our case before then," he grumbled, glaring up at the judge, who had grabbed his gavel and banged it down, declaring the day's proceedings over.

"Yeah," I said slowly, staring at Houston as he trudged out of the room. "About that...I think I have an idea of what might be going on there."

Chapter 21

After that first, not-so-great day in court, I called Wren when I got back to my hotel room. I had an idea about what was going on with Judge Houston and I wanted to run it by him. Sitting on the bed with my heels kicked off and my suit jacket hanging over a chair, I waited as the phone rang. And rang. When it kicked me to Wren's voicemail, I ended the call. I hadn't been prepared to leave a message and hated the impromptu, awkward way I always spoke when I didn't have something figured out in my head first.

"I'll call him back later," I said to the empty room. I was a little hurt that he wasn't around to answer my call; he knew that him being away from all this, when we'd gotten to this point together, was a sticking point for me. The least he could do is be around his phone at the end of the day.

Dropping my phone on the bed, I shucked off my clothes and showered, running my theory about Houston over and over through my head. The obvious tiredness he was fighting, his disinclination to rule in our favor, the lack of spit and fire he usually brought with him to the courtroom...they all added up to one thing: the mob was after him.

Drying myself off, I wiped a clear passage in the foggy mirror and looked at myself. Was I jumping to conclusions? Seeing the boogeyman around every corner just because my rental car had been messed with? I plugged in the hair dryer and began blowing the hot air over my hair. Houston could be having other personal problems that didn't involve the mob. His mother could be sick, his dog could be missing, he could be having money troubles.

"That doesn't explain why he's so dead set against letting us win an objection every now and again," I told my reflection over the sound of the hair dryer. Some of them had been legit and we'd deserved what he'd ruled, but when almost every single objection was in favor of the defendant? That wasn't right. Wasn't fair.

I finished drying my hair and pulled it back into a braid for the night. Checking my phone, I saw that Wren had called while I was cleaning up. Tapping the screen, I sat on the bed and rehearsed what I'd gone over in the shower.

"Maya! How was your first day in court?"

"It wasn't as good as it could have been," I said, tightening the ties of my bathrobe. "But I have a theory as to why that is." I explained everything, telling him about how exhausted Houston appeared, how he kept ruling in favor of the defendant. I concluded with, "And that's why I think he's being threatened by the mob."

Wren was silent. I knew that it was a lot to digest so I gave him a moment before saying, "Thoughts?"

"It feels like a pretty big jump," he said, his voice apologetic.

Sighing, I leaned back against the headboard. "I know. I keep second guessing myself but it makes sense." I paused. "Doesn't it?"

He blew out a breath. "Yeah, it does. The only thing to do is approach Houston and ask him about it."

I was afraid he'd say that. "How is that going to come up in casual conversation? 'Oh, hey, Judge Houston, have you been threatened by the mob? Because there are some underhanded connections between the defendant and Luca Rossi I can't exactly prove that you should know about.' He'll kick me out of his office faster than you can say disbarred."

"It's the only option," Wren said. "I don't know what else to tell you. Your hunch isn't enough to take to the police and you don't even know if Houston is getting harassed or threatened. You're going to have to ask him."

I sighed.

"How is the trial going otherwise?"

I waved a dismissive hand in the air. "It's going okay, I guess. Our witnesses have been cooperative and giving their testimonies like they've been told to. There's just so much that even I still don't understand about Christopher's arrest that it's hard to nail down whether we're convincing the jury or not."

"Talk it through," Wren said. I got the impression from his voice that he was settling back into a chair, getting ready for a long talk. "What don't you understand?"

"The FBI agent we questioned today said that he saw Christopher going for his pocket." I shook my head. "Everything we know about Christopher has pointed to his savviness. A pocketful of pills just doesn't seem like something he would do. He's too smart for that. He'd have one or two tucked into the cuff of his shirt and let them drop just before handing Collins his drink. No one would see a thing." I ran a hand over my forehead. "It doesn't make sense."

"Even the best make mistakes," Wren replied. "Maybe it was an off day for him."

"You don't last as long as he has and have off days," I said. "Something isn't right."

"Don't take on too much," Wren said. "Just focus on the trial and let everything else take care of itself. Are you going to be able to pull it off even with Houston giving you trouble?"

"It's all going to depend on whether or not Houston lets us use the information TJ gave us." I didn't want to talk about the fact that I was still pretty put out by Wren's unwillingness to testify or even be present at the trial, so I sped past this topic and moved on. "I think we're having a meeting with him at the end of the week to discuss the inclusion of new evidence. But the biggest issue is whether or not Paul is going to keep disregarding everything I say."

We talked for another half hour—well, I talked and Wren listened and when the conversation finally wound down, I said, "I won't keep you up any longer. Thanks for listening to me complain. Hey, I didn't even ask about how things were going at work. Did they miss you when you were gone?" I'd monopolized the whole conversation and didn't want Wren to think I was so obsessed with myself and my problems that I didn't care about him. Because I did. I missed him.

"The library isn't the busiest hotspot in town, so I don't think they were too inconvenienced by me being gone for so long. One of my regulars gave me a hard time, but Mrs. Horton has always had a crush on me."

I raised an eyebrow. "Oh, really? This Mrs. Horton, she's happily married, right?"

"Yes, and about eighty years old, I'd guess," Wren said with a laugh. "I always save the daily paper's sudokus for her and she said when I was gone her brain had gone soft without them. She's a sweetheart."

"Sounds like it," I said, absurdly relieved that Mrs. Horton was an octogenarian and not some young, good-looking soccer mom with too much time on her hands. "Well, I guess I should call it a night. I have some notes to take before going to bed."

"Alright. Thanks for calling, Maya. It was good to talk to you. Call me tomorrow, okay?"

"I will." I opened my mouth to say goodnight but something else came tumbling out instead. "I miss you, Wren."

There was a long moment of silence that I filled with mentally slapping myself. When Wren's voice came through the speaker, it was low and slow, almost sensual.

"I miss you too, Maya. I wish I could be there for you. I really do."

"I know," I said, barely above a whisper. "I'll talk to you tomorrow."

"Tomorrow," he replied.

After tapping the screen and ending the call, I tossed the phone on the bed and flopped down next to it. "I can't believe I just said that," I told the empty room. "Next thing you know, I'll be professing my undying love and asking him to father my children."

Shuddering at the thought—and the very cute mental images that accompanied it of Wren holding our newborn baby—I pushed myself up and grabbed my notebook, resolved to get some work done before going to sleep.

When I woke up in the morning to the harsh sound of my alarm, my cheek was pressed against the notebook, the spiral edge digging into the soft skin of my face.

"Shit," I said groggily, tapping the alarm off and trying to rub away the aching pain in my cheek. I'd fallen asleep and, checking the notebook, hadn't done a thing to prepare for today. "Double shit."

Mentally forcing away the dreams I'd had, of Wren and I on a beach much like the one outside of Christopher's cabana, playing frisbee with a daughter that looked just like me, I sat up. Since I'd showered the night before, I just combed my hair and put on my makeup before pulling on my pantsuit. As I was arranging my briefcase, the door to my hotel room jiggled, the handle bucking up and down as though someone was trying to open it from the other side.

"Hello?" I called out. Had I ordered some kind of room service the night before? After my tours of duty in the Middle East, I'd done some weird things in the middle of the night without remembering but that kind of thing hadn't happened in years. "What is it with me and hotel rooms?" I muttered to myself when no one answered my call and remembering an incident in the near past. "I must put out some kind of 'come mess with me' vibe."

The door rattled violently and I began to think that it was going to break open. I quickly scanned the room in search for a handy weapon. I couldn't bring my pepper spray on the airplane, so I was at the mercy of what was available to me. I saw my belt, still stuck in the loops of my jeans, and whipped it free, smiling in satisfaction as the heavy metal buckle whistled through the air. To my left I could see my laptop charging cord dangling from the desk and knew I could use that as a garrote, if need be. There was also an empty glass bottle on me bedside table; one whack and I would have a needle-sharp stabbing implement.

Swinging the belt around in a circle, I called out, "I'm armed. If you come inside this room I will shoot you." I wasn't exactly as armed as I wished I was, but they didn't know that.

The door stilled and I heard the sound of muffled voices. Bringing my ear closer to the door, I heard someone say, "Excuse me. I said, what do you think you are doing?"

An explosive *oof* followed this demand and I heard steps running down the hallway. Unlocking the door, I pulled it open and peeked out. A uniformed man was pushing himself to his hands and knees, looking over his shoulder at a figure fleeing down the hallway. The door at the end of the hall banged open as the man—I could see from this distance that the figure was male—pushed through and disappeared behind it.

"Are you okay?" I asked the young man who was now standing beside me, his arms wrapped around his stomach. I recognized the uniform as being that of the hotel. I wanted to chase after the guy, but knew that I'd better make sure the poor hotel employee was okay first.

"Yeah, I think so. Jeez, that guy hit me hard."

"What was he doing?" I asked, my belt dropping loosely to hang by my side. *Nothing to see here, just a fashionable makeshift killing tool.*

"I think he was trying to break into your room," the man said, bending over slightly at the waist. "Ugh, I think I'm going to throw up."

I checked him out. "You'll be fine. It's probably just the adrenaline. Let me get you some water." I brought him a plastic cup filled with water from the tap and watched as he downed it. "Did you get a good look at him?" I asked, once he'd finished drinking.

"Not really," the man said, shaking his head. "I had just been called to a room down the hall," he gestured behind us, "to check out the plumbing and saw him trying to open your door with a crowbar. When I walked up to him and asked him what he was doing, he hit me in the stomach and took off. He was bald, I remember that."

I winced. A crowbar to the stomach sounded painful. Then, I realized what his story meant. A man had tried to break into my room. A man with a crowbar and a bald head. Could it be one of the guys that had messed with my rental car brakes? I growled under my breath, wishing I had decided to chase after the guy; it was too late now, he was long gone.

"Hey, are you going to be okay? I have to make a call," I said, not even waiting for his response before I ran back into my room. Picking up the hotel phone, I dialed Paul's room number.

"This is Paul," came his voice over the receiver.

"Are you okay?"

"Yeah, why wouldn't I be?"

"Whew," I let out a relieved breath. "I'm glad you're okay. Look, a guy just tried to break into my hotel room. Have you noticed anything weird outside your door?"

"No, I haven't noticed anything. What do you mean, someone tried to break your door down? How?"

I told him what had happened When I was finished, I paused to catch my breath and heard him say, "Wow. Well, that's certainly an interesting story."

I straightened. "No, it's not." He was making it sound like something I made up. I was getting so sick of his patronizing me.

"I'm sure it was just some drunk coming in after a night of partying. He picked the wrong door and got mad when his key wouldn't work. The same thing happened to me last year, except it occurred at two in the morning at a conference in Las Vegas. I almost knocked the guy's head off."

"But why would he start beating the door with a crowbar?" I asked angrily. "Was it a construction workers convention he was getting back late from?"

Paul's tone changed from wry to soothing. "You're right, Maya. That is strange."

"It's not only that," I said, still pissed off. "I think that Houston has been getting threatened too. That's why he kept ruling against us yesterday." I had planned on waiting to tell Paul about my suspicions face-to-face, but the pieces all fit. We were being targeted.

"Um, Maya, let's just cool down a little bit. Tell you what, how about we meet downstairs for breakfast and go over this new theory of yours."

I scowled. He made my "new theory" sound like a fairytale, a make-believe story I was trying to pass off as truth. But, I couldn't jeopardize my standing as second chair so I swallowed my pride—again—and agreed to meet him in the lobby in ten minutes.

Grabbing my jacket and briefcase, I marched out of the room, slowing down as I passed by my door. There were deep gouges in the wood, surrounded by jagged splinters. Taking pictures of the damage with my cell phone, I zoomed in on the image and let out a deep breath. If the guy had made it into my room and had done that kind of damage to my body...I closed my eyes, working to control the emotions coursing through me. I felt anger and concern and, what really bugged me, vulnerability. Gritting my teeth, I opened my eyes, closed the door, and strode down the hall toward the elevator. I wasn't a victim. I was a fighter. If he would've made it into my room, he would have regretted it—if he'd lived long enough.

Chapter 22

The day before had been relatively uneventful, with Paul and Colby examining and cross-examining others who had been present at the art gala, from Christopher's fellow waiters to those who had been present to admire the art and celebrate Tim Collins's wife. The day hadn't been won by either side; the waiters had noticed little besides the amount of tips they'd been able to make and the gala attendees were more concerned with acting too well-bred to have observed anything that would sully the glamor of the evening than offer any evidence.

Today, however, was going to be different. Today was the day we were going to ask the medical expert to come forth and testify as to Tim Collins's heart condition, and this afternoon we were scheduled to meet with Houston in his chambers to discuss the inclusion of TJ's findings. I woke up early and popped out of bed before my alarm went off, hoping as I headed toward the shower that my new room—comped by the hotel, whose manager was aghast that something as incredible as an attempted break-in had happened under his watch—would remain unmolested.

When I got out of the shower I texted Wren.

Meeting with Houston today! Cross your fingers!

I dried my hair, arranging it in a neat chignon, and donned my business suit. Looking at myself in the mirror, I blew out a deep breath. Today had the potential of making or breaking our case. So much was riding on the evidence that TJ had provided us with that I wasn't sure how our prosecution would fare without it. Colby had done a very competent job of cross-examining our witnesses so far that I thought the jury was most likely still riding the fence, unconvinced one way or the other concerning Christopher's guilt or innocence. But, with the emails and other evidence TJ had collected, all doubt would be erased, with each piece of evidence, from his multiple identities to his connections to the mob to his correspondence with Ryan Gorst all acting as nails in Christopher's coffin.

I blew out a breath as I left the room, glancing up and down the hallway before heading toward the elevators, trying not to psych myself out about how important the meeting with Houston was. I was toying with the idea of also using the private consultation as an opportunity to approach Houston about his possible contact with unsavory characters like Luca Rossi. It would be an ideal...my phone buzzed from within the depths of my purse and I hauled it out, pushing the call button for the elevator before checking the screen.

It was a text from Wren. *Check this out and, please Maya, watch your back.* There was a link included and as I tapped on it, the elevator arrived. Stepping inside, I waited for the link to load and pushed the button for the lobby. When the headline of the news website he'd sent me popped on the screen, my eyes widened.

"Holy shit," I breathed as I read about the recent death of a San Francisco inmate named John Esposito. He'd been attacked in the showers with a makeshift shiv but the wounds that he'd suffered weren't the cause of death; the guards who discovered the body had noticed a sizeable lump in Little John's throat and the ME who had examined him later identified it as a bar of soap. Little John had been choked to death with soap while being stabbed repeatedly. I wasn't squeamish when it came to violent death but the thought of anyone, even someone as unlikeable as Little John, having a bar of soap shoved down their throat was disturbing. It looked like Rossi was cleaning up loose ends, exacting revenge on his one-time employee for snitching. How had he known? As the elevator arrived at the lobby and the door opened, an even more pressing question followed...was I next or was this a warning?

This thought accompanied me through the hotel lobby and into the cab, haunting me as I stared unseeingly out of the window at the sun-drenched, Texan metropolis. Rossi had managed to kill a man who was supposed to be under the protection of the California correctional facility he was imprisoned in, which meant he'd pulled strings, paid off guards, and managed to infiltrate a tough-to-crack institution—and I was just one woman with no protection, no around-the-clock guards. The knowledge unnerved me, but by the time I'd arrived at the courthouse, I'd told myself that the fact the Rossi was on the rampage didn't matter. What *did* matter was that my father's killer was brought to justice. I could look after myself; the United States Marine Corp had made sure of that. But, the Brazilian Jiujitsu classes I usually attended had fallen by the wayside, what with the case, and maybe I should think about finding a dojo in Dallas.

I pushed thoughts of Rossi and Little John aside as the cab pulled up to the courthouse, focusing on the day to come. First was the physician who would testify as to Tim Collins's heart condition. Then the meeting with Houston...yeah, I didn't want to think about that right now either.

One thing at a time, I told myself as I entered the auspicious building. *One thing at a time.*

"The prosecution would like to call Dr. Aditi Patil to the stand."

I watched as the stately older woman walked to the witness stand, her dark hair and complexion set off by the rose-colored suit she wore.

Paul walked around our desk and approached the doctor. "Dr. Patil, could you please state your qualifications and experience for the court?"

She rattled off an impressive list of university degrees, certifications, awards, and years of experience in her field. When she'd finished, she sat back and folded her hands in obvious self-satisfaction; Dr. Patil was a woman who'd excelled and she liked being able to share that fact with others.

"Thank you. Is it true that you are Tim Collin's personal physician?"

"Yes, it is. I've been Mr. Collins's primary physician for the past twelve years."

"Before we proceed, have you been given permission by Mr. Collins to share his medical history? I understand there are privacy laws that you must adhere to and I wouldn't want to put you in a professionally compromising position."

Dr. Patil nodded. "Yes, Mr. Collins had agreed to me sharing his personal information and diagnoses. He's signed documentation acknowledging and waiving his HIPAA rights."

On cue, I rose and handed the document to Paul, who handed it to the bailiff, who handed it to Judge Houston. Some days, the theatrics of the courtroom seem the height of laughability—especially on days where I've just learned that an informant had been choked to death with soap.

Houston glanced at the page briefly before letting it drop to his desktop and gesturing for Paul to continue his questioning.

"Dr. Patil, without getting into details that don't pertain to this trial, can you tell us about Tim Collins's health? Does he suffer from any disorders or illnesses?"

"Mr. Collins has a serious heart condition and had a pacemaker surgically attached to his heart five years ago."

"I see," Paul said, assuming a concerned expression. "And how does that affect Senator Collins's daily life?"

"It doesn't," Dr. Patil answered. "As long as he exercises moderately, eats a diet low in cholesterol, and monitors his blood pressure, Mr. Collins shouldn't even be aware of the fact that his heart is damaged."

"Are there any substances besides cholesterol that he should avoid? Anything that might cause his heart condition to worsen?"

"His alcohol consumption should be closely monitored and supplementation that directly affects the heart should be avoided."

Paul walked back to our desk and picked up a sheet of paper, studying it intently. Looking from it to Dr. Patil, he asked, "What about oleander, bitter orange powder, and St. John's wort? Could those be considered dangerous supplements?"

"Objection!" Colby shouted, getting to his feet. "As the doctor has said, her experience lies in the medical field, not herbalism."

"Your Honor," Paul said quickly, before Houston could sustain the objection, "Dr. Patil is certainly qualified enough to say whether or not her patient's condition could be worsened by specific supplementation."

"Sustained," Houston said. The semi-circles beneath his eyes were even more pronounced today, the skin hanging there looking bruised and heavy.

Paul sent me a meaningful look, one eyebrow raised, before nodding regretfully and turning back to Dr. Patil.

"What kind of supplementations are dangerous for those suffering from heart conditions similar to that Tim Collins is afflicted with?"

"Anything that specifically affects the heart." Dr. Patil held up a hand and started ticking off fingers. "Raises or lowers the heartrate. Increases or decreases circulation. Thins or thickens the blood, vessels, or lining of the heart's walls."

Paul hurried to me and sorted through the papers on the desk. I knew which one he was looking for and found it first, handing it to him.

"Our medical expert testified to the constituents of the substances found within the capsules FBI agents found on the defendant," he said, scanning the paper, "and she said that the plants and herbs contained within, oleander, bitter orange, and St. John's wort, would directly affect someone with a heart condition. From your experience, do you know of any evidence that would refute that?"

Dr. Patil shook her head. "There are numerous studies that support the contention that the plants you mentioned would be detrimental to someone with a heart condition." She paused. "*Very* detrimental."

"To the point where the person's life would be in danger?"

"Objection! Conjecture," Colby said.

Paul gave the doctor a quick, surreptitious look and she nodded in understanding, speaking fast, "Someone with a heart condition could very well die after ingesting those substances."

"I object!" Colby said, at the same time Houston opened his mouth and spoke.

"Sustained! Counselor, you will abide by the rules of this courtroom and not goad your witness into speaking when it is not appropriate." Judge Houston was glaring at Paul. "If you do that again, I will hold you in contempt."

"I apologize, Your Honor. It won't happen again."

I knew why Paul had done it. He'd figured that every objection would be ruled against him and in order to give the jury the information we wanted them to have, he would have to bend the rules a little bit. He turned his attention back to Patil.

"Thank you, Dr. Patil. No further questions."

Colby stood and stormed around his desk, his hands clasped in front of him. "Dr. Patil, are you a trained pharmacologist?"

She shook her head, an amused look on her face. "No, but I did graduate from Imperial College in London at the top of my class and have served as the top cardiologist physician at Baylor University Medical Center for the past ten years. So, it's safe to say that when I give a medical opinion on something, I'm far from guessing or speaking based upon pure conjecture."

Colby scowled. "If you could please stick to yes or no answers, Dr. Patil."

Shrugging, she nodded.

"Thank you. Do you ever subscribe herbal supplements to your patients?"

"Very rarely. I believe in science, and medication that has been exhaustively studied for side effects and possible complications. I don't think enough scientific inquiry has been performed on herbal supplements to support their being helpful."

I winced. She'd walked right into a trap.

Colby folded his arms across his chest. "If there is not enough scientific data supporting the benefits or dangers of herbal supplements, how can you assert that oleander, orange bitter, and St. John's wort are dangerous, regardless of whether or not someone has a preexisting condition?"

Dr. Patil pursed her lips, seeing that she'd taken the bait. "Though the harmful effects of those substances might not have been proven without a doubt, there is still enough empirical data to support—"

"But you just said there was a paucity of scientific inquiry, Dr. Patil. Now you're saying with that being the case, you'd chance your reputation on the contention those substances are dangerous?"

"You're twisting my words around. What I said was—"

"I can ask the court reporter if I need a reminder of what you said. Dr. Patil, are you one-hundred percent certain that oleander, bitter orange, and St. John's wort would've caused Tim Collins adverse symptoms?"

After a long silence, Dr. Patil blinked and said, "Nothing is one hundred percent except death and taxes, Mr. Colby."

I wanted to stand up and cheer. It was the best maneuvering I'd ever seen in the courtroom by someone on the witness stand, and I could see that the jury had been charmed by her answer.

As though feeling the change in the atmosphere, Colby gave a short nod and muttered that he had no further questions.

Paul stood. "I'd like to ask one more question before the witness is dismissed. Dr. Patil, is it possible that someone with a pacemaker and a serious heart condition could die if they ingested these substances?"

She nodded. "Yes. Very probable, actually."

"Thank you. No further questions."

When Dr. Patil walked past our desk, I gave her a wink and she dipped her head at me, a smile playing at the corners of her lips.

A recess for lunch was called, and Paul and I walked to a nearby deli to go over our upcoming meeting with Houston.

"And remember," he said, when we were finished eating and he was neatly dabbing at his mouth, "let me do all the talking. Your involvement with TJ has to be downplayed as much as possible so that Houston doesn't think that undue measures were taken to get access to the evidence against Christopher. One whiff of anything that will call into question the lawfulness of how the evidence was gathered and he won't let us use it. Got it?"

I didn't roll my eyes until he'd turned from me to pay the check—but it was a close one. How many times since we'd started working together had he reminded me that he was in charge of the trial and that my involvement was merely the result of him doing someone a favor?

We walked back to the courtroom and waited outside of Judge Houston's chambers, his assistant letting us in after a few minutes. Dark wallpaper and wooden paneling gave the room an old-fashioned, twentieth-century aristocratic feel, with book-lined shelves and an ornately carved table holding crystal decanters full of mahogany colored liquid only further-ing the Victorian vibe of the room.

"Counselors, to what do I owe this pleasure?" he asked from behind a wide, stately wooden desk. His elbows were propped on the desk, his fingers steepled in front of his face with his eyes barely visible atop them.

"Your Honor, we have vital evidence that is integral to our case that we are here to ask you to allow."

Houston's eyes narrowed and his hands fell to the desktop with a slap. "Gathering evidence should've already taken place. With that in mind, why do you feel the need to ask me for permission? Is there something amiss with it?"

Paul cleared his throat. This was the tricky part.

"The evidence was collected under rather...unusual circumstances." He proceeded to explain TJ and the incidents that led to its use, leaving out Wren's involvement as the nameless technological wizard who had developed the program. It had been a condition that I'd insisted on, knowing that Wren wanted to stay as far away from anything to do with the trial as he could.

Houston's face darkened as Paul spoke, his expression getting even more dour than it usually was. When Paul paused to take a breath, he interrupted, raising a hand.

"This is highly unusual, counselor," Houston said. "Let me get this straight. You used a computer program to hack into the defendant's computer, after finding his name on a list of people who owned an expensive watch? That is all the proof you possess that Christopher McLaughlin is an assassin who was hired to kill Tim Collins?" He looked to the side, his eyes moving so fast before returning to Paul that I almost wasn't sure they'd moved at all. "What did you find on his computer that is so important you want me to admit it as evidence?"

"Much more than I can tell you about before we're due back in the courtroom," Paul said, shaking his head. He glanced at his watch. "Which is in about twenty minutes."

Houston raised an eyebrow at him. "You forget that I set the schedules here, counselor." He leaned back in his chair. "In what form is this evidence? On paper, a computer file, a disk of some sort?"

"Everything we'd like to admit as evidence is on both Counselor Hartwell's computer and mine. Once we have your okay, I'll print out the evidence for formal admission into our case."

"I see. Well, as I said, this is highly unusual. I'm going to need some time to think about it." Houston squinted at the tall, freestanding clock on the far wall. "I won't be reconvening this afternoon, due to personal reasons, but meet me here early Monday morning, before proceedings begin, and I'll have an answer for you."

Paul nodded and we stood, each of us shaking Houston's hand. I was so wrapped up in thinking about the possibility of him letting us use TJs evidence that I couldn't think about anything else until we were outside of the building.

"Oh, man! I was going to ask about whether or not Houston is being harassed by the mob." I slapped my forehead. "I can't believe I forgot that."

Paul shrugged. "Maybe it's for the best. I'm sure it would've alienated him, at best, and pissed him off, worst case scenario. If you're still set on asking him, save it for the Monday."

I nodded reluctantly. It would have to wait until after the weekend, then. But for now, I was thankful that he hadn't denied our request outright. Maybe things were finally looking up.

Chapter 23

That night, Paul and I met for dinner in the hotel's restaurant. It had been my idea, a kind of mea culpa that sought to cross the divide between us and hopefully help us work past this lingering resentment that existed between us. I was feeling magnanimous after the meeting with Houston. I knew that the inclusion of TJs evidence would mean us winning the case; there was no way the jury could hold onto any idea of Christopher's innocence after learning what was in his personal computer. No way.

I held onto this thought throughout our meal, even though the ebullient high I'd been feeling dissipated as Paul and I tried to navigate awkward conversational gambits. Before the hors d'œuvres had been consumed we'd gone over his family and mine, our various hobbies and interests, and ended up sitting in silence as the main course was served.

I'd ordered the filet mignon and Paul the fish, and as we tucked in, I asked, "How's the lemon pepper sauce? Is it as good as it looks?"

He nodded, not bothering to inquire after my meal, so I ate the tender beef in silence, reminding myself that a workout in the hotel room come morning would be appropriate after eating all this protein. Push-ups and maybe some squats, with a few—

"Maya, I have something to confess," Paul said, interrupting my planning.

I set my fork down, the seriousness of his tone perking my ears. "You do?" I thought that maybe he was planning on apologizing for being such an ass to me and looked forward to dragging out his apology; he owed me at least a couple minutes of groveling.

"When Jack called me and asked me to allow you to second chair the case, I fought against it. Hard." He shook his head, not seeing the expression of confusion I knew to be on my face. "I have a team of highly experienced and professional lawyers I work with on a regular basis and I wasn't looking forward to dealing with someone new. But," he sipped his wine, "I think it's turned out okay."

I didn't know which to address first, the fact that he thought I was "okay" or the fact that he clearly thought I was here only on Jack's credentials and not my own.

"How do you know Jack and Rebecca?" I asked, assuming that to know one was to know the other. I wanted to seethe, wanted to lash out at the fact that Paul didn't respect me, but knew I had to let it go.

Paul waved a hand, sitting back in his chair. "I go way back with both of them. I went to law school with Rebecca and met Jack through her." He shrugged. "He and I never really hit it off. I got the feeling that he was really possessive over her and never liked it that we were friends." He drank his wine, finishing the glass and signaling to the waiter for another. His cheeks were slightly flushed and his tone was way more friendly than I was used to hearing, and I was glad that tomorrow was Saturday. I didn't relish the thought of babying a hungover lead.

After his wine was replenished, he continued. "I don't know what went on between you two, but Rebecca did not have many nice things to say about you. She said you were too personally involved to be a competent lead."

I ground my teeth. Too personally involved to be competent? *What a bitch.* "Wow. She must have been trying really hard to come up with nice things to say about me." I couldn't help my sarcasm, I never claimed to be perfect and knowing that Rebecca had bad-mouthed me to a business associate was infuriating.

Paul laughed overly loud, his hand slapping the table and rattling the plates and glasses. "She said that you and the computer wizard you're working so hard to keep under wraps had crossed the line when it came to how you managed to gather evidence against the defendant but that she couldn't begrudge you too much, as the capture was going to make her look good when it came time to dole out promotions."

"How nice for her," I managed to say through my clenched jaws. "What else did she say?" I figured that we may as well hash this out now, since wine had loosened Paul's tongue.

"That you couldn't help but throw yourself at every guy you came across, that it must have been physically challenging for you to climb the corporate ladder at your firm laying on your back, that you—"

"Okay," I interjected, holding up a hand. "That's enough. I change my mind, I don't want to know what else she said about me."

Paul shrugged. "I'm just repeating what she told me. I didn't believe any of it. You know how catty women can be."

I pursed my lips, my fingers curling around the steak knife next to my plate. *Do not stab him. Do not stab him. Do not stab him.* When the mantra had finally slowed my heartbeat and calmed me enough that I wasn't itching to jump across the table and attack him, I met Paul's wandering gaze. "Thanks for being truthful, I guess." I released the knife and set my hands firmly in my lap. "I think I'm going to call it a night. Call my room tomorrow when you're ready to do some prep for next week." When he nodded in agreement, his attention on an attractive woman at the next table, I stood and left the restaurant, sticking him with the bill. It did little to cool my temper.

My hotel room was undisturbed and stayed that way all night, which was becoming a novelty that I didn't take for granted, and I woke the next morning refreshed and energized—and ready to work out some of the animosity left over from the previous night's conversation with Paul. I found a local BJJ dojo and found that they had a morning class for intermediate students. Since I wanted to stop at the local library to do some research after the class, I stuffed my laptop into my gym bag before heading out. I walked to the dojo, as it wasn't far from my hotel, and spent a wonderful two hours grappling with strong, tanned Texans who took the craft of indestructability seriously. After spending a couple of hours at the library, hunched in front of my laptop screen and trying to stay away from other patrons—I'd showered after my class but hadn't thought to bring a change of clothes—I walked back to the hotel, stopping along the way to grab some coffee and a pastry, and turned my thoughts to the case. Though things were at a standstill until Houston came back to us with his decision regarding the TJ evidence, there was still one witness left who could make or break the case: Christopher.

I desperately wanted to be the one to question him, and spent the last ten minutes of my walk thinking of ways to convince Paul to allow me to do so. After his comments last night, I knew it was going to be an uphill battle; I thought that he respected me a little bit more than Rebecca did, but she'd done little to help my cause with her malicious gossip. After hearing what Rebecca had said about me, I was surprised that Paul had agreed to work with me at all. Had that been the whole point? That Rebecca hadn't wanted me on the case so she filled the lead attorney's head with lies? I didn't care whether she liked me or not, but she had to see that my past experience and dogged determination would be an advantage to the trial, rather than a hindrance.

Was it really jealousy about my supposed relationship with Wren that made her hate me or was there something else going on there? I wiped a bit of pastry from the corner of my mouth as I stepped into the hotel lobby, thinking that maybe I would call Wren before meeting with Paul, to clear my head of this annoying new puzzle. Moving toward the elevators, I saw a flash of movement out of the corner of my eye and saw Paul in the hotel restaurant, waving at me. He had a plate of eggs and pancakes in front of him and his laptop open and booted up next to his food. He mimed that he'd call me after he was done. I nodded and raised a hand in acknowledgement before getting into the elevator and riding it up to my floor.

Unzipping the side pocket of my workout leggings, I retrieved my room card as I walked down the hallway. Intent on wiping the sweat from the card onto my shirt—I felt like my whole body had been dipped in lukewarm, salty water—I didn't notice the fact that the door to my room was open until I was only a few feet from it.

"Are you fucking kidding me?" I muttered under my breath as I sidestepped next to the wall, sliding along it and peering into my room, hoping that I was just the victim of an industrious maid. *What is it with me and hotel rooms?*

Inside, I could see my room was trashed, my clothes strewn all over the floor and the bedsheets torn from the mattress. The contents of my briefcase had been tossed around the room, papers that had been crumbled and torn littered the floor and desk, the rolling chair that was usually tucked into it on its side. Even the mattress of my bed had been tossed aside, the box spring beneath bared. The grim frown that had spread across my face eased when a man stormed out of the bathroom, flinging towels around and growling under his breath. He sounded frustrated. When he came to stand in the middle of the room, his hands on his hips, I saw his head swivel around, as though he were unsuccessfully looking for something. I couldn't tell if he was the same man from before, with the crowbar, but I was *very* glad to see him. A morning spent grappling had worked to raised my testosterone levels and the fact that my personal space and belongings had come under attack—again—also served to send spikes of adrenaline through my limbs, erasing the lingering tiredness and suffusing me with the familiar flight or fight rush. Oh, and flight? That was the last thing on my mind.

Gripping the card tighter in my fist, I entered the room on the tips of my toes, moving toward the man, who was still peering about the room as though expecting whatever he was looking for to jump out at him. I rubbed my thumb over the edge of the card, enjoying the feel of the hard plastic as I came to stand directly behind the man.

He must have felt me, some primal instinct alert to the fact that a predator was near, because he started to turn toward me. I moved first, jabbing out with the hand holding the card and striking his face. The edge of the card sank into the soft skin of his cheek, scoring across it and opening a wound that immediately started oozing blood.

"What the hell?" he screeched, slapping a hand to his face as he stumbled back. Lifting his hand, he saw that it was covered with blood and turned his gaze to me. His dark eyes glittered with hate and pain as they met mine. "Bitch," he snarled.

"What are you looking for?" I asked, not taking my eyes from him. He'd clenched his hands into fists and squared his feet, readying himself to attack me.

"You," he growled, taking a menacing step toward me.

I assumed a fighting stance, letting a smile lift the corners of my lips. "Well, you found me. Now what?" I knew he wasn't telling me the truth. He wouldn't have trashed my room if he'd been looking for me.

Blood dripped from his pointed chin, running along his jawline and falling from the lowest point of his face. "I'm going to make you pay for this." He gestured at his face before taking a step toward me.

I smirked. "Do you accept credit cards?" I brandished the blood-smeared card clenched in my fist. I took a step toward him, intent on dropping and taking him down at the knees.

"What the hell happened here?" came a voice from behind me. I recognized Paul's voice but didn't take my eyes off of the man in front of me. "Who are you? Maya, what's going on?"

His close-set dark eyes flicking from me to Paul, the man shifted from foot to foot, silently acknowledging the fact that he was outnumbered. Faster than I thought he could move, he bolted forward, using his shoulder to knock me to one side. I pivoted, using the momentum to lash out with my foot, hoping to trip him. I made contact and his ankles collided, but not enough to take him all the way to the floor. He stumbled and caught himself, just before crashing into Paul, who was standing in the doorway with an aghast expression on his face. The two men pitched out of sight into the hallway.

I'd dropped to my hands and knees after kicking the intruder, but pushed myself to my feet as I heard sounds of battle from outside the room. Running past the bathroom toward the door, I slowed just long enough to grab the hair dryer from the counter, swinging the heavy appliance on its cord as I entered the hallway.

Paul lay on his back, gasping for breath. Looking up and down the hall, I just managed to catch a fleeting glimpse of the man before he crashed through the door leading to the stairwell. It was only the fact that Paul sounded as though he were dying that made me stay by his side rather than chase after the trespasser.

Running my hands along his chest and trachea, looking for a puncture wound or some other reason for his distress, I heard him wheeze, "I'm...okay...just..."

"Got the breath knocked out of you," I finished for him, sitting back on my heels. I pushed down the impatient frustration I felt upon finding out that he was just a little out of breath rather than seriously injured. I could've caught that guy, made him tell me what he'd been looking for and who he was working for, ending this ridiculous series of break-ins once and for all.

Paul put his hands against his sternum and grimaced. "Ugh."

"Do you think he was working for Rossi?" I asked, more to myself than to Paul, who was writhing around on the floor as he recovered his breath. After checking to make sure that he was on the mend, I stood and left Paul in the hall, intent on trying to find clues as to what that man had been after. Money? Some incriminating evidence to blackmail me with?

Putting my hands on my hips, I looked around the room. It was in shambles. My purse had been upended on the bed, its contents strewn about but seemingly all present and accounted for. Even my wallet had been dumped out, bills and coins in small disordered piles. I couldn't believe he hadn't taken any of it. I'd pushed the mattress back on top of the box spring and was just about to sit on the bed when I remembered the one thing that I'd brought with me before leaving for my jiujitsu class this morning.

I pulled out my laptop out of my gym bag and sat down, setting it down beside me. Looking at it, I wondered if that had been what the intruder was looking for. Such things were often hidden beneath mattresses; hell, sometimes I hid my laptop beneath my mattress when I stayed at hotel rooms. I had too much sensitive documentation and too many important files on my computer for me to lose it and it wouldn't fit in the safes hotels often provided. It looked like my decision to bring it with me this time had paid off. Looking down at the silver-colored rectangle, I remembered that Paul had had his laptop in front of him when I'd seen him in the hotel's restaurant that morning.

Hmmm.

Walking back out to where Paul was getting himself into a sitting position, I asked, "Did you stop by your room before coming here?"

He shook his head, still breathing heavily. "I came right here from breakfast."

I looked around the floor. "Where's your laptop?"

Paul looked at his empty hands, as though expecting to find it there. "I don't know."

"Well, you didn't drop it," I said.

"Oh, shit," he said on an exhale. "That guy must've taken it."

Shaking my head, I reached up and pinched the bridge of my nose. "Oh, shit," I echoed. We were lucky. If we had lost both of our laptops, most of our work concerning the evidence Wren and I had gathered through TJ would have been lost. I could always buy a new computer and have Wren send me the files again, but I'd added so many notes and comments to them that we would've lost months of work.

A thought occurred to me but I didn't voice it aloud, as Paul was still recovering, not only from his collision but from the knowledge that his laptop was gone. Was it coincidence that our laptops had been the target of a raid the day after we'd met with Judge Houston? Pressing my lips together in a grim line, I resolved to speak to Houston about it first thing Monday. It was time to take off the kid gloves and deal with this head-on.

Chapter 24

After sending Paul on his way, the man had obviously never been in a physical confrontation in his life as he was inordinately fragile after his brush with violence, I went back into my room and started cleaning it up. I didn't want to deal with hotel staff again—I was pretty sure the manager might start thinking about ways to kick me out after yet another break-in—so I rearranged the furniture that had been tossed aside, made the bed, and cleaned up the personal belongings that had been strewn across the room before settling down at the desk and pulling out my phone. My time spent at the library this morning had given me some ideas about how to keep Wren involved in all of this without him having to give up his privacy.

After Wren had answered his phone with a cheerful, "Hey, Maya!" I got right down to business.

"Wren, I have some things that I want you to look into. I was at the Dallas public library today—"

"You went to another library? I feel like a cuckolded husband."

I gave this the minor chuckle it deserved before continuing. "Yes, I've been cheating on you with other librarians. Anyway, I was looking into Texas laws concerning the inclusion of evidence gathered using programs like TJ and started to think that maybe we should have a backup plan."

"Why? Are the laws strict there?"

I shrugged. "Actually, Texas is pretty lenient on that kind of thing. They allow a lot of clemency when it comes to putting bad guys away. Must be a holdover from the Texas Ranger days, I don't know. But, Houston has been such an asshole lately, that I started to worry about what would happen to our case should he not allow TJ's evidence, so I'd like you to do some digging and see if you can't come up with something more concrete."

In the silence following this, I could practically feel the gears of Wren's mind churning away. When he finally spoke, it was with a distracted tone that told me he was already mentally engaged in something other than our conversation.

"I could get back into the dark web, try and see if I can come up with a clearer version of that video Concerned Citizen sent. If Christopher's face is shown anywhere on that video, maybe I can narrow down a snippet and enhance it until there is no question that he was there the night your father died." His voice was low and abstracted, as though he were talking to himself more so than to me. "I mean, it won't help in getting him convicted for trying to kill the senator but it might give enough background motive to prove that he is indeed a contract killer, and it might help in the future if we ever want to go after him for other crimes."

"Exactly," I said. "Getting him into custody for the whole Tim Collins thing is the immediate goal, but I still plan on nailing him for what he did to my father. And if you can prove that he was at the scene of my dad's accident, I think that would go a long way toward keeping him in prison forever."

"Yes, yes. First I'll conjure up a troll profile that will allow me to surf the dark web undetected, then I'll sift through the different video files that the Concerned Citizen had access to, just to see if there is another version of the video he obtained, then I'll—"

Getting the feeling that this was going to be a protracted description that would go right over my technologically inferior head, I interjected. "Okay, thanks Wren, for getting on that. It means the world to me." Remembering that it was a Saturday and that other people actually had personal lives, I added, "Do you have any plans for this weekend? I mean, *did* you have any other plans before I gave you a bunch of stuff to do?"

"I'm sitting at the circulation desk of a completely empty library right now, working on a crossword puzzle, and that was the extent of my weekend plans. Of course, the library is closed tomorrow, so I would've had to steal the paper and bring it home with me to finish the crossword from the comfort of my kitchen table. So, really, you giving me something to do has saved me from having to commit a crime. I should be thanking you."

I smiled, feeling the now-familiar internal warmth of Wren's friendship. "Anything I can do to help curb the rampant crime sprees of Landsfield Ridge."

As I didn't want him to worry about me, I didn't tell Wren about the break-ins or my concerns about Houston; he had too much to deal with already without me piling on more of my own personal baggage. But before I said goodbye, there was a heavy, awkward silence that spoke of words unsaid, of repressed emotions that could only be contained for so long before they'd explode from the confines of suppression and restraint.

The words, when they came, were a little hoarse. "I miss you, Wren."

"I miss you too," he said somberly.

With a final goodbye, I ended the call and dropped the phone on the desktop. I didn't know what the future held for me and the mysterious librarian, but I was starting to suspect that there *would* be a future, whether I was ready for it or not.

When Monday finally arrived, I was ready to do battle with Houston. I'd spent the rest of the weekend mentally preparing for our meeting, developing both my arguments as to the relevancy of TJ's evidence and how I was going to voice my suspicion that Houston was not on the up and up, that he was being coerced by forces intent on squashing the proceedings and stopping this trial before it ever went to a jury vote.

Paul looked no worse for wear as we waited outside of Houston's chambers. He'd opted out of most of the preparatory meetings I'd suggested we have, saying that his stomach hurt or that he had a headache. I no longer harbored any suspicions that he was working against me on this case, that he had any hidden agendas. I had, in the beginning, thought that he was a little too outspoken against me to be honestly engaged in the trial, but now I knew that he was just a wimp, a soft man who hid behind verbal machismo to conceal the fact that he was vulnerable and insecure. He'd been spoon-fed for too long and when push had come to shove, when faced with a phys-ical confrontation rather than a sedate courtroom, he'd been unable to deal with it and had retreated into the relative safety of his own little world. I didn't blame him, exactly, but I did resent the fact that he was unable to live up to my expectations of how a person should conduct themselves when faced with adversity.

The only good thing that had come of the weekend's events was that Paul was more willing to allow me to take control. One of the first things I'd said when we'd met outside Houston's chambers had been, "I've been working on this all weekend and have somethings to go over with you before we go in."

"Why don't you take the lead in there?" he said, gesturing toward Houston's closed door. "I wasn't feeling well enough to do much in the way of preparation."

My eyes wanted to roll in their sockets, but I managed to keep them fastened on Paul's. "Of course," I said with a nod. "Whatever you think is best."

When Houston's secretary finally let us into his chambers, I walked straight toward the large desk he was sitting behind, not waiting for Paul to follow.

"Judge Houston, how are you? How was your weekend?" I asked as I sat in one of the chairs on the opposing side of the desk. He looked the same, maybe a little more fatigued than he had the week before. Dark semi-circles still hung beneath his lidded eyes and the skin around his mouth sagged with weariness.

Without waiting for him to answer, I extracted my laptop from my briefcase and set it on his desk, carefully adjusting it until it was front and center, my motions intentionally slow and methodical. Turning my attention to Houston, I said, "I had a visitor this weekend, Your Honor, and although I'm not positive, I think he trashed my hotel room looking for this." I narrowed my eyes as they bored into his. "Is it a coincidence, do you think, that my laptop would become an object of attention directly after speaking to you about what evidence was on it?"

Paul, who had finally joined the party, cleared his throat. "Uh, Maya? Don't you think we should—"

"Absolutely," I interjected, not taking my eyes from Houston. I took a deep breath before continuing. "Judge Houston, are you being threatened in any way? Being coerced or influenced by outside parties who might be negatively impacted by the outcome of the trial? Because if you are, I can help you—"

This time it was Houston who interrupted. "I'm not sure what you are insinuating, Ms. Hartwell, but I *think,*" he injected a healthy amount of sarcasm into the word, "that you are trying to imply that my judgement is unclear, that I can be swayed by anything other than truth, justice, and the evidentiary findings that it's your job to provide. Is that what you're saying?"

"Your Honor," Paul said, his voice higher pitched than it usually was. "What I think Ms. Hartwell is trying to say is that if you have been..." he trailed off when Houston looked at him, his teeth bared.

"I know exactly what she is trying to say, thank you very much, counselor." Houston stood and walked around his desk. He came to stand before it, looking down on me as I sat in my chair. "Even if I had been, how did you put it? Threatened or coerced? Even if I had been, you are probably one of the very last people I would look to for help, Ms. Hartwell. Now get out of my office."

My jaw fell open. "Judge Houston? But what about—"

"Request to enter evidence denied. I thought about it, counselor, and cannot abide by the unlawful way in which it was gathered." He pointed toward the door to his chambers. "Don't make me tell you again."

I was in shock as I stood and gathered my laptop before moving to leave the room. This meeting didn't go anything like how I had planned. I hadn't thought that he would gleefully confess and we'd put our heads together to figure out how to get him out of the mess I'd been so sure he was in, but I had entertained the idea of him eventually admitting to being coerced and agreeing to seek protection for the rest of the trial. And what I really hadn't seen coming was his refusal to allow the TJ evidence. During my research at the library, I'd found previous cases in which such had been conditionally allowed by the presiding judge. It seemed like such an unjust rejection that I turned, almost running into Paul, who'd been following close behind me.

"Your Honor, you have to reconsider. The evidence is vital to our—"

"Get. Out." Each word was spat out, his voice carrying enough venomous dislike that my feet were moving before I was aware of it. When Paul and I were in the hallway outside Houston's chambers, the thick wooden door between us and him shut, I dropped my briefcase onto the floor, letting it fall heavily from my shoulder. My laptop was still safely tucked under my arm, but its safety was the farthest thing from my mind at the moment.

"Thanks for your help in there," I snarled at Paul. "You did a great job of backing me up."

"Maya," Paul replied reproachfully, having regained some of his composure, "we talked about dealing with the matter carefully, slowly. You marched right in there and started making demands. What did you think would happen?"

"I thought that you would have more of a backbone, that's what I thought." I rubbed my temples with the tips of my fingers. "What are we going to do now? Our whole case was reliant upon that evidence."

Paul straightened his shoulders. "Give me some credit, Maya. The outcome of this trial hasn't been decided yet, regardless of whether or not that evidence is included." He turned and walked down the high-ceilinged hallway, speaking over his shoulder at me. "Come on, court is going to be convened soon and we have some prep to do."

I stood by the door, indecisive. I wanted to barge back in there and demand some answers. It wasn't coincidental that we had approached Houston about sensitive information contained in our laptops the day before Paul's had been stolen and mine had almost been; and Houston's attitude and appearance were atypical, even Paul, who was skeptical about my theories, agreed with that much. And the mob was known for the way they leaned on those involved in litigious matters affecting themselves or their business ventures. It all added up, all made sense. Houston was being threatened to throw the case the defendant's way, he'd given up the knowledge of what evidence we had against Christopher, and...there was nothing we could do about it.

I growled deep in my throat as I gathered up my briefcase, put my laptop inside, and followed Paul. My phone buzzed and when I saw Wren had sent me a text, I paused to reply.

He'd written, *Are you still with Houston? How's everything going? Let me know when your meeting's over.*

Meeting over. Not good. I'll call you when I get the chance. Any luck on your end? I hoped that he'd been able to find something, some speck of evidence that we could use moving forward.

Not yet. Still working on it. I'll talk to you later.

Sighing, I slipped my phone back into the pocket of my suit jacket and continued walking, my mind full of misgivings and disappointment. It felt like there were so many loose ends to keep track of that the most important threads were in danger of slipping through my fingers. Picking up my pace, I reminded myself about the big picture. Nothing mattered more to me than putting Christopher safely behind bars until I could gather enough evidence to put him away for good for killing my father. Nothing.

Chapter 25

Finally, the day had come. I woke up early that morning feeling a mix of excitement and trepidation, anxiety and exhilaration; today was the day Christopher would take the stand. Ever since my confrontation with the intruder, Paul had been more and more willing to let me get involved in the trial. I think more than his ass had been bruised that day, I think his ego took a hit too, and he'd finally managed to open his mind to the possibility that I was capable of doing more than taking notes and bringing him coffee in the morning. It had taken me little effort to badger him into letting me be the one to question Christopher. The feeble arguments he'd thrown at me seemed to be more for appearance than anything else, and I started to get the feeling that Paul just wanted this whole experience to be over so he could go back to his safe and normal life of prosecuting bad guys during the week and golfing on the weekends.

I spent extra time on my appearance, making sure that not a hair was out of place as I rehearsed the questions I was going to ask. I had a very smart black dress which I felt very comfortable wearing, it was professional looking and it seemed to have a knack of putting me in the right head space. The night before, Wren and I had stayed up late going over the highlights, the questions and intonations that were most important, and I'd remembered to bring up something that had been niggling at me before we hung up.

"Wren, something's been bugging me for about a week now. Paul told me that Rebecca had been the one to convince him to let me join the case. You were there. Don't you remember Jack being the one to say that he was going to put in a good word for me?"

Wren made a thoughtful noise before answering. "To be perfectly honest, I don't remember that conversation."

"We were near the interrogation room. Christopher had just been taken into custody." I let this sink in before asking, "You don't remember?"

"Sorry, Maya. I don't. Why? What's bugging you?"

I shook my head. "It's just that I got the impression that Rebecca despised me, and I couldn't figure out why she would try to influence Paul to let me second the trial—especially since I had a better connection with Jack and he'd been the one to tell me that he knew the lead."

"A better connection with Jack, huh?"

Rolling my eyes, I said, "Oh, never mind. I guess it's not important now. It's just been something that's been on my mind."

"I haven't talked to Jack or Rebecca since before the trial started, but I can reach out and ask about it, if you want me to."

I thought about it for a few seconds before shaking my head. "No. You've got more important things to work on, like that video on the dark web. Have you had any luck with that yet?"

"Not yet. But I'm hopeful."

We ended the call and I'd gone to bed alternatively thinking about Christopher and Jack, the worries separate but connected, as they both revolved around this case and my desire to put the former in jail.

Now, as I glanced at my reflection once more before collecting my briefcase and leaving the hotel room, I only had enough room in my mind for one thing: Christopher.

"The prosecution would like to call the defendant to the stand," I said, on my feet and addressing a judge who looked sullenly at me. Houston hadn't been exactly hostile since that botched meeting in his office, but his style hadn't changed: he was still overwhelming ruling in favor of the defending attorney when objections were raised.

Christopher rose to his feet and strode toward the witness stand, his shoulders back and his head held high. After he was seated and sworn in, I walked around my desk and come to stand before him, trying to control the nervous thrills emanating from my stomach and coursing through my arms and legs.

"Before we begin," I said, tilting my head questioningly at Christopher, "could you enlighten me on how to address you? Your current passport says your name is Christopher McLaughlin, but that can't be right."

"Why not?" he asked, one eyebrow raised as though he were amused.

"For several reasons," I replied, ticking the points off with my fingers. "First, it's a UK passport and there are no records of you ever living or traveling in the United Kingdom. Second, it was issued within the past year after being declared lost...which is only interesting because the person who this passport belongs to is currently lying in a cemetery in Scotland and has been for the past ten years. So, I'll ask you again, how should I address you?"

He shrugged his shoulders, a smile playing at the corners of his lips. "However you feel comfortable, I guess. There are a lot of people named Christopher, so I'm not surprised to learn that one is buried in Scotland. I'm sure there are a lot of people named...What's your name again?"

I narrowed my eyes. I wasn't going to answer that. I'd been hoping that having to clear up his name would trip him up, force him to reveal the fact that he had multiple identities, but he seemed completely nonplussed about the matter. Since the proof of his many names and addresses was considered part of the TJ evidence, I decided to drop this line of questioning and move on.

"How long have you been employed by Lucca Rossi?"

"Objection," Colby said, rising to his feet. "Relevance?"

I turned to Houston. "The fact that this man," I gestured at Christopher, "is employed by Lucca Rossi, a well-known leader of a crime syndicate, is certainly relevant to the character and actions of the defendant."

"Sustained," Houston said, glaring at me.

Trying not to roll my eyes, I nodded and attacked from a different angle. "Who told you to drop the pills in Senator Collins's drink? How were you approached?"

"I was contacted through a mutual friend."

"And did this mutual friend tell you that you were going to take part in a prank? Or did they tell you that you were being paid to murder a well-known public figure?"

"Objection! Leading the witness."

I held up a hand before Houston could sustain the objection. "Let me rephrase. Did your mutual friend tell you what your objective was?"

Christopher nodded. "I was told that some friends of the guy whose drink I was supposed to spike wanted to embarrass him, that the pills were supposed to make him look like he'd drunk too much."

"And you didn't question this at all? Didn't wonder what kind of *friends*," I accentuated this with finger quotes, "would want to embarrass a man at his wife's birthday celebration?"

"Have you ever been hungry?"

This non sequitur caught me off-guard. "Yes," I said slowly.

"Have you ever been unable to buy food for yourself?"

I barely managed to not roll my eyes. I saw where this was going and it was nowhere good. He wanted to make it sound as though he'd been down on his luck, only agreeing to put the pills in the senator's drink because he had no other choice. I silently cursed Houston for not letting me use the TJ evidence. If I had been able to, I could have proven that Christopher had millions of dollars in several different bank accounts—he was *very* far from being down on his luck.

"No," I said. "Let me remind you that I'm supposed to be the one asking questions here, not you." Speaking of questions..." I wanted so badly to ask him if he'd ever owned a ridiculously expensive watch, one that only a minute percent of the population could afford but knew that such a question was destined to go nowhere, lead to nothing. Colby and Houston would jump so far down my throat that I wouldn't be able to take a breath for months. I continued my sentence, revising as I swallowed what I had been going to say. "...how much were you paid to spike the senator's drink?"

"Definitely not enough, viewed from where I'm sitting now."

That got a weak chuckle from the crowd, and I clenched my hands into fists so tight that I could feel my fingernails digging into my palms. *Keep your cool.*

"Please, if you could answer the question."

"I was offered two thousand dollars, with only half paid up front and the second half due upon completion of the job. And since I was apprehended before I could get the second half, I only ended up with a thousand dollars for my trouble."

I quirked my brows up in an expression of surprise. "Only a thousand dollars? That won't buy a lot of groceries, not in this day and age. I'm surprised you agreed to so little."

Christopher shrugged. "Every little thing counts when you're destitute."

I couldn't stop the snort of derision that this little gem produced. He was looking at the jury as though seeking leniency, searching the faces of those sitting in judgement of him for empathy or pity. To my disbelieving chagrin, some were nodding as though they understood his hardships, as though they knew what it was like to have nothing but desperation to eat for dinner. Seeing it made my stomach heave. I had to change courses.

"Tell me about the people who hired you. You said there was a mutual friend. Who was that? Where did you meet?" I couldn't resist adding, "At the local soup kitchen?"

"Objection!"

I was expecting this so I waved away that last question. "Did you ever meet the people who hired you?"

He shook his head. "Everything was done over the phone. They wired the money into my account. I never saw any of their faces."

"Does the name Luca Rossi ring a bell?"

Christopher shook his head. "Nope."

I gritted my teeth and turned to the side, looking away from Christopher. As I did, he said, "You look familiar. Have we met somewhere before?"

My head swiveled back and I stared at him. There was no way he would've recognized me from—

"Have you ever been to Mexico?"

The question sent liquid spurts of adrenaline through me. My eyes fastened to his and I could feel my face redden. I could see amusement in the depths of his green eyes and knew that he thought this was all a big game, an interesting pastime that he was being forced to experience before getting back to his life.

"As I said, I'm the one asking—"

"Are you sure? Because when you turned to the side, I could've sworn that I'd seen your profile before. With the jungle on one side of you and the beach on the other. No?" he asked as I shook my head. "Huh. I guess I'm mistaken. Wouldn't be the first time," he said, assuming a winning smile as he glanced self-depreciatingly at the jury.

"Who do you think you are?" I demanded, the question tumbling out of my mouth before I even knew I was going to ask it. I cleared my throat, trying to regain some of my self-possession, and saw Paul gesture at me in the corner of my eye.

"I *think* that I'm exactly who you say I am," Christopher said, his smile dimming to a slight grin. "Do you have any other questions for me?"

I raised a hand in Houston's direction, asking for a moment, as I back tracked toward the prosecutor's table, knowing that I was in for it. Sure enough, Paul glared at me as I walked toward him.

"What do you think you are doing?" he hissed, his teeth bared.

"I'm sorry. I'm—he rattled me."

"Sit down. I'll take it from here."

Feeling dejected and embarrassed that I'd let Christopher get to me, I nodded, taking a seat as Paul stood to take my place.

"Were you at all worried about the senator experiencing any adverse side effects from the pills you were supposed to feed him? Did they tell you exactly what was in them?"

I barely heard Christopher's answer. I was too busy wallowing in self-pity. I felt like I'd blown it. This had been my chance and I'd let Christopher get the better of me. I was frustrated and furious at my lack of professionalism. The rest of the questioning played out just as I'd feared it would, with Christopher looking like he'd been in the wrong place at the wrong time, interested only in making a little bit of money without knowing the full consequences of his actions, and Paul looking like a bully who'd never known the meaning of poverty. It was a travesty of justice.

Colby threw Christopher a couple of soft ball questions, letting him lob the answers out of the park, before returning to his seat with a satisfied expression on his face.

Houston looked at me, an unreadable expression on his face, as the courtroom fell into silence. "Let's adjourn for the day and listen to closing arguments tomorrow."

The bailiff called for everyone to rise as Houston left the courtroom, a trailing wake of black fabric following him out the side door. Paul wasted no time before turning to me.

"Wow, Maya," he said, a disgusted sneer on his face. "You really botched that. And after begging and begging to be the one to question him, too. I never should have allowed it. You lost the case for us, you know that right?"

I hung my head, knowing that I deserved the tongue lashing. "I'm sorry, Paul. It's just...you don't know what that guy has put me through."

"Oh, I know exactly what he's put you through. You made sure to tell me over and over again. And now he's going to walk out of here a free man. All because of you." Paul gathered his briefcase and notes, avoiding eye contact as though unable to look at me any longer. "I'll be giving the closing arguments tomorrow. I hope we both can agree on that."

I nodded. It seemed that the kowtowed Paul was gone, his self-assurance given back to him by my misstep. Even though I desperately wanted to give the closing argument, I knew that nothing I could say would change his mind, not now, not after what I'd done today.

As I walked from the courtroom, replaying the day's events over and over again in my head, I felt an overwhelming sense of dejection come over me. Christopher was going to go free and it was all because of me.

My phone buzzed and I pulled it out of my pocket. I saw Mr Richards name flash up on the screen but could not face talking with him at this time so let is go to voice mail. Then the phone buzzed again hoping for some good news when I saw that Wren was calling.

"Hey, Wren. Please tell me something good."

He sighed. "Sorry, Maya. I've searched and searched but I haven't been able to find a version of the video that shows Christopher's face. I'm not giving up, but it's been harder than I thought."

Groaning, I lifted a hand to cover my face.

"Are you okay?" he asked, his voice full of concern.

"Wren, I made such a mess in the courtroom today."

"Hey, it's going to be okay, Maya. One way or another, I know that justice will win. You just have to believe in the process. That's what you always say, right? Believe in the process and it will come through for you?"

"Yeah, don't listen to me, Wren. I don't know what I'm talking about and I never have." I ended the call and threw my phone into the depths of my briefcase. Feeling tears threaten to come spilling out of my eyes, I dug into a side pocket of my purse and pulled out a tissue—right before bumping into a large, hard body.

Looking up, ready to apologize, my mouth dropped open when I saw that the person I'd run into was Jack Miller.

"Jack? What are you doing here?"

He smiled down at me. "Just checking on how everything is going. I watched the proceedings today." Raising one eyebrow, he said, "Not going too good, is it?"

I pressed my lips together in annoyance. "No, it isn't."

Leaning down toward me, Jack spoke in a low voice. "I knew you'd be just the person for the job."

"What is that supposed to mean?" I asked, frowning.

He looked past my head, at something or someone behind me, and moved around me. "I've got to go. Talk to you later, Maya."

I opened my mouth, to ask him about whether he had rec-ommended me for the second chair, but didn't get the chance to speak before he was gone, disappearing into the crowd coming out of a courtroom on the lefthand side of the wide hallway.

That was weird, I thought, rising up onto the tips of my toes to try and catch another glimpse of Jack. *What had he meant about me being the person for the job?* My thoughts muddled, I continued walking through the courthouse, intent on going back to my room and taking a long, cleansing shower. Maybe things would look better, afterwards.

Chapter 26

The shower helped, marginally, in clearing my head and making the outlook of the case less dreary. I still couldn't figure out what Jack had been doing at the courthouse or what Jack had meant by his offhand comment.

I knew you'd be just the person for the job.

What did that mean and how did that keep with the fact that Rebecca had been the one to recommend me and not Jack? Realizing I was going around in mental circles, I dropped that line of thinking for now and concentrated on tomorrow's closing argument—not that Paul was going to let me within ten miles of its delivery. I still couldn't believe that I'd let Christopher burrow his way under my skin. Where was the calm and cool Maya who sliced an intruder open with a room key? What had happened to her?

I sighed as I toweled the dampness from my hair. Christopher had happened, and even though he'd managed to push buttons I hadn't even known I had, I would never let him get away with his crimes. Any of them.

I returned some phone calls I'd missed during the day, touching base with my paralegals and my mother, who'd been calling me incessantly since the trial had started, wanting to stay up to date with its progression. I told her very little, mostly just that the trial was going fine and yes, I was getting enough sleep and eating regularly. She was invested in the trial but I didn't want to fill her mind with too much—her life had settled back down after I'd told her that her husband had been killed and I didn't want to disrupt it until I had good news to share.

Sliding into bed, I grabbed my notepad and a pencil, intent on continuing to work on the finer points of our case's final arguments—and had to fight to keep my eyelids open. The hot shower and the emotional exertion of the day had finally caught up with me, and all I wanted to do was go to sleep. I forced myself to jot down a couple of notes, more in defiance of my tiredness than actual need, before putting the pad and pencil on the desk beside the bed and turning out the light. Maybe things would look better in the morning. Thinking wry-ly to myself that I'd thought that same thing about my shower, with indecisive results, I snuggled into bed and was asleep in minutes.

When someone banged on my door at six the next morning, I groaned. Checking the bedside clock and seeing how early it was, I pulled on some shorts and a t-shirt before stalking to the door, intent on letting whoever had decided to wake me up know that they had better have a good reason for it—or else.

Jerking the door open, halfway hoping that one of the guys who'd busted into my previous rooms was outside, my jaw dropped when my eyes fell on Wren.

His eyes were puffy and rimmed with red, his cheeks lined with stubble, and his thin hair was disheveled, but I still felt a surge of joy at seeing him on my doorstep.

"W-what are you doing here?" I exclaimed, stumbling over my words in my excitement.

"I took a red-eye last night," he said with a shrug. "It sounded like you needed a friend last night so," he paused, grinning at me, "here I am."

I threw my arms around him, pressing my cheek against his shoulder. "You have no idea how happy I am to see you." I pulled back. "But what about staying under the radar? You didn't want anything to do with the trial."

"I still don't. I'm not going with you to the courthouse but I can stay here, at the hotel, and be available when you need me."

I shook my head in amazement. "I can't believe you're here. They gave you more time off of work?"

Wren nodded. "They don't have much choice. No one wants to work at a library in the middle of nowhere, and when I said that I would quit if she didn't give me a few extra days, my boss agreed to give me a little bit more time to take care of things." He cocked his head to one side. "I think she thinks I'm taking care of an elderly relative or something."

"Well, whatever she thinks, I'm so glad you're here." I pulled him into the room. "I have so much to tell you."

I closed the door, grabbed his backpack from his shoulders, and sat Wren down on the bed before picking up the phone and ordering room service. After making sure that the woman on the other end of the line understood that I wanted two extra-large cups of coffee, I hung up. I sat beside Wren and proceeded to tell him about everything that had happened recently, from the intruder to Paul's mental recovery. After relating the fact that I suspected Houston was being coerced and that he'd sent the man I'd slashed across the face, I cocked my head to one side and said, "Speaking of which, how did you know what room I was in? I asked the manager to keep my personal information, like my name and room number, a secret."

Wren smiled. "It took me all of two seconds to find your hotel and room number yesterday after hacking into the hotel reservation system."

Being reminded of his technological wizardry made my stomach go sour. "I wish we'd been able to use the evidence you worked so hard to gather. It would've made what happened yesterday not matter so much, in the grand scheme of things."

With a sigh, Wren nodded. "I know. It was a huge step backward, but it's not over yet. You still have the closing argument today plus the fact that Christopher admitted to the intent of putting those pills in Collins's drink. He's not going to just get off scot-free."

"Yeah, but if he's convicted of a lesser charge, he'll be out within a few months, a year at most." I stood and paced back and forth across the room. "Can you imagine? My father's killer enjoying three hots and a cot for six months before he gets out and continues on with his hitman life, enjoying fabulous wealth while leaving a trail of death in his wake?"

"Three hots and a cot?" Wren repeated, his forehead wrinkled.

I waved a hand. "Three hot meals and a bed. Prison's like being on vacation, except you don't have to pay for anything."

"And you can't leave," he quipped.

A knock sounded at the door, room service with our coffee, and when I sat back down next to Wren, I had a big cup of piping hot coffee for him.

We sat, sipping in silence for several minutes. I relished in the fact that we were back in action, together again. It was so nice to know that he was in my corner, though I had to beat back feelings of culpability; I hoped that his job wasn't in danger because of his coming here.

When my phone started buzzing from where I'd left it on the bedside table, I stood and grabbed it, turning off the alarm that I'd set the night before.

"I have to get ready for court," I said. "Why don't you lay down and try and get some sleep?"

Holding up his half-empty cup of coffee, Wren shook his head. "Not going to happen any time soon. But go ahead and get ready to go." He reached over and grabbed his backpack from where I'd set it by the bed, pulling his laptop from it. "I'll get back to work."

I showered again and dressed halfheartedly, not putting nearly the same effort into my appearance as I had the day before, hoping that changing up my routine would result in a different outcome. By the time I was ready to go, Wren was fast asleep on the bed, his open laptop perched on his stomach. I smiled at him, gently picking up the computer and setting it aside, careful not to wake him. He was always coming to the rescue when I needed him the most. How would I ever repay him?

Leaving him a note saying that I would be back after the day's proceedings and exhorting him to sleep and get room service, on me, I grabbed my things and quietly slipped out of the room. I felt better knowing he was here; nothing seemed as dismal as it had yesterday. I could only hope the feeling persisted throughout the closing arguments.

When I entered the courtroom, my head was clear and my limbs were free of the nervous jitters that had plagued me every day as I'd walked through those doors. Now that Wren was here, I felt different, as though I'd been preparing for this case for six years, ever since my dad's death, rather than merely watching from the sidelines as the outcome was being decided for me by Houston and Paul. I didn't even harbor any anger toward Paul for his decision to give the closing argument; he was right in that I was too closely tied to the outcome. His speaking, after what had happened yesterday, was for the best.

When the judge called for the prosecutor's closing arguments, Paul stood, smoothing down his suit jacket, before moving to stand before the jury.

"Ladies and gentlemen of the jury, we're here today to decide the guilt or innocence of that man." He pointed at Christopher, who was staring at nothing, completely expressionless. "We've shown you exhibit after exhibit proving the fact that he masqueraded as a waiter that night in Dallas, and was in possession of poison capsules with the intent on putting them into the drink of a United States Senator. He has admitted to accepting money for his role in what could have been a deadly prank." Paul paused, letting the whole of the evidence against the defendant sink in. "Outside of letting the man actually kill the senator, I don't know how much more evidence we could provide that would point to his guilt. Throughout the course of this trial, we've laid out a trail for you, the members of the jury, to follow. Each signpost, from the testimony of our medical experts to the fake moustache and tattoos the defendant donned as part of his disguise, has pointed you toward a singular destination: the defendant's guilt."

I looked at Christopher in the hopes of finding some expression of guilt or remorse, but found that he didn't even seem to be paying attention to what Paul was saying. He was looking into the audience, his dark eyes intent.

I followed his gaze and saw that it was directed at a thickly bearded man with a dark complexion. The man's expression was questioning, his dark eyebrows raised in an unspoken inquiry. My eyes darted back to Christopher, whose lips were pressed together in a grim line. When he shook his head with the barest of movements, I glanced back at the bearded man. He shrugged and nodded, as though acceding to something, offering a grin that showed large white teeth.

I was pondering what the exchange had meant as Paul finished up our closing argument, wondering who the man was and what he'd been offering—and what Christopher had turned down. Was he an accomplice? I didn't think so. Nothing TJ had produced pointed to anything but Christopher being a lone wolf.

"I hope that you, the members of the jury, will carefully consider the ramifications of the defendant's actions. A man, a husband and father, could have died from ingesting the pills that the defendant, by his own admission, had been tasked with putting in Tim Collins's drink. The United States of America could have lost an important political figure, a visionary who believes in the very ideals that people like him," Paul pointed at Christopher, "are trying to undermine. Please, don't forget that, as you retire to your quarters for deliberation. Thank you."

As Paul walked back to our desk, I snuck a glance at the jury. Some were nodding sympathetically, while others were staring down at their laps, their faces either uncertain or unreadable. Nothing had been decided, one way or the other. Not yet.

Colby stood and replaced Paul, his posture relaxed.

"Ladies and gentlemen of the jury, the man sitting before you is guilty of nothing but needing to fill his empty stomach. We've all experienced hardships and privation, we all understand what it is to be hungry and destitute. How can you fault a man for decisions he's made out of desperation? Especially when those decisions have been based upon the assumption of perpetrating nothing but a harmless joke?" Colby paced across the expanse between the lawyers' desks, Houston's raised platform, and the jury box, his hands clasped behind his back.

"That man," he said, pointing at Christopher, "made a bad choice, did something that he shouldn't have done. He knows that and is sorry, but he never agreed to kill anyone, never had any intention of causing the senator any lasting harm. The prosecutor would have you believe that my client purposefully tried to kill Tim Collins. That is far from the truth. The truth is that my client was paid to put a harmless pill into a man's drink—and that he suffered egregious bodily harm before he could do so."

Colby continued on in this same fashion for another few minutes, reiterating the fact that Christopher had been a man put in a hard situation and that he'd done what anyone else would do when facing the same hardships: survive at all costs.

It was a good argument, but it didn't change the fact that Christopher had committed crimes of which he'd confessed to being guilty. I hoped that the jury wouldn't lose sight of that amidst the rhetoric. They did, sometimes. They got caught up in the emotional whirlwinds of pity and empathy, and disregarded the fact that the person they felt sorry for was still guilty.

When Colby closed with, "Don't forget what it's like to be hungry, to be desperate, when you retire to your deliberations. A man's life shouldn't be over simply because he sought to ease some of his hardship with the execution of a harmless prank. Everyone deserves a second chance," I was tempted to clap my hands. What a performance.

Judge Houston reminded the jury of their sworn duty before excusing them to their deliberation room. Standing, he also excused the rest of us before walking out of the courtroom, and as he moved I saw that he was limping and trying to hide it. Pressing my lips together, I watched as he disappeared into a side door. Not even bothering to congratulate Paul on his closing argument, I strode from the courtroom, turning right in the hallway and hurrying to Houston's chambers. I was relieved to see that his secretary wasn't in residence yet. Glancing around, I approached the door, intent on getting in and catching Houston so off guard that he wouldn't have time to erect the walls he'd chosen to hide behind.

When I got close to the door, I heard the muffled sound of voices from inside and put my ear to it, trying to make out what the voices were saying.

I heard Houston say, "I did everything you asked of me. What more can I do?"

A deep, male voice replied, "You had better make sure that the jury votes in the right direction, or you will have hell to pay."

"How am I supposed to do that? Go in there and hold them hostage until they vote how you want them to? That's preposterous!"

"What's preposterous is that you still don't understand who you're dealing with. Do you want your daughter to be found dead in the Trinity River, drowned and bloated beyond recognition? Is that what you want?"

"Of course not!" Houston shouted. "That's why I've been doing all this, to keep her safe!"

"Then see this through. That's all you have to do. See this through and your daughter will be just another college sophomore, rather than another statistic. Dallas can be a dangerous town for pretty young girls."

I heard footsteps approaching the door and quickly backed away until I was standing behind an American flag hanging limply on a short flagpole against the wall. It wasn't great cover, my head and feet were clearly visible, but it was all I had.

The door to Houston's chamber opened—and Jack walked out of the room, a grimly satisfied expression on his face.

Chapter 27

I have my military training to thank for my composure. If self-containment hadn't been drilled into me for years, I'm sure that my jaw would've dropped and my eyes would've opened wider than they ever had before. Before I knew it, I was moving from behind the flag and standing in Jack's path.

Upon seeing me, he assumed a grim expression, one that was both expectant and forbidding. He'd known this moment would come, had prepared for it, but just hadn't been expecting it to happen *now*. I could read his countenance with an easiness that surprised me; even though I'd always been gifted with being able to scrutinize and interpret witnesses with aplomb—one of my greatest strengths as a lawyer—Jack had always been a walled fortress, only exhibiting whatever emotion he wanted me to see. I'd noticed it during the few meetings we'd had, chalking it up to his profession. Special agents of the FBI had to be circumspect or they wouldn't last long. But today was different.

"So, you're threatening to murder young girls now?" I asked, squaring my feet and mentally preparing myself for a fight. My briefcase was heavy, full of notepads and my laptop, and I knew that launching it at his face would slow him down considerably, should I need to do so. It might cost me the information on my laptop, but Wren was here now, and he had more access to the TJ evidence than I did.

"You don't understand who you're messing with, Maya. You never have."

"I know exactly who I'm messing with, thanks to you. I'm messing with a crooked FBI agent, a judge who's being blackmailed, and a crime syndicate that doesn't want to lose their greatest asset. Did I miss anything?"

The corners of Jack's lips lifted in a smile. "Maybe you do understand, after all. The only thing you're missing is the complete comprehension of what my employers will do to keep what's theirs. They value Christopher highly and will go to great lengths to keep him out of jail. Very great lengths."

"What did they threaten you with?" I asked, lifting a brow.

He shook his head. "Nothing. I had nothing to lose. What they did do is offer me more money than I'd make in a lifetime of working for the government." Shrugging, he continued, "Everyone has a price, Maya."

Thinking back to all of the phone conversations we'd shared, the video chats spent laughing and talking about our shared interest in catching the assassin, made my stomach roil. He'd played me. He'd acted like an all-American guy who had nothing but my best interests at heart, commiserated with me when I'd complained about the months-long wait we'd had to endure before Christopher made his move, kept me informed about the inner workings of the investigation. In the quietest space of my heart, I could acknowledge the fact that he'd charmed me, had me second-guessing my attraction to the quiet, intelligent librarian with unwavering loyalty and imagining what life would be like if I were to have a relationship with an exciting, good-looking, well-built agent of the FBI. It was my own foolishness that gave rise to the flush of anger and embarrassment suffusing my cheeks.

"I hope it was worth it, Jack, I really do. Because I'm going to expose you. Expose everything."

He lifted his thick eyebrows in amusement. "Oh, really? With what evidence?"

Clearing my throat, I lifted my chin. "I've got plenty."

"Maya, Maya, Maya," he said, chuckling and shaking his head. "You've got nothing and we both know it. You aren't even going to win this case. You know that too. Even without your bungling your examination of the witness the other day, you were never going to win. I made sure of that."

"What do you mean?" I was hoping to goad Jack into a confession, provoke him to give me something concrete I could use against him, give me evidence I could bring to the authorities.

"Tell me, do you think an experienced assassin would do the things Christopher did? Would mishandle the situation so badly?"

I opened my mouth to object but found that I couldn't. Jack was repeating the thoughts that had been going around and around in my head for weeks. The circumstances around his arrest had felt off from the very beginning...and with a flash of clarity, I knew why.

"You told him he was going to be a target at the gala." This was said on an exhale, the accusation breathy and soft, not the ringing claim I wanted it to be. "That's why he was so clumsy with the pills, so careless. He knew he was going to be arrested—because you told him."

Jack grinned down at me. "A little slow, but you got there eventually. Good for you, Maya. Now, if you'll excuse me—"

"You betrayed me," I said, sidestepping to stay in front of him as he tried to move around me. "You betrayed your country."

He rolled his eyes. "Spare me the patriotic rhetoric. Do you know what the United States government pays its *special agents*?" Air quotes accompanied the term. "Barely a living wage. If I had a wife and kids, she would have to work full time too, just so we could put food on the table, cover the mortgage, and pay for the kids' school supplies—and we'd still be up to our eyeballs in debt. So don't start throwing accusations around."

"If you had a wife and kids, I'd pity them. I'd pity them because I'd make sure that their husband and father would be spending the rest of his life in jail."

This got a laugh out of Jack. "You can't even put a fairly notorious hitman in jail for the rest of his life, Maya. How do you suppose to put me there?"

I gritted my teeth. He was right.

This time when he moved to go around me, I didn't get in his way. My limbs felt preternaturally heavy, the knowledge that I'd been betrayed making my legs feel unsteady, my feet encased in concrete.

"You won't get away with this," I said to his retreating back, my voice hoarse.

He looked over his shoulder at me. "I already did."

I watched him walk away, part of me wanting to tackle him to the ground and the other wanting to go back to my hotel room, burrow under the covers, and not come out for a week. Remembering that Wren was waiting for me, that he had more invested in Jack's betrayal since they'd supposedly been friends, I spared no more than a quick glance at the door to Houston's chambers before hurrying away. If his daughter's life was in danger, there was nothing I could do to convince him to change course. I couldn't offer her any protection, had no evidence with which to imprison the people threatening Houston and his daughter. I was powerless—and I hated it.

Resolving to talk this over with Wren, and mentally chastising myself for the fantasies I'd harbored about Jack, I hurried from the courthouse, looking over my shoulder as I got into a cab. I thought I might have painted a target on my back during my confrontation with Jack, and the last thing I wanted to do was bring Wren into the crosshairs too.

The cab pulled up to the hotel and I sent Wren a quick text saying that I was on my way up before climbing out. Continuing to keep my head on a swivel, I eyed everyone I passed on my way through the lobby, looking for familiar faces or furtive, cagey expressions. Seeing nothing but innocent bystanders, I got into the elevator and went to my floor, walking swiftly down the hall to my room.

I was looking forward to hashing all that had happened out with Wren. He was my sounding board and, I realized as I walked down the hallway, one of my best-friends. He was intelligent, kind, and, most importantly, loyal.

When this is over, I resolved, *my life moving forward is going to include him. I don't know how we're going to make it work. All I know is that I* am *going to make it work.*

The next day, the jury started their deliberation and our presence in the courthouse was more a matter of habit than necessity. Paul and I made small talk while I debated on whether or not to tell him what I'd discovered about Jack. I'd thought he and Paul were close friends but wasn't sure anymore. I wasn't sure about anything or anyone. So, based on that indecision, I kept the newest developments to myself. I didn't know who to trust, other than Wren.

He'd been appropriately shocked when I'd told him about the things I'd overheard outside Houston's chambers the day before.

"I can't believe Jack betrayed us!" he'd shouted, rising to his feet, his face flushing. "I've known him for years!"

"How did you meet, again?" I'd asked, unsure if he'd ever shared the story of how and where he'd managed to make friends with two FBI agents.

He waved this away, as though it were unimportant. "I'm going to call him right now. Make him explain himself."

I moved to stand in front of him, shaking my head. "No. I don't want him to know you're here. It might put you in danger."

"No more danger than you're in!"

"I need you, Wren. You're my technological eyes and ears. I'm not in any danger, not anymore."

He frowned. "Why do you say that?"

"Because of the way the trial is going." I blew out a breath. "There is no way that Christopher is going to be found guilty."

"Oh, come on. It's not that bad, is it?"

I nodded. "Yes, it is. Okay, maybe he'll be found guilty of the lesser charges," I conceded, "but nothing that's going to put him away from any length of time. He'll be out again in no time." I put my hands on Wren's chest. "Which is why I need you to stay safe. With your help, I know we'll gather the evidence we need to put him in prison for good."

"What are you going to do about Houston's daughter? The fact that he's been throwing the case to keep her safe?"

I sighed. "Nothing. The damage has been done. We're going to lose the case. Houston will have done his job and his daughter will be safe."

Wren gathered me to his chest, hearing the defeat in my voice. "It's not over yet, Maya. Don't give up."

Now, back in the courthouse awaiting the jury, I harbored a small hope that the jury might have seen past Christopher's smarmy demeanor, that they hadn't been distracted by the poor job I'd done with his questioning. Juries had surprised me before and there was a chance that they—

"Maya, the jury's back."

Paul's voice brought me fully back to the present—very reluctantly, as I knew the fact that the jury was back already was not a good sign. Unanimous guilty decision usually came after days of deliberation; it was the not-guilty verdicts that took no time at all. If all of the jury members didn't think that the suspect's guilt had been proven beyond a reasonable doubt, then there was little for them to talk about.

We were brought into the courtroom, standing until Houston came in and sat. The jury was then brought in and as I looked at them, I knew my suspicions were going to be confirmed. I could tell just by looking at the expressions on their faces.

The preliminaries were gone through, the charges against Christopher restated, before Houston asked for the jury to reveal their verdict. As the bailiff took the folded piece of paper from the head jurist and walked it to Houston's bench, I allowed the tiniest bit of hope to soothe the forceful beating of my heart. Maybe, just maybe...

Houston's face was unreadable as he opened the folded piece of paper, glanced inside, and refolded it, handing it back to the bailiff. As the uniformed man gave the paper back to the head jurist, I glanced over at Christopher. He was leaning back in his chair, his hands folded in his lap, looking as though he were perfectly content to sit there all day long. A tourist watching the goings-on of a rather uninteresting local attraction, but happy to be on vacation, all the same.

The jurist stood and read the verdict.

"On the count of assault, we find the defendant not guilty. On the count of reckless endangerment, we find the defendant guilty. On the count of conspiracy to commit murder, we find the defendant not guilty. On the count of attempted manslaughter..."

I held my breath. This was the big one, the charge that would keep Christopher behind bars for a long time.

"...we find the defendant not guilty."

My breath let go in an audible whoosh. Paul glanced over at me, as though checking my emotional status, before turning back to the proceedings.

Houston, who'd been nodding his head as the verdicts were read, banged his gavel. "I sentence the defendant to six months in prison and will add an additional three months and a fine of ten thousand dollars to his sentence for the charge of reckless endangerment. This court is adjourned."

Amidst a swirl of black cloth, Houston stormed from the courtroom. Even from my compromised vantage point, I could see that he was relieved. The skin around his eyes and mouth had loosened, making him look even more tired—but much more happy.

Even though I'd been expecting the verdicts to drop the way that they had, I still felt as though the whole trial had been a sham from start to finish. I hadn't lost it with my questioning of the witness, I knew that now. I'd lost it from the very beginning, thanks to Jack. It wasn't much of a consolation but it was something. There was only one thing that I wanted to do now.

I stood and walked over to the defendant's desk, holding a hand up toward the pair of uniformed guards who'd come to take Christopher away.

"Just one moment, please."

They stood back, their hands hanging loosely at their sides, on the ready.

"I'd like to speak to you, once you've been returned to custody," I said, holding Christopher's gaze. "Will you allow me that?"

Looking up at me, one eyebrow lifted, Christopher pursed his lips. When he didn't respond, I thought that he might deny my request, but it seemed that such wasn't going to be the case.

"Yes."

Dropping my chin in recognition of his acceptance, I had almost turned to go before he said, "And bring that man you were with, the one you brought to my beach house, with you."

I swallowed. Clearing my throat, I said, "I will."

As I walked away, I wondered at the intelligence of my request. What was I going to gain from speaking to Christopher? Was I just going to be putting a big target on my back? Leaving the courtroom, I realized it didn't matter. I wanted him to know that I knew he killed my father. And I wanted him to know that he wasn't going to get away with it.

Chapter 28

After the trial, I went home to San Francisco and Wren went back to Landsfield Ridge. We promised to see each other as much as our schedules allowed. I said this platitude with the utmost sincerity; I wanted Wren in my life and although I wasn't sure yet what exactly that life was going to look like or how it would work, I didn't care. We'd gone through too much and had too many connections to let time and physical distance keep us apart.

Other cases took over and time passed, though I never forgot Christopher and my burning need to keep him behind bars for good, the yearning lessened as time passed, drowned out by other pressing obligations. The morning Wren called me with the news, I was running late for work but still froze when I heard what he had to say.

"Maya, you won't believe it, but I've got him dead to rights."

"You've got who dead to rights?"

"Christopher. I found video footage from a traffic camera—after scrolling through all of the footage within a three-mile radius of where your father's car was found—and found a speeding camera had been triggered, providing a clear picture of Christopher and the license plate of the van he was driving. We've got him, Maya."

Wren's voice was a combination of cheerful glee and somberness that made my beating heart fill with warmth. I knew what it meant to him, to be able to provide me with the evidence we needed, and respected him for his reticence to show how excited I knew he must be.

"Oh, Wren. I don't know what to say."

"You asked Christopher for visitation rights, correct?"

I nodded, then realized he couldn't see me. "Yes."

"Let's go see him and tell him what we've got. I'm hoping that he'll be willing to give up information that will help us take down Rossi. I hate the thought of that man getting off scot-free, especially since he's so close to you. He might get a wild hair to get revenge on you for leading the investigation into Christopher's background."

I opened my mouth to protest but shut it again without speaking. Wren was right. I was actually kind of surprised that Rossi hadn't made a move against me—he wasn't the kind to let go of a grudge and he had reason to hold a big one against me.

"That's a great idea, Wren. I'll set it up. How soon can you travel?" My schedule was more than full but my paralegals were more than capable of handling things for a couple of days so I could fly to Dallas, where they were keeping Christopher in a minimum-security facility for the duration of his sentence.

"Tomorrow. The second I found the files I told my boss that I might have to take a couple more personal days."

Thinking that the library system offered way more benefits than my highfalutin law firm—which only offered the bare minimum of paid sick or personal days—I told Wren I'd arrange our travel, as long as he could drive down and fly out of San Francisco.

We agreed to leave in two days' time, giving Wren enough time to drive down on short notice and me to wrap up some things at work. After ending the call, the very next thing I did was contact the proper authorities to set up a meeting with Christopher. All I could do was put the process in motion, Christopher would have to agree to the meeting before a time and date could actually be set, but I wasn't worried. I thought that he was curious about me and my interest in him, especially since he'd recognized me outside his Mexican beach house. And since his impressive intelligence would have been far from taxed during his months of incarceration, I was betting on his willingness to meet with me, merely to enliven the boredom of his daily existence.

His boredom is definitely going to be enlivened, I thought with a grim smile as I walked to my bedroom to start getting ready for work. *He won't know what hit him.*

***

After going through the laborious process to gain access to the interior of the prison, a process that reminded me of our ill-fated meeting with Little John, Wren and I waited in the visiting room for Christopher to appear. The facility was large and surrounded by razor-wire fencing, painted the neutral tan color that such places are usually found in. I wasn't exactly nervous, but I felt fidgety, and had to consciously keep my knees from bouncing up and down beneath the desk we sat at. The meeting room smelled of stale sweat and whatever the guard had had for lunch. It'd been loaded with garlic, whatever it was, and added to the general stench of the place.

When he walked in, I was again reminded of someone just casually marking time until they had to be somewhere. Christopher ambled over, eyeing Wren curiously as he sat down across the table from us. Since this was a minimum-security prison, he wasn't wearing handcuffs, and the only thing that marked him as a prisoner was his gray uniform.

"I was glad to hear that you wanted a meeting," he said, using one hand to smooth back a lock of hair from his forehead. It had grown back during his stint in prison, his once-shaved head now covered in thick brown hair. "You would not imagine how frustrating it is to have a decent conversation with the people in here. I would be surprised if any of them has even a high-school education."

"Yes, how trying for you," I said, not bothering to keep the sarcasm from my voice. "But, unfortunately, you had better get used to it because you're not getting out of here anytime soon."

He filled a plastic cup of water from the equally break-proof pitcher on the table and sipped at it before responding. "Actually, I'm to be released next month." He set the cup down and grinned at me. "I'm getting out early due to good behavior."

Wren spoke for the first time. "I've got something to show you." He pulled out his laptop, which had been a bear to get through security, and opened it, tapping on the keys for a few seconds before turning the screen toward Christopher. He tapped it one more time, to bring up the file I'd seen many, many times already. To add to this, Wren pulled some stills he'd taken of the speeding camera out of his laptop bag, sliding them across the table. They featured Christopher driving the van, with his face and that distinctive watch clearly visible. Everything was time stamped and incontrovertible.

I watched Christopher's face as he stared at the screen. I was expecting to see consternation mar his even features, but the slight grin on his face only widened as the video played.

"Interesting," he said, turning the laptop back toward Wren. "Say, could you refill my water for me?"

He directed this at Wren, and as Wren obliged, Christopher's hand snaked out and grabbed his wrist. Turning Wren's wrist over, Christopher revealed a tattoo that I had noticed in passing but hadn't thought of asking him about. It was a small triangle with a six-pointed star inside. I'd assumed it held some religious connotations, maybe a Mason emblem, but hadn't given it much more thought than that.

As quickly as he'd grabbed Wren, Christopher released him again, sitting back in his chair with a self-satisfied expression.

"I know you," he said to Wren, quirking an eyebrow. "How strange that fate has brought us back together."

Wren's face paled. "I don't know what you're talking about."

"No? Hmm."

I looked from Wren to Christopher, waiting for someone to explain what was going on. When no one spoke, I interjected.

"Does someone want to tell me what's going on? Wren?" I reached out and touched Wren's shoulder, trying to bring him back down to earth. The look on his face was abstracted, distant, and it scared me a little.

Christopher's eyes darted from me, to my hand on Wren's shoulder, to Wren, before coming back to me.

"It's like that, is it?"

"Like what?" I snarled, keeping my hand on Wren for a moment longer before slowly pulling away. I didn't want him to think he was able to orchestrate my gestures, no matter how uncomfortable it made me to know that he could.

"Never mind." He leaned forward over the table, his eyes on Wren. "I know who you are and I know that your name isn't Wren." Adopting a sneer, Christopher continued. "I mean, what are you supposed to be? A bird? They couldn't come up with anything better than that?"

Blinking, I tried to assimilate what Christopher was saying. If Wren's name wasn't Wren...then what was it? And who was 'they'?

A guard entered the room and said we had five more minutes.

"Listen to me carefully," Christopher said after the guard had retreated, his voice dropping low. "If you want to stay in hiding, that's fine with me. I don't care about you anymore. What I do care about is getting out of here." Turning his attention to me, he continued. "If you want to guarantee *Wren's* continued safety, you'd better listen carefully. You are not to give that video or those photographs to anyone. You are not to share what you know with anyone. I'm going to contact you in a week's time with further instructions and until then, you had better keep your mouth shut if you want him," he pointed at Wren, "to stay alive."

The guard returned and started walking over to us. Christopher stood, his eyes holding mine.

"Remember. If you want your boyfriend to continue to be counted amongst the living, you are not to show anyone else what you've shown me today." The corners of his lips lifted. "*A bientôt.*"

I watched Christopher being led away, unable to formulate a single coherent thought. Once he exited the room, Wren and I stood to leave. My movements were clumsy, my mind a blur. I looked at Wren once as he walked out of the room, but he shook his head and mouthed *Later.*

Once outside the facility, I turned to Wren and crossed my arms over my chest.

"What's going on? What was that all about?"

"Maya..." he shook his head. "I can't tell you." His expression was pained but I felt no pity for him.

"What do you mean you can't tell me? What exactly can't you tell me? Is Wren your real name or not? Who are you?" All of a sudden, all of the irregularities of his character came crashing down on me. His technological savvy, his acute preparedness, his "friends" in the FBI. I'd suspected he was much more than a simple librarian—but now, faced with the reality, I didn't know what to feel, what to do, how to respond.

"Maya, it's...complicated."

I turned from him and climbed into our rental car. Even though I wanted to start the engine and drive away without him, I waited until he was seated before heading toward the airport.

We didn't speak as I headed west, into the setting sun. I didn't know what to say. All I knew was that I had evidence against Christopher that I couldn't use because Wren, the man I'd come to know and love, had secrets. *Love?* Was I really thinking that? Even in the private depths of my mind? Did I really love him or was I just grateful that he'd done so much to help me throughout this long process? Pushing aside my confusion, I continued with my original train of thought. Secrets. Secrets that he, even after all we'd been through, was intent on keeping from me. The trajectory of my future had suddenly veered off course. I couldn't be with a man who was lying to me, no matter how much he'd meant to me, how supportive and giving he was. Could I?

The only person I can trust is myself. It had always been that way and now it seemed as though it always would be.

I shook my head, silently rebelling against the idea. I'd spent my life wrapped in loneliness, and Wren offered me an alternative to the never-ending cycle of work and social isolation that I always found myself in. He'd been there for me, watched my back, helped me and had given himself completely to my pursuit of justice, with nothing in it for him other than non-stop research and the uncertainty of international espionage. I owed him something for his willingness to sacrifice his time and effort in helping me. And it looked like what I owed him was my loyalty, even in the face of his secretive, undisclosed past.

Without speaking, I reached out and grabbed Wren's hand, gripping it tightly in mine.

I was a Hartwell, and I always paid my debts.

Epilogue

Christopher sat down in front of the phone and cracked his knuckles, wishing he had a tumbler of whiskey in front of him. Sighing, he pushed the thought aside and lifted the receiver, dialing a number he knew from memory.

"This is Maya."

"Hello, counselor. How are you doing today?"

"Who is this?"

"I'm sure you know from the caller ID that this call is from a correctional facility in Dallas. You know exactly who I am. I'll ask again. How are you?"

"Let's skip the niceties. What do you want?"

Christopher smiled at her harsh tone. He wondered if the little hints he'd dropped in her lap during their last meeting had become an itch she'd been unable to scratch.

"I have a proposition for you. But first, I need to lay some groundwork. The man you know as Wren is actually Kit Davidson. He, as I'm sure you already suspect, is not a librarian. He is a federal agent with an active $2.5 million dollar contract out for his life. I was one of several people offered the job, but he disappeared into the Witness Protection program before I got the chance."

Silence followed these pronouncements, so Christopher filled it.

"My proposition is this: I will take care of the person who initiated the contract on Kit's life—on one condition. I want that evidence you showed me destroyed, along with any copies you've made, and your promise that you'll drop any and all charges against me. You will stop following me—I know it was you and Kit that day outside my home in Mexico—and will stop gathering evidence with which to convict me."

"What do I get in return?" I asked, my voice strained and hoarse.

"Taking care of the person responsible for the contract will be my last job. I promise you that. I want to retire, enjoy my freedom. I don't want to continue looking over my shoulder, always expecting to see you chasing after me."

"I repeat, what do I get out of this deal?"

"You'll get the reassurance that Kit is safe and will remain that way. I sense you two have a budding romance going and I would hate to see you hurt in the crossfire, in a relationship with a man who isn't who he seems and always on the run." Christopher hardened his voice. "If you refuse, I will divulge Kit's new identity to the man holding the contract. He will be hunted mercilessly and anyone with him will be targeted as well, deemed necessary collateral damage."

"You killed my father. I can't just let you go free."

Christopher straightened. "I did? Who is your father?" He shook his head. "No, it doesn't matter. If I killed him, he probably deserved it."

"He was a loving father and devoted husband. A lawyer who always sought out justice and lived with the utmost integrity. He did *not* deserve to die."

He could hear the emotion in her voice, and took a moment to go over the jobs he'd done, mentally ticking them off. He'd only killed two lawyers—and one had definitely deserved it. The other...

"Ah, yes. I believe I know who you're speaking of." He sighed. "You're right. His was a job that I'm not proud of. It was a difficult time in my life and I was forced to make hard decisions. Nevertheless, my offer stands. My life for Kit's. You have three days to decide."

"What happens in three days?"

"Why, that's the day I'm to be released. Didn't I tell you I was being released early for good behavior?"

"You've only served three months of your sentence. How could you be getting out already?"

"I've been a very good boy. You have three days, counselor. Use them wisely."

Christopher hung up the phone and rested his chin in a cupped hand as he reviewed the conversation in his mind. He knew exactly the conundrum he'd dropped in her lap. He had been able to spot the bond between the two of them the second he'd entered the meeting room. Once he'd realized that the man sitting in front of him was the target of an old contract, a fact given away by the distinctive tattoo on his wrist, Christopher had immediately started formulating a plan of how to exploit the situation.

He thought he'd come up with an admirable proposition, one which had the potential of benefiting all three of the interested parties. The two lovebirds could live happily ever after, knowing that Kit-slash-Wren was out of harm's way, and they wouldn't have to live looking over their shoulder. And he would not go to the hell hole they would probably put him in, if he was convicted of murdering Maya's father. He would gladly live out the rest of his days on his island cabana in the South Seas. It was a win-win, really.

The only caveat was that he had strong suspicions about how ideologically stubborn Maya Hartwell could be; if she'd been willing to travel all the way down to Mexico to spy on him, had been tenacious enough to track down the evidence she'd shown him last week, Christopher wondered at her readiness to drop her pursuit of him—especially upon learning that he'd killed her father. It was regrettable, the fact that the one job he actually felt some measure of contrition about was coming back to haunt him. Risks of the trade, he supposed. It was a trade he was happy to leave behind.

It was hard to quit something that had brought him so much financial and personal success, but one had to know when it was time to call it quits, especially when his line of work was so dynamic, so dangerous.

Knowing that his time was nearly up and that the next in-mate in line was anxiously waiting his chance to use the phone, Christopher stood, adjusting his drape of his pants before opening the door to the private conversation room—one of the few perks of the minimum-security facility he was currently stuck in.

As he walked back toward his cell, Christopher spoke softly to himself.

"What shall it be, Ms. Hartwell? The pit or the pendulum?"

Up Next for Maya Hartwell

Book 4 in the (Quest for Justice) Series - Coming to Amazon Q2 2024 or sooner!

Newsletter Sign Up

You can find out more about my books and any up coming news at my website via this link **www.gabbyblack.com** or indeed just sign up for my newsletter by going to the website.

About the Author

Get ready to embark on an exciting journey into the captivating world of mystery, courtroom drama, crime, and investigation with Gabby Black's thrilling novels. As an ardent enthusiast of these genres, I pour my heart and soul into weaving stories that will keep you eagerly turning the pages, filled with suspense, unexpected plot twists, and enigmatic mysteries that will keep you guessing until the very last word.

With a background spanning nine years in the Justice System, I draw upon both my vivid imagination and real-life experiences to craft gripping tales that will leave you absolutely spellbound. When I'm not immersed in writing, I'm out there exploring the world through travel, connecting with diverse people, seeking out new adventures, and drawing inspiration for my next novel. Oh, and did I mention I'm a lover of fine wine, well, let's, be honest it's actually most wine! You might have picked up on that from the pages of my books.

So, won't you join me on this exhilarating journey into the unknown, where every page holds the promise of discovery and excitement? Grab one of my novels and let's dive into a world where thrilling stories await, and unforgettable adventures are just a page turn away. Cheers to the mysteries that lie ahead!

Thank you so much for reading and I sincerely hope you enjoyed the third book in the new 'Quest for Justice' series. As an independent author, I am incredibly grateful for your support. I would love if you could take just a few moments to write a review. Your reviews are immensely helpful and I do genuinely read each and every single one. For those of you who are reading from an ipad, phone or pc here is a direct link to leave a review **https://rebrand.ly/1d6iumz** otherwise kindly log into your Amazon account, find the book and leave a review. I truly appreciate your time and feedback. Thanks immensely!

You can find out more about me and my books at my website via this link **www.gabbyblack.com**

Printed in Great Britain
by Amazon

42049988R10165